The Emissary

by Marc Pietrzykowski

The Emissary

ISBN-13: 978-0615-891-89
ISBN-10: 0615-891-85

for more books, visit Pski's Porch:
www.pskisporch.com

Printed in U.S.A.

- For Ashley -

The Emissary

Chapter 1

Buildings, like the people who raise and inhabit them, are most interesting once they grow old and start to fall apart. Not so old that we abandon them to vines and gravity, they must be in use, worn but still serviceable, crumbling under the weight of their stories and, thus, lovely. Abandoned buildings have the power to fascinate as well but their appeal is morbid, a reminder of what lies well beyond the death of the body, and so most of us would rather look at pictures of them, or at least view them from afar, be it through the lens of a camera or through the tunnel of epochs, the romance of archeology, of the ruin. Tile missing from a wall in a well-used public rest room is a sign of life, of activity, whereas the same missing tile in an abandoned hospital bespeaks rot, transmutation, maggotry. New buildings, stinking of paint and concrete and drywall patch, have nothing to offer but a false sense of sterility and, perhaps, a sense of potential, of lives that might be lived through them, stories that will someday bend their stiff angles into curious warps, droops, and curls.

Case in point: the ElderGrove Residential Living Facility, built in 1972. When this 14 bed, concrete-block-and-steel-roof edifice was erected in a gone-to-seed alfalfa field 15 miles north of Candler City, it was called the Candler Home For Retirees. It looked about as comfortable amongst the weeds and scrub pine as a newborn in an abattoir, white and moist and shining in the summer sun, the only rectangle for miles around. By the time the Aames ElderCare corporation bought the building in early 1997, suburbs had surrounded it, a strip mall sold shoes and Chinese food across the street, and all the rooms inside had worn soft as an old shoe. Aames added a second building with 16 more beds in 1998, and that building looked just as gawky and useless as the first, though it was larger and covered with speckled fake brick and weirdly sparkling grey vinyl shingles. But the second building, known administratively as the West Wing, degenerated so quickly that the East Wing, the older sister, soon looked the newer of the two. The rapid decline of the new building might be attributed to the cheaper building materials Aames used, but most of the residents of the East Wing assumed it was because the West Wing was a de facto hospice facility, the dark side that East Wing residents crossed over to when they could no longer even minimally care for themselves.

The floor plan of the East Wing still followed, in 2013, the plan devised for it in 1972, with a series of seven apartments lining either side of a long hallway that led into the day room, at one end, and a large bathroom and shower area, at the other. The kitchen was in one of the upper corners, opposite the nurses' station and was just large enough for a counter, a mixer, four-top burner, a double oven, a microwave, and a small dishwasher, and a walk-in cooler at the back. The dining area flanked the kitchen and held the coffee maker and toaster and a cabinet full of dry goods, leaving barely enough room for the residents to sit, elbow to elbow. As a result, most of them chose to dine in the day room, or in their apartments. The day room itself was sparse and transitory, equal parts hospital and cheap hotel lobby: a large flat screen TV dominated one wall, surrounded by a semi-circle of chairs and throw pillows and worn-shiny blankets. On the other side of the room were three round tables, each with three or four chairs surrounding them, a sanitary station, and shelves full of books, board games, and more blankets. It was at one such table that a current resident of ElderGrove, Mrs. Treadwell, sat, comparing her toes, which peeked out of the ends of her slippers, with the papery yellow that showed through spots where the floor tile had worn away from years of chair legs rubbing against them. They were nearly the same color, her toes and the underlayment. She knew she could hide in that color, if it came to that, that it was the same color that underlay everything, the tile, the foolish wallpaper, the pocked ceiling tile marked with ominous stains, the grass outside, the sky. "Ok, are you ready to go, Mrs. Treadwell?" Cameron, a carefully bearded young man with sleepy, benevolent eyes put a small, black, digital recorder on the table and placed an equally small microphone on a tripod beside it, pointing toward her.

"What, oh, yes," she said, lifting her head. Her voice had an odd rattle to it, like wind pushing through a broken basement window.

"So," Cameron continued, sitting back in his chair, "you were going to tell me about the pickle factory."

Mrs. Treadwell stared blankly for a moment, then sighed. "Oh, the pickle factory, of course. Yes..." she folded her hands together in her lap and looked at them, nodding crookedly. Cameron was used to her routine at this point: once she had a hold on the memory she wanted, she needed a minute or two to rock back and forth and coax the past into the present in full regalia.

"Yes," she continued suddenly, "Papa was a great one for taking us, myself and my sister and my two brothers, on tours, little trips he thought would educate us to the ways of the world. He was a funny man, my father, in many ways, he wore a little mustache just like Hitler's until the war started, then he had to shave it off so he wore a Van Dyke instead, do you know what that is?"

"Um, like a goatee?" Cameron answered.

"That's right, I think that's another name for, yes, and when he wore his Van Dyke he curled his mustache with wax, he was very fanciful, loved wearing hats, but he was very practical too, very practical, he was a cold man. Mother was very different, but she was also practical, and also cold, a difficult woman to know, but she loved us, they both loved and cared for us. Ah, but the pickle factory, yes. One day Papa heard a new factory had opened on the East side of the city, and so mother bundled us all up, it was the late winter or early spring, and Papa took us all to the streetcar. I hated the streetcar, but everyone else loved it, it was like a circus ride for them, I hate rides, all that jostling. You know there were men that would touch you on the streetcars, just rub against you with their hands..." she shuddered and fell briefly silent. "But, yes, the factory truly was a wonder, an engineering marvel, my father called it, and he knew something about engineering and factories. I remember we stepped off the streetcar and walked blocks, it was chilly and a cold wind blew us and father in the lead, like he was marching us in a parade. We turned a corner and there it was, bright green, glowing green even, all the other buildings near it, they were all factories, were brown or grey, dull colored, and here was this glowing green building, three stories, each smaller than the other like a wedding cake. A green wedding cake..." she chuckled to herself. Cameron smiled and scratched his nose.

"We were frightened, of course, even father was a little

taken aback, but onward through the fog! And looking back, I know of course he had an appointment with the foreman or manager, he was not the sort to drop by uninvited, even in his own house. Yes, a man came to meet us at the door, I remember, he popped his head out as we were coming up the sidewalk, he was very red, his hair and his face were all red. I don't remember his name, if I ever knew it, but he and father shook hands and off we went into the factory. We all stopped first in a small room and put on galoshes that were much to big for the children and some kind of goggles, too, I think, or maybe little masks for our mouths, we had to put something on our mouths. Yes, it was probably our mouths, because we went through a big door and then another door and phew! Did it stink. Like vinegar, and like blood, too, and rotting meat. Not like the pickles I knew! Dolly, the youngest, grabbed my hand, and asked, what did she ask, 'are there elephants in here?' something like that, she had a great fear of elephants and thought they would sneak out from under her bed at night and terrorize the house. Father shushed her and we all listened to the red man explain how they made the pickles, how the raw pickle came down into the enormous vat in the middle of the room through tubes, there were thousands of them, tubes leading down to the vat from the walls and ceiling, and how they mixed with vinegar there and then were spit out from other tubes, depending on what kind you wanted: a tube for sweet pickles, and one for dills, and one for sliced pickles, and how the men standing at the end of the tubes had to chop or pinch the pickle at just the right time to get the right size, and they dropped into jars and moved down the conveyor belt to the lid screwers, who screwed them on. Then they went into the vacuum room, but we didn't get to see that because it was a trade secret. While he was talking, and I remember this very well, Dolly wandered off, it was my hand she was holding and then she was gone, father was looking up at the bottom of the vat with the red man, Amos and Charlie were kicking at each other, like boys do, so of course, I had to go and find Dolly.

"Well, I wandered forever, it seemed, no one paid me a speck of mind, the workers just bustled everywhere, not caring that a very young girl was lost in the factory, or even noticing I was there, it seemed! I started to get scared myself, I remember I was in a long hallway, there were tubes on the ceiling and in the walls, and workers just walking right past me. Then I saw Dolly up ahead, pushing her way through a swinging door, or maybe one of the workers was leading her by the hand, so I ran, I ran down the hallway and pushed through the door and, oh my I can see it even now, there was Dolly, and she was laughing to herself, she had this way of laughing so hard that no noise came out, do you know the way I mean? Yes, she laughed that way all her life, it wasn't a very long life, but in any case... she was, yes, she was laughing, and I said 'Dolly! I have been looking everywhere for you,' or something sisterly like that, and she just laughed harder and said 'funny babies!' and that's when I looked around and saw so many babies hanging from the ceiling, hundreds, maybe thousands, of little green and yellow and brown babies, hanging in these harnesses, kind of like swings, their little fat legs were poking through, oh my.... and the tubes, all the tubes were connected to the harnesses, and some of them were connected to their fingers, and these little masks some of them had on, like feed bags for horses, but smaller and with tubes coming out. Such wonderful architecture! The building and the tubes and the babies, all of it. I, I just stood there with my mouth open, it was the strangest thing, and then one of the workers grabbed Dolly and I, hard, and pushed us out of the room and down the hallway and then down another hallway, and there was Father and Amos and Charlie and the red-faced man. Father was very angry, he told us we were very bad to wander off and were in trouble and I tried to tell him about the babies and that I was only trying find Dolly but he was too angry to listen, or he was trying to make the red-faced man think so, anyway. Amos and Charlie were happy, I was in trouble, and so I never told anyone about the babies, just Dolly, of course, and always when it was dinner time and Mother passed the pickle tray around we would look at each other and never, ever eat a pickle. I have never had a pickle since that day and I never will." She sighed, then let her hands, which had started to jump and flutter near the middle of the story, float down together into her lap.

"Wow, well, that," Cameron said, reaching out to press the 'stop' button on the recorder, "is one heck of a story, Mrs. Treadwell. You've outdone yourself, I think."

"Oh, no, it's just one of those strange things that happened, when you live as long as I have, you see just about everything there is to see, architecturally speaking. You'll think twice about eating a pickle now, I think! Especially Vlasic, the red-faced man's name was Vlasic, I recall, because years later Father tried to make me marry him, but I ran away to Chicago instead—"

"Really, that sounds like a great story for next time," Cameron replied. "Can we save that one?"

"Yes, of course, yes, yes, I think it's getting close to supper anyway, I must go get ready." Mrs. Treadwell stood and smiled again at Cameron. "I do have the best stories, don't I?"

"Yes, you are the queen of stories, no doubt," he answered.

She beamed. "Oh stop, you're making my head swell. We have an appointment for next Tuesday, then?"

"Same time, same channel," he said.

"Channel? I'm sorry?"

"It's just a saying, yes, I'll be here, Mrs. Treadwell. One o'clock?"

"Indeed," she replied.

She smiled once more before shuffling out of the day room toward her apartment. Cameron shook his head and started putting away his equipment. "Hey Cam," said a voice, and he turned in his seat to see a young, dark, heavyset woman in nurses' scrubs standing behind him, one hand on her hip, one holding what looked like a deflated enema bag. "Hi Angela," he replied.

"You really make her happy, you know? Make a lot of these folks happy, but her, well, you just a good man," she said, wagging the tube of the bag at him for emphasis.

"Yeah, well, she's really got some crazy stories, I dig hearing them."

"Oh yeah, she just plain crazy, but sweet, even when it get dark she don't lose it, like a lot of the peoples here." She sighed. "So what you do with the recordings?"

"Ah, I animate, make cartoons for them, and then I put them up on YouTube. I'm way behind, actually, I got some good war stories from Eddie just before, um, he passed, and I really need to get those up, I always try to—well, it's good for them, and it's good for me, I like making the movies, you know?" He felt, as he always did, lost when trying to describe his motivations for this project. He felt funny even thinking of it as a 'project.'

"Sure, I think so," Angela said. "I mean, everyday I go home and feed my kids and I say, Angela, you got to get yourself a different job, something with good pay, not so many headaches, not so much... sad stuff, but then I wake up the next morning and I know I'm doing good for people's lives, you know? And then my girls see me doing that, they know all that stuff they hear in Church on Sunday means something, even if some people be deaf when they sit and listen and look at each other's clothes..."

"Yeah, that's kinda it, working here before college really turned me on to the whole thing. But I gotta go Angela, sorry, got my own job to get to, drinks won't serve themselves." He knew if he didn't interrupt, Angela was likely to continue talking until the sun swallowed the cold, dead earth, and he couldn't be late again, not this week. Well, maybe he could, no one was storming the Lost Lake Shopping Center to apply at Applebee's, not so he'd noticed, and he did like listening to Angela, she had a nice way of moving, even doing the simplest things. Mrs. Treadwell's latest story really was a good one, he already felt some ideas floating around as he walked out the front door to the parking lot; maybe he'd use some of the same cutouts he used to animate from her last recording, the story where she claimed to have kicked Hubert Humphrey in the balls and caught some foot fungus from him that her husband killed with turpentine. But those cutouts really looked too much like old Monty Python era Terry Gilliam stuff, Clyde was right. He shoved the snow off the windshield with his glove and arm and fell into the driver's seat, suddenly drained of energy. The cold air outside was metallic, and as his car warmed the air, he could feel himself nodding, sagging into the blast of the heater vents like a dog finding shade on a hot day. No time for a nap, no time for a quick call to Cookie for some weed, no time no time, he'd worked hard to make sure that was not his life's refrain, but there it was, creeping in, an uninvited choir.

****

Angela checked the charts, making sure the newest resident, Thomas Kinney, was included on the printout. She'd not met him yet, he'd been in his room since he arrived, before her shift started, and showed no sign of joining the others in the cafeteria, so she put his medication and food tray on the cart with the others. She hoped he was not another shut-in, that's the last thing they needed.

Her phone vibrated at her hip and she glanced at the text, from Rosie, her eldest daughter, saying she needed cookies for Thursday—cookies for what? Angela wondered, sighing. Every day she reminded herself what a blessing they were, Rosie and Alison, and how lucky she was, and how her bamabalan ex-husband managed to contribute to the DNA of two lovely girls was beyond her—"Ms. Padilla?" a voice at her elbow said, softly. It was Mrs. Treadwell, already dressed and ready for supper, her knobby cheeks yellow against the blueish white skin of her cheeks.

"Yes, Mrs. Treadwell? You look very nice," she added.

"Oh why thank you," Mrs. Treadwell said, looking down at her shoes. "When you're done flattering me, can I sign up to use the kitchen tomorrow? I'd like to make some brownies for our new guest."

"Oh I think that would be ok," Angela replied, "as long as you make me some cookies for Rosie to take to school." Mrs. Treadwell was the only resident who regularly used the kitchen, though any of them were welcome to. Mr. Klickinoi occasionally reheated pots of goulash that his daughter brought, but several months ago he'd fallen asleep and burnt a pot and set off the fire alarm, so now he could only use the kitchen when one of the orderlies was available to help him. All the residents were supposed to have an aide help in the kitchen if Eddie the cook was unavailable, as he worked diligently to be—actually, that was the purpose of signing up, so Eddie could absent himself and one of the PCAs could mind the burners and so forth, but Mrs. Treadwell not only needed no supervision, she made wonderful baked goods at least once a week for both residents and staff.

"Oh, of course, how many would you like me to make? Four dozen?"

"It's a joke, joking, Mrs. Treadwell, really. I'll sign you up for tomorrow, after breakfast."

"It would be my pleasure, truly, I love to bake, you

know," Mrs. Treadwell pleaded.

"Well, all right, let me bring the ingredients, though, ok?"

"Ah, very good, yes, I will make a list after supper and give it to you before you leave for the evening."

"You really are melaza, Mrs. Treadwell, did anyone ever tell you that?"

"Oh," she frowned, "not since 1933, I think." She slipped off toward the dining room, stepping carefully, almost mechanically, in the dull yellow shoes she wore for supper. Angela watched her go, barely noticing her odd gait, her way of gliding along while keeping her arms and hands stiff, like she was using invisible railings to guide her, so deliberate she almost seemed like a puppet, albeit one that floated. Angela knew that part of finding one's way in a new situation involves absorbing all the strange habits and peculiar rhythms of people quickly, so that they no longer seemed strange, and she prided herself on her ability to assimilate, to become part of a community rapidly, so that others were surprised when they were reminded how new she actually was. It was her second month at ElderGrove, and already the residents were making cookies for her daughter.

****

Tom woke and listened to the strange noises coming from the other side of the door. Coughs and rattles, squeaking wheels, a sudden burst of dry laughter: none of the noises were wholly alien, but they were also not his, they were not played by the orchestra that had supplied his life's sound track for the last thirty years. He peeked around the room, at the stained dresser top, the cheap wooden chair, its arms worn to a dull shine; he felt the lowered bar at the side of the bed he lay upon and remembered. He'd always sworn never to end up like this, in one of these places. He and Hector had sworn together, taking an oath in the bleak first years of AIDS and funerals every weekend, watching their friends crumble one by one: I promise to help you die, to keep you out of assisted living facilities, to help you along and keep hold of your hand as you go down into darkness rather than let some little white girl wipe your ass. And help Hector he had, but then he was alone, like Jesus trying to pound the nails in himself, one hand bound by fear, confusion, a lack of will... a lack of faith. Someone knocked on Tom's new door. He rolled over and faced the wall, despite a sudden compulsion to talk and talk..

He heard the door crack open, felt a sliver of light on the back of his right ear. "Mr. Kinney?" a voice called softly, then the door was all the way open and something wheeled was pushed into the room. "Mr. Kinney, I'm Ms. Padilla, I brought you some dinner." He heard her standing in the room, could feel her staring at him, wished she would just go away.

"I know sometimes it's hard to get adjusted to a new place, so I'm just going to leave your tray here on the dresser. I'll be back later to pick it up and see if you need anything else, ok?" She placed the tray on the dresser and backed the cart out of the room, closing the door quietly after her.

Tom rolled back over and turned his head toward the dinner tray. It was a hospital tray, set with a carton of milk, some plastic silverware and a napkin, wrapped in plastic, and a brown plastic dome set over a plate. The smell of corn leaked through a hole the size of a quarter set in the top of the brown dome. The smell reached his nose and his stomach knotted. He fell asleep and woke and the whole room reeked of corn. He started crying softly, noticed he was crying, and rolled back over to face the wall again, then started pinching his thigh with his thumb and forefinger, again and again, beneath the covers.

Chapter 2

The following morning, the smell of cake drifted from the kitchen to the day room, lifting nostrils as it went. Nurse DeFazio frowned as the scent reached her, she had enough trouble keeping the dietary charts straight without Mrs. Treadwell's weekly butter and chocolate infusions, but the woman certainly could bake, and the residents always perked up for an hour or two after 'tea,' as Mrs. Treadwell called the small feasts. Then the sugar worked its way out of their systems and they peed and fell asleep, so, perhaps the diet and medication tweaks were alright after all. And not everyone needed adjustments, really, she just had to learn to relax, stop sweating the small stuff like Maggie kept telling her. Oh Maggie, jamming the apartment full of self-help books, crystals, magnets, ankhs, little vials of colloidal silver... but she still made Carol Ann quiver after twelve years together, cooked a great tomato and cheddar omelet, and played the piano late at night to help Carol Ann sleep, so there was really nothing to complain about. Well, a few things maybe. "Nurse DeFazio?" a hoarse voice interrupted Carol Ann's reverie. A small, frog-lipped man in a light pink sweater stood at the other side of the counter, trying hard to blink his eyes.

"Yes, Mr. Zimmerman, what can I do for you?"

"Ah, the television is not behaving again, and I can't

find the orderly, that Chinese boy—"

"Yes, I understand, Mr. Zimmerman, let me find Chris and get things squared away for you as soon as I'm done checking things back here, ok?" She smiled and tilted her head.

"Thank you, I'm so sorry to bother you, but it seems like the, uh, tea will be ready soon, and of course *Andy Griffith* will be on, so everyone is expecting the television to work and I can't find the boy—"

"Don't worry, I'll take care of everything," Nurse DeFazio interrupted, and she would take care of everything, as Mr. Zimmerman knew, as she knew, as everyone knew, that's what she did, took care of things, put them in order. She even looked like the kind of person created to make crooked things not so crooked: her broad, high forehead bespoke an intimidating intelligence, and her small eyes were bright beneath her bushy eyebrows, like baby squirrels hiding beneath a hedge. The rest of her face fell away unassumingly, leading Maggie to compare her more than once to an alien. Like she could talk, when those ears caught the wind she'd blow down the block—

"Nurse DeFazio?"

"Yes, Mr. Zimmerman?"

"The boy fixed the TV, it was just the plug! Ha!" Mr. Zimmerman grinned and slapped his thigh.

"That's good to hear, now make sure you find something that everyone wants to watch, no fights."

"No fights, no fights, we'll put on *Andy Griffith* and turn the sound down low for tea so Dorothy can't hear," he answered, chuckling as he shuffled away toward the television. Carol Ann shook her head and went back to checking the numbers on her clipboard with those on the computer monitor. There was no need to check, she knew, she'd printed off the charts herself on Monday, nothing could have changed, but just in case, she had to make absolutely sure they were straight. She knew this was obsessiveness on her part and also that it served her well, that her job and her neuroses worked together to assure the numbers added up. After rechecking the med log, her next item was introducing herself to the new resident, Thomas Kinney, perhaps trying to coax him out of his room. New residents reluctant to leave their rooms were the norm, but she also knew that her chances of helping him integrate with the community were much better in the first weeks. If he didn't come out after that, chances were good he would stay in his room, decline, and only leave when he was shipped to the West Wing. She looked at his file: born in 1928, so he was eighty-four, born in Mississippi, was in jail for a time for manslaughter, oh dear, well, seems he cleaned up his act after that, piloted tugs in Ashtabula for 30 years, one daughter, Helen, no mention of other family, asthmatic, suffers from hypertension and gout, also severe arthritis in hands, legs, and spine. Nothing that would necessitate his presence at ElderGrove until the bottom of the list, where Carol Ann noted he'd suffered three minor strokes in the last six months, causing him to become "withdrawn." Well of course, Carol Ann thought, I'd be withdrawn too after three strokes in six months, minor or not. A sudden crash sounded from the day room, and Carol Ann glanced up to see Mr. Zimmerman picking up his chair, grinning toadily at her. He must have been arguing with Ms. Newell again and leaped up to make some point, knocking his chair backwards in the process. It happened at least once a day. She turned to get a welcome packet for Mr. Kinney and caught a glance of herself in the mirror beside the wall clock: brown hair beginning to go grey at the temples, parted at the side, the same haircut she'd worn for 20 years, ever since she met Maggie at the jazz festival and was swept off her feet. Her bare feet—was that right? She hated going barefoot, did she like it before, when she was young and woozily swaying to Sonny Rollins? Probably so, she found it hard to remember the person she had been, then, though her face was the same, of course, more lines around the grey eyes, more lines around her sharp nose, her too-large nostrils, her small, thin-lipped mouth. Alien indeed, why do they never show old aliens in the movies? Only the young ones, flush with alien hormones, scrubbed with some kind of alien moisturizer. She brushed the front of her shirt violently, as though it might smooth out some of the wrinkles in her soul, then opened the bottom drawer of the filing cabinet to assemble a welcome basket for Mr. Kinney.

The "welcome basket" was one of her first innovations at ElderGrove, as was calling all the residents "Mister" or "Misses," or "Miss," if that was preferred. They were modest changes to be sure, but she liked to think they helped improve the quality of life of the residents, and the aides as well. She knew the welcome basket helped new residents feel more at home, many of them had told her as much. Each basket contained two packages of sugar-free cookies, an official ElderGrove brochure, a calendar of scheduled activities for the month, a list of nearby businesses and a shuttle schedule, earplugs and eye shields for residents who had trouble sleeping, and a small fleece blanket, blue for the men and pink for the women. By far the most important item was the welcome card, which she had all the aides, nurses, and residents sign. She checked the card quickly a final time before putting it in the envelope: all three nurses, all nine aides, and all thirteen residents had signed, and no one had signed more than once, which had happened before and still stuck in her craw. Nurse DeFazio forged Dr. Small's name, as usual.

She smiled at Mr. Zimmerman, busy arranging cups and place setting for their afternoon "tea," held whenever Mrs. Treadwell decided to bake something. It was a tradition in place well before Nurse DeFazio had arrived, and if it wasn't Mrs. Treadwell's idea—she claimed to have "absorbed" the ritual from a previous resident—she had certainly taken charge of it. "Doesn't it smell wonderful, Mr. Zimmerman?" she asked as she passed by.

"Sure does, better than Dorothy's pants, anyway!" he sniggered and then drew back a bit, as though expecting a blow.

"Shut up!" Dorothy cried from her wheelchair.

"Really, Mr. Zimmerman. Respect, remember? We give respect and we get respect in return."

"I'm sorry, I know, but really she went in her pants."

"Shut up!" Dorothy turned her chair and started rolling toward Mr. Zimmerman. Nurse DeFazio could smell that Dorothy had, indeed, lost control of her bowels again, and she put the welcome basket down on a table and grabbed the wheelchair handles, steering Mrs. Newell—the title she preferred to use, and which she tried to get Mr. Zimmerman to use, without much success—toward the bath and shower room at the end of the resident's hall. "Ms. Padilla?" she called down the hall, and Angela popped out of one of the rooms, one gloved hand holding a rectal thermometer.

"Right here, Nurse DeFazio," she answered.

"Ms. Padilla, could you help Mrs. Newell, I think she'd like to get cleaned up before tea."

"Yes, please," said Dorothy in a whiny, little-girl voice.

Angela smiled. "Of course, let me just finish with Mr. Gladwell first." She popped back into Mr. Gladwell's room and pushed the door nearly shut. Nurse DeFazio pushed Dorothy into the bath and shower room and bent down to her: "Ms. Padilla will be in in just a moment to help you clean up and be nice and fresh for tea. And don't worry about Mr. Zimmerman, he's just being a bother."

"Huh!" Dorothy snorted, "He just wants the same thing they all want. All men want the same thing." She shifted in her chair and stared at the tile floor.

"Ok, well I'll leave you to Ms. Padilla," she replied as Angela came through the door.

Carol Ann exited swiftly, Dorothy already railing at Angela, hiding her embarrassment in a barrage of invective too anonymous and rambling to really cause the aide serious injury. She moved briskly down the hall and stopped to rap lightly on Mr. Kinney's door. "Mr. Kinney?"

"What is it?" came a muffled reply. She cracked the door open and called again.

"Mr. Kinney, it's Nurse DeFazio, I'm here to say hello and give you an ElderGrove welcome basket."

"A basket? Oh, well then, fine, fine, come in. Ooo, a basket." His voice was mockingly confident, even sharp. She pushed through the door and saw Mr. Kinney sitting up in his bed, fully dressed in slacks, a yellow shirt, and a herringbone suit coat. His socks were the same color as his shirt, and he peered at her under bushy white eyebrows, over a pair of rimless glasses.

"Well hello, miss—what did you say your name was?"

"I'm Nurse DeFazio, I'm the director here at ElderGrove. At the East Wing, that is, Nurse Pinsky is the director of the West Wing, but you won't have much contact with her, I'm sure,—" she felt herself rambling nervously, without knowing why, which made her ramble further: "though of course she does a fine job, very professional and very thorough, but in any case, I brought you this—" she deposited the basket on the table beside Mr. Kinney's bed and sat stiffly in the chair beyond it. "Did you sleep well, Mr. Kinney?"

"Not really, but thanks for asking nurse—what is your name, your given name?" he answered, setting the book on his lap.

"Ah, well, Carol Ann, but here at ElderGrove—"

"Carol Ann, very good, very country, if you don't mind my saying, in a good way of course. I'm Thomas, though I much prefer to be called Tom, and no I didn't sleep well, I had very peculiar dreams that kept me awake most of the night." He sighed, rested his hands on his chest, and closed his eyes.

Carol Ann continued feeling unaccountably flustered. "Well, ah, I'm sorry to hear that, but let's back up a bit here, at ElderGrove, we all refer to one another as 'Mr.' and 'Mrs.,' not by our first names, so—please, if we could do that."

"Of course, Carol Ann, I understand, you can call me Mrs. Kinney, in that case."

"Mrs. Kinney?"

"Yes, is that not right? My significant other passed away some years ago, but it is not the habit of widows to revert to the pre-lapsarian 'Miss', is it?" He chuckled lightly. "I'm joking, of course, my dear, so sorry. You will soon learn that old Tom has little left that works aside from his sense of humor, his sense of smell, and of course his impeccable dress sense." He smiled primly at Carol Ann, tilting his head backwards to spy her reaction through his glasses.

"I see. I really would prefer Nurse DeFazio, it helps so much to make all the residents feel—to feel worthwhile, I think, if the staff and residents refer to one another with the proper titles. But I won't make you do anything you don't want to do. Just don't be surprised if I fail to answer to 'Carol Ann', no one calls me that except my mother. Even my significant other doesn't call me that."

"Really," Tom replied, "and what does she call you, if I may be so bold?"

"Annie. She calls me Annie."

"Well, Annie, so glad to make your acquaintance, and happy we could reach this understanding."

"Certainly, Mr. Kinney. Is there anything else I can do for you? Some of the other residents will have tea soon, it's kind of a tradition here, and I'm sure, with your exceptional sense of smell, you noticed the wonderful smells coming from the kitchen?"

"I have, and I would be glad to join everyone shortly. Do you know why?"

Carol Ann began to suspect Mr. Kinney could get very annoying very quickly. "Why?"

"Because of the dreams that kept me up all night long. Should I tell you what they were about?"

"Ok, if it doesn't take too long, I'm really very busy today."

"I promise to be concise. But first, let me tell you that when I arrived last night, at the behest of my daughter, who claims I am unable to take care of myself and need the kind of 'assistance' you provide at this wonderful facility, baskets and whatnot, well, I did not want to be here, not in this room, not in this building, not on this earth. No, she didn't coerce me, I came as a favor to her, she has a very difficult and confusing life, as do so many people these days. I almost think it's harder to be a black woman today then it was 40 years ago. Well, no, I know that's not true, but it is hard in different ways. Regardless, I was here, and I didn't want to be, and then one of your employees deposited some terrible imitation of food on that same table where your basket now sits, so I fell asleep with the reek of it in my nose. That might account for the dreams which followed: I found myself falling, as so often happens in dreams, but then I slowed, and was falling like Alice down the rabbit hole, watching bits of my life float by me. I won't bore you with those, but at some point I stopped falling and was simply floating in the air, and I heard a voice ask me if I wanted a chair. 'Yes, please,' I said, and a chair appeared and I was already sitting in it and there was Hector, my love, my partner, my beautiful mocha man, standing in front of me, but he had no head. 'How are you, Tom?' he said, but he had no head, as I said, and I looked and his face was in the center of his chest. 'I'm fine, why is your head—'

'I'm so sorry you ended up here,' he told me, and then he said 'I am waiting, you know, but you have work to do,' and I realized he was now talking from my earlobe, he had apparently metamorphosed into my earring, this one," and he touched a small gold hoop in his right hear. "It was very strange, but then I always have very strange dreams."

"Yes, sounds like it," Carol Ann said, and stood to go.

"Wait, wait, I'm almost done," he continued. She remained standing, a hand on her hip. "Then I heard music, and I was still sitting but I was in the Copacabana, do you remember that place?"

"A little before my time, I'm afraid, but I know of it."

"Well, there was this sister there who did a Carmen Miranda routine, exceptional talent, Puerto Rican, I think, before all this silicone and botox. 'You have work to do here. Later we can be together,' Carmen said, but with Hector's voice, and her lips didn't move, I mean she wasn't a ventriloquist, she was a drag queen! And I looked, and Hector's face was on one of the grapes in her hat!"

Carol Ann smiled. "Nice place for a rest."

"I'm sure he thought so, he loved fruit. 'What kind of work,' I asked him.

'You have to race,' he said. Now this was confusing, I mean, I can walk to the corner store, but really.

'I don't think I'm really able to do that, love."

'Yes, a race toward understanding. Once you understand, the race is over. What happens afterward is up to you.' Now this is very vague, and very unlike Hector, did I mention he was Professor of Classics at the University of Toledo? No? He was, and as a result, he was a very particular, very direct, very concrete person, he wasn't prone to speaking in parables, unless he was quoting someone. But, it was a dream, he was trying his best to oracular. So I asked him a questions: 'How long will I waste away in this place?'

'What happens afterward is up to you,' he repeated.

'What does that mean?'

'Whatever happens will be your decision,' he said, and then poof! I woke up and smelled the stink of corn coming out of the wastepaper basket." He stopped and laced his fingers together across his chest.

"Well that is a very involved dream, indeed. Will be you be joining the other residents for tea?" Carol Ann said, opening the door to leave.

"I will, I said I would, but first, please, one more question."

Carol Ann sighed. "Ok, Mr. Kinney."

"What, Annie, do you think it means?" He tilted his head and narrowed his eyes.

"Honestly, Mr. Kinney, I haven't he foggiest idea."

"Neither have I, my dear, neither have I," Tom answered, and swung his legs off the bed into a pair of wingtips waiting on the rug beside his bed. "Perhaps we will both find out soon enough."

"Maybe so, Mr. Kinney. Please enjoy the welcome basket, it has schedule of activities, a welcome card—well, you can peruse it at your leisure."

"I certainly will."

Need to keep an eye on that one, Carol Ann thought as she left the room and navigated the small crowd gathering near the day room tables. In his room, squinting at himself in the woefully inadequate mirror, Thomas Kinney thought the same thing.

****

Mr. Zimmerman loved tea. He also loved Mrs. Newell, who he insisted on calling Dorothy, despite Nurse DeFazio's insistence on the use of titles. He loved her because she reminded him of his first love, a trick rider named Vera who introduced him to the wonders of human lovemaking on a hay bale in the backyard, behind the tents and trailers, following the last night of a week-long stint flaking the rubes in Macon, Georgia. He was fifteen years old, short and skinny, and had been traveling with the circus for little more than a year, having fled his drunken father's roaring fists and begged his way onto the caravan the same night he first saw the charivari, the mad spilling out of clowns, stumbling and kicking and hitting one another. "I can do that," he thought, and he did, though his apprenticeship would last two more years. He was primarily a character clown, usually Paddy the Cop, though later he just did the come in and small gags for the kids. He knew Dorothy was not Vera, but sometimes he got confused and damn if she didn't look just like Vera, and other times he just liked poking at her, calling her "possum belly queen," making faces at her while she tried to watch television, and prank calling her cell phone, pretending he was Publisher's Clearinghouse or the United Underwear Inspection Association. His affection for her was the reason he was so glum at afternoon tea, since Dorothy had declined to attend after her accident. He wasn't glum enough to decline a hefty slice of Mrs. Treadwell's red velvet cake, of course, and so he sat, shoveling forkfuls into his mouth, while Tom folded his body into an empty chair near the window.

Mr. Zimmerman looked side-eyed at Tom, filled his mouth again, and said "Humpphheedo."

"Hello," Tom answered.

"Mr. Kinney, so glad you could join us," Carol Ann called from across the table, where she stood plating pieces of cake. "Angela, this is Mr. Kinney," she continued, a signal for Angela to introduce him to the other residents. But Angela froze instead, as did most of the residents, forks poised in mid-air. Carol Ann glanced around, confused.

"Is something wrong?" she asked.

"Wha, ah, you called me 'Angela,'" Angela answered.

"Oh no I surely did not," Carol Ann replied. The residents

answered as a group, oh yes, you did, you sure did, we heard it, everyone mumbled and nodded at one another.

"Well," Carol Ann reddened, "I'm so sorry! My own rule and I just absolutely forgot! How awful. Ms. Padilla," she said, dragging the vowels out, "this is Mr. Kinney, our new resident." She finished with an awkward sweep of her hand.

"Hello, Mr. Kinney," Angela said, nodding her head.

"Hello, Tom, please," he answered, pinching at the sugar bags with his fingers, bent inwards with arthritis.

"What's that?"

"Tom. I would prefer to be called Tom. Is that alright with everyone?"

Thus did the residents of the ElderGrove Residential Living Community, East Wing, separate themselves into two tribes, those who preferred to retain the honorific "Misters" and "Misses" and those who preferred to use their first names. It was extraordinarily confusing at first, and not much less confusing afterward, but everyone grew accustomed to being called the wrong sort of name once in a while and so didn't get too bent out of shape about it. Tom was Tom, or "Mrs. Kinney," if you forgot and used "Mr.," Angela was happy to be Angela, Dorothy was Dorothy, and Cameron, who didn't even work there anymore, had always been just Cam, as somehow he had eluded the whole titular convention from the start. Mr. Zimmerman chose to stay Mr. Zimmerman, which surprised many people, and of course Carol Ann was Nurse DeFazio. There were a few outliers: Mrs. Treadwell claimed she couldn't remember her first name, Mr. Gladwell asked to be called "Frank," though his given name was Albert, and Chris Park, to further his dream of becoming the first Korean-American rapper from the greater Toledo area, insisted on being called "C-Spot," though no one ever remembered, no matter how often her reminded them.

Now allied in two tribes, some of the residents began

competing with one another in small, friendly ways: Frank and Mr. Zimmerman's weekly Parcheesi game, for example, grew into a heated, team-based, best-of-five series that left everyone exhausted. Often, without intending to, the Misters and Misses would sit together in the dining room by the door, while the first-namers would gather closer to the entrance to the kitchen. There was talk of t-shirts and bowling jackets, of trips to play shuffleboard, of scavenger hunts; then someone's granddaughter brought her a Wii, and bowling tournaments were the rage for several weeks, until Mr. Zimmerman broke it trying to do a magic trick Just as quickly, the tribal competitions ceased, though the naming conventions stuck, and every new resident and employee was asked, upon arrival, which they preferred. Carol Ann took it all in stride, though she never could get the hang of using first names and so stuck with titles. Except when speaking with Tom, that is. When she told Maggie about the new resident and his refusal to use "Mister"—and his salty insistence on being called "Misses," if it came to that—her love nearly choked on a piece of kiwi, so hard was she laughing.

"It's not that funny," Carol Ann said, wiping Maggie's mouth with a napkin.

"Yeah, yeah, it really is," Maggie answered. "You take yourself too seriously. Your chi is seriously blocked, my friend. You need to loosen up." She dipped her spoon back in her bowl of fruit.

"I'm plenty loose, I just thought it helped them with self-respect issues."

"Right, see," Maggie pointed her spoon at Carol Ann, "that's what I mean. Who has the self-respect issues, really? Come on Annie, don't you think you're projecting?

"Don't do that, don't analyze me, You're not an analyst."

"Nope, you're right, I'm not." Maggie rose and went into the kitchen. Carol Ann wondered why she'd been so prickly lately, digging into Carol Ann, then leaving the room, leaving the conversation unresolved, the jibes hanging in mid-air. She's been this way before, always just before she cheated on me, felt awful about it, and came home crying, admitting all, wanting redemption from Carol Ann. It's the redemption part she wants, not the sex, she just wants to be forgiven. Now who sounds like an analyst, Carol Ann thought. "I'm going to get some wine," Maggie yelled from the kitchen.

Carol Ann called back "ok," softly enough, she hoped, that Maggie would hear the pain in her voice and come back and kiss her, hard and long. She heard the door open and close, breathed deeply, and pulled a blanket off the back of the couch to wrap around her shoulders.

Chapter 3

The snow had melted from the tops of the little brown hillocks beside the East Wing when, three weeks later then he'd promised, Cam returned to ElderGrove. The wet matted grass and mud rising from the snow looked to him like the backs of whales arching up out of the water, or blisters on dark skin, like when he got sun blisters as a kid and they popped and stung. Or, it could be Cam hadn't been getting enough sleep and was smoking way too much weed. He'd dutifully left messages for Mrs. Treadwell each time his dickhead boss had scheduled him for double shifts after first Mandy, then Jill, both quit. The boss's constant stream of sexual innuendo surely had something to do with their leaving, though he was entirely too pathetic for anyone to take seriously, even as a creeper. He treated Cam with locker room camaraderie, despite Cam's lack of reciprocation, and often, comprehension: what the hell was a "sko," anyway? He kept meaning to look up some of the slang that fell out of the guy's mouth, but once work was over, he always found something better to do. Clyde might know what some of the words meant, and Cam's brother Dylan would definitely know, but that would mean talking to him, something Cam tried to avoid at all costs. Trying not to think about Dylan reminded Cam his Dad's birthday was coming up, which reminded him he'd forgotten his Mom's birthday until his Dad texted him to say he'd gotten her a card and a gift certificate to Bed,

Bath, and Beyond and signed it from the boys. So much guilt, so little time.

The sun ricocheted off the front windows of the East Wing and blinded Cam as he made his way to the door. The West Wing loomed darkly to his right, blocked from direct sun by a row of pine. When Aames ElderCare presented architectural drawings of the proposed new wing to the Candler City Council, the two buildings looked like two welcoming hands, as though you could drive up the traffic circle and have a hug as you helped your loved ones out from the back seat and said goodbye. When it came time to build, the expense of shifting the driveway proved too great, and the West Wing was built slightly more than perpendicular to the East, so the West Wing now appeared to be staring disapprovingly at the East Wing's front door. Hence Cam's sensation, every time he visited, that someone was staring at him from behind his back.

"Hi Cam," said Angela, sitting behind desk in the lobby.

"Hi Angela," Cam answered. Angela's beauty froze his brain, and the distance he perceived between their lives—an impossibly sexy single mother of two who liked mofongo and baccalaitos, and a pasty animation geek from the suburbs who had to look up mofongo and baccalaitos on the internet after she mentioned them—kept it frozen most of the time she was around, until it got annoyed at being frozen, and made him mad at her.

"You haven't been around for a while. Here to see Mrs. Treadwell?"

"Yeah, I mean, yes, her and maybe some other folks too, I have the whole night off."

"Well," Angela leaned over the counter conspiratorially, causing Cam's spleen to twitch, "you want some good stories, we got two new peoples in here that are just wild." She glanced to the side as she said wild, as though someone might hear and take offense. Cam's spleen twitched again.

"Oh yeah? Two?"

"Oh yes, one, Tom Kinney, he make Nurse DeFazio call him Tom, do you believe that? He's a riot, very crafty, I like him right away. And then just yesterday, this new guy, Bob, Bob, um... well I can't remember the last name but he want everyone to call him Magoo!" She laughed silently to herself.

"Magoo? Wow. No more mister and missus?" Cam squinted down the hall, curious and, unaccountably, a bit frightened.

"No, Mr. Tom, I mean Tom, you know, he just said, 'no, I'm Tom, and if you want to call me something else, you can call me Mrs. Kinney!" An audible laugh escaped Angela this time.

"Mrs. Kinney? I don't—"

"He's funny, you know, he's gay."

"Oh, right." Cam's Uncle Garret was gay, and also a minister at the First Unitarian Church of Toledo, and also a distinguished philatelist, and Cam had a hard time imagining him demanding to be referred to as "Mrs. Casey."

"And then the Magoo man gets here yesterday and oh my god, a lo loco. The mouth on that one." Cam felt the front door open and Angela smiled quickly at him, then looked over his shoulder at whomever had just entered. "Hello, welcome to ElderGrove Residential Living Facility!"

Cam went down the hall and entered the day room, wondering what penance Angela was serving by working the front desk. She was a nurses' aide, not a receptionist, but this wasn't the first time he'd seen her there. DeFazio moved her staff around a lot, he'd noticed. She probably thought it made them happier. She had a lot of ideas about what made people happy, for someone who seemed not very happy herself—not unhappy, just not really firmly grasping what happiness meant. And there she was, behind the counter of the nurses station, separated by a wall and swinging door from the reception area. Cam looked blankly at the grey filing cabinets, the medicine locker, the small brigade of trolls and teddy bears, and the dry-erase board scrawled with arcane palimpsests.

"Hello, Cameron." Carol Ann nodded and squinted her eyes. She was wearing glasses, Cam noticed, did she always have glasses? "Here to see Mrs. Treadwell?" Before he could answer, a hoarse, drunken voice bellowed from the back of the room behind him:

"Where the fuck is my headband!"

Carol Ann's face shrunk to an edge. "Excuse me, Cam. I'll see if Mrs. Treadwell is awake."

"What the shit...." Cam turned and saw Rae, one of the new nurses' aides, handing a tall, pantless man in a wheelchair a brownish handkerchief tied in a loop. He plopped it on his head with one hand and tried to pull down one side, then the other, until the left side hung over his eye. Rae quickly adjusted it for him before he could bellow again, and then Carol Ann was at his side, talking quietly, very close to his ear. "Yeah, yeah, sure thing, Nurse Ratchett," he mumbled, loudly enough for everyone to hear as Rae led him back down the hall. Carol Ann followed them through the doorway. At the day room tables, an ocean of whispers began to ripple.

Cam smiled and waved "hello" to Frank, who had raised his own hand in greeting, then gone back to whispering with Mary Rose. Cam knew all the residents in the room, and a few of them—Frank, Mary Rose, Eustace—had been here since he had first volunteered here, his senior year of high school, six years ago. Man, six years and what have I done. Carol Ann came down the hall with Mrs. Treadwell in tow, frowning faintly, as always, beneath her wispy shawl.

"Here she is Cam," Carol Ann said, presenting Mrs. Treadwell with a flourish, a bit like a game show model. "And I'm sorry for the, ah, the noise before, someone's just having a little trouble adjusting to ElderGrove is all."

"He's an ass," Mrs. Treadwell added.

"Well, he should be just fine as soon as he..." she searched the ceiling for a better word, and found none: "adjusts."

"He's one of the new residents Angela told me about?" Cam asked, once Carol Ann had settled Mrs. Treadwell into her chair and gone back to the nurses' station.

"Yes, he's a big jerk. A blowhard. I don't like him."

"Who's the other new guy?"

"Oh Tom? He's very nice, he's very quiet. He stays to himself quite a bit, he likes to stay in his room and read, he says, but he's colored so you never really know. What he's up to, I mean. Strange architecture. And he comes to tea and is very nice, that's the only time he comes out and mixes, except sometimes at breakfast. Oh and he likes to watch Project Runway with Dorothy."

"Really? He sounds interesting, maybe he'd like to do a recording." Mrs. Treadwell's stories were bizarre and thus interesting to Cam, but their very oddness was becoming predictable.

"Oh maybe, I don't know, well you know I have the best stories anyway."

"Yes, you do, you really do. What are you making for tea today?"

Mrs. Treadwell darkened. "Nothing. We can't have tea today because of that man, that awful man. And because Talisha quit, the stupid girl, and because Kent was fired, you know the skinny man with the things on his neck?"

"Yeah, I remember, he wasn't here very long."

"No, not long at all, now he's gone. They caught him stealing, I think."

"Oh. Well that's sad." Stealing what, Cam wondered. No one here had anything to steal.

"Never mind, at least we can have a story. Did you bring your machine?"

"Sure, yes," Cam answered distractedly, watching as Rae wheeled the bellowing man, now quietly fiddling with a pile of beads, into the day room. He turned back and smiled at Mrs. Treadwell and took out his recorder and microphone, setting them in front of her expectant face.

"So, do you have a story in mind?"

"I do, I do, more than one, oh my... you didn't visit me for a while but I knew you would come, I wrote notes to myself so I would remember them," she replied, taking some folded, wrinkled papers out of the pocket of her robe.

"Great. Well, let's start," Cam said, pressing the "record" and "play" buttons.

"Yes, just let me think for a minute." Cam waited for her to collect herself. She seems to go into a kind of trance, he thought, it still gives me a shiver, I can feel her getting far away but more present too, somehow. "The hell is this panty-eater?" The bellowing man bellowed again suddenly, startling Cam and Mrs. Treadwell both. Cam turned in his chair and saw the man staring at him. "Pardon?" he asked.

"Pardon? What are you, a canuck?"

"A what now?"

"Canadian, are you from Canada, panty-eater?"

Cam stared unsteadily for a moment before replying. The man was quite tall and so was folded into his chair painfully, sitting largely on one hip, his legs thrust out at different angles. His head was colossal, mangled like a boxer's but sharply defined all the same, nose bent in three places, one cheekbone rising, the other crushed nearly concave, dark eyes twitching ferally beneath monstrous white eyebrows, like a cat hiding under a hedge.

"Jesus are you a retard, too?" Cam snapped out of his daze.

"No, I'm not retarded, I'm not Canadian, and I don't think we've met," he said, tightening angrily. Like his father, he grew more formal when confronted, which made him seem more aloof, which usually made his antagonist more confrontational, which made him grow even more formal. He often attributed his lack of a steady girlfriend to this behavior.

"He's a louse, is who he is," Mrs. Treadwell said over his shoulder.

"And you're a scabby old bitch," said the man in the wheelchair. "And my name's Magoo, that's who. If you ain't Canadian and you ain't retarded, what the fuck are you?"

"My name is Cam. I come here to, ah, record people's stories, like Mrs. Treadwell here." He patted Mrs. Treadwell's hand and both of them recoiled. He'd forgotten how cold and papery her hands were.

"Stories? Well shit, what kind of stories can a dried up skank like her tell?"

"I told you he was a louse. Foul-mouthed and foul-minded, buffoon architecture," Mrs. Treadwell answered.

"And you can kiss my hairy, shriveled asshole, sister," Magoo bellowed, arms starting to flail.

Carol Ann appeared suddenly at the table. "Mr. Magoo. Please calm down, we've spoken about this before," she said, interjecting herself between Magoo and Cam.

"Ah shit," Magoo mumbled as Carol Ann rolled him toward the back of the room. Mrs. Treadwell sat, hands folded in her lap, shaking softly. "I'm sorry," she whispered to Cam.

"Sorry? Oh no, it's not your fault," Cam replied, almost putting his hand on hers again, "he interrupted you, I'm sorry I didn't handle it better."

"He's scared, a scared man with not much left other than fear to cling to," she answered. They watched as Carol Ann spoke quietly to him, then walked back to the table where Cam had set the recorder. "Cam, could I ask you a favor?"

"Sure," he nodded.

"I know you promised Mrs. Treadwell you would meet with her today, but do you think you could spend a little time with Mr. Magoo first? Recording him, I mean. I just think it's so wonderful what you do, it helps everyone so much, isn't that right Mrs. Treadwell?"

"But it's my turn! I have some stories!" Mrs. Treadwell shook the small pile of wrinkled notes in the air.

"I know, I know it is, and if Cam has time he can work with you afterward, buy I really think it would help Mr. Magoo cope, I mean, he needs help adjusting or things will continue being hard on us all." She smiled sharply, a smile that demanded compliance.

"Sure, ok, if that's ok with Mrs. Treadwell, I'm good with that," Cam folded.

"But it's my turn!" Mrs. Treadwell demanded, then huffed, rose more quickly than Cam thought she could, and brushed by into the kitchen.

"Thank you, Cameron," Carol Ann said. "I'll go get Mr. Magoo."

Magoo seemed sedate again, almost catatonic, as she wheeled him to the table. His eyes were unfocused, watery, under droopy lids. "Mr. Magoo, Cam here is interested in collecting oral histories, isn't that what they're called, Cam?"

"Uh, sure, I just call them stories, we can talk about whatever."

"Right, well, Mr. Magoo, I think Cam would like to record some of your, of your reminiscences, if that's ok with you."

Magoo wobbled his head upwards to look in Carol Ann's general direction, then nodded crookedly.

"Wonderful, ok then, I'll just leave you to it. Do you need anything, Cam?"

"Nope, I'm good, thanks."

"Wonderful," Carol Ann repeated to herself as she drifted away. As soon as she was out of earshot, Magoo fixed Cam with a glare. "Jesus, she gives me gas."

"Ah, well—"

"Can you get me some dope?"

"Pardon?"

"Cut the 'pardon' shit, panty-eater, you said you ain't Canadian so cut it. Dope. Smoke, reefer, weed, grass, pot, mary jane—"

"Yeah, yeah, I know what it is."

"So can you get me some? How much is a half ounce?" Magoo twisted his head to look at Cam with just his right eye.

"Um, yeah, I can get you some—wait, you're joking, right?"

"Not joking. Want dope. This place is fucking boring enough without it. Legs don't work, palsy makes me shit myself, left eye nearly gone, DOPE!" He thundered the last word and several residents turned to look, then remembered they'd decided to ignore him.

"Ok, yeah, a half is usually one-sixty."

" A hundred sixty dollars! Christ, what's it grown in gold flake and watered with pussy juice? Ok, how 'bout just a quarter then. A hundred and fucking sixty dollars, criminal. You know I'm on a fixed income, right?" Cam suspected he was joking, but wasn't sure if it was at his own expense.

"I figured, sure."

"And some papers. And a lighter," Magoo added.

"Fine, I can get those. If you start a fire—"

"I won't start a fire, and I won't snitch. Do I look like a fucking snitch? " Magoo turned his head back so he was looking straight at Cam.

"I don't know what a snitch looks like," Cam admitted.

"Well they usually have a big fucking scar right here," Magoo replied, drawing a line with a bent finger from the corner of his mouth to his ear.

"Really, I never heard that," Cam replied, and reached to turn on the recorder.

"What what, what are you doing with that?" Magoo belched.

"I'm going to record you, remember?"

"Fuck that, I just wanted some dope."

"Ok, I'll get you some weed, but you have to tell me a story in exchange, like how you know about the squealer scar."

"What? Everybody knows that, everybody who ain't panty-eater," Magoo shifted in his chair.

"Well where did you learn it?"

"Fucking prison, what do you think? Boy are you thick."

Cam pressed the "record" button. "Why were you in prison?"

"Which time?"

"Ok, how many times were you in prison?"

"I spent three years in juvie, three years in Riker's island, five years in San Quentin, and eleven years in Pleasant Valley. After that stretch, I decided fuck prison, never went back." Cam felt himself staring again.

"Why did you go? If you don't mind my asking."

"I don't give a fuck what you ask, panty-eater. I was in juvie for stealing cars and shit, the usual, then did the Riker's stretch because I didn't do nothing, not a goddamn thing, I took the fall for some bitch, stupidest thing I ever did. San Quentin because they caught me with a shitload of speed, then Pleasant Valley because someone else was gonna drop a dime on me and I beat his ass for it, some little wetback shithead thought he could get over on me."

"You—what did you do to him?"

"Manslaughter, 'cept he wasn't a man, he was a pussy."

"Wow." Cam sat, transfixed by the tiny red "recording" light.

"Yeah, whatever. That enough to get me some dope?"

"How did you not go back, after that? I mean what did you do?" Cam plundered on.

"What do you mean what did I do? I didn't go back, I stopped running with the Red and White, married a good bitch, worked on bikes and kept my nose clean. Well, pretty clean," he chuckled to himself. It sounded like someone farting in a bathtub.

"What's the 'Red and White'?" Cam asked. Magoo squinted.

"You don't know anything, do you? You a Catholic school boy?"

"Me? No," Cam answered.

"Red and White is the Angels, baby, the one percent of the one percent, my family, the best fucking motorcycle club in the universe."

"You were a Hells Angel?"

"Fuckin' right."

Cam began to think of an avatar for Magoo, started storyboarding in his head. This could get good.

"So you must have some crazy stories, then, like—I don't know, when were you in the Hells Angels."

"I'm still a fucking Angel, ain't no retiring from the Angels. I just couldn't hang, fucking parole kept me away from my brothers. I got prospected in '61, went out to Cali after I got outta juvie, had enough of fucking New York so I got on my bike and rode. Went Full-Patch in '62."

"Full patch?"

"Full member, voting rights, got my colors all straight, Eight and one."

"Wow."

"Yeah, you said that."

"You must have been to some kick-ass parties."

Magoo's eyes squinted even more, and Cam wondered if he'd fallen asleep. After a long pause, his voice came, weary and distant. "Tell you what, Canuck. I'll tell you a story, a story about how I met my lady, goddamn, that was a party alright."

"Ok."

Magoo shifted his hips, let out a little strand of drool,

and settled into the chair. "First met Jeanie in '66, she was my brother Danny's lady, course I knew Danny already and maybe they wasn't really together...no, they was together, Danny was just a crazy fucker. Bit a guy's nose off once and later PJ says to me, 'Magoo, you see Danny bit that fucker's nose off?' and I says, 'yeah, so', not so big a thing, but then he says 'yeah, you see him spit it out?' And no, I sure didn't, the fucker chewed it up and ate it. But he was my brother and I wouldn't let some pussy get between us, but... wait, anyway, where was I, oh yeah, they had this big party out on Kesey's place, down in La Honda, we drove down from Burdoo and it was fucking wild, man, half the fucking people were naked and half were, I don't know painted or something, skinny little bitches dressed as clowns, making it with anyone, and of course it was Kesey so the fucking wine, the fucking wine was loaded with acid, everybody was flipping out and just—"

"Wait, you mean Ken Kesey?" Cam interjected.

"No, Casey at the bat, of course Ken Kesey, one flew over the cuckoo's nest but most of'em just stayed there, in the nest with the cuckoo, eating fucking acid and staring at the clouds. And all this weird noise, like they hid speakers in weird places, I was talking to Cheater and we heard some kind of evil fucking head on fire music coming out of a tree, Cheater climbed up there and pulled the speaker down and we stomped on it and set it on fire, all these fucking naked little girls just standing around going, 'wow'..." Magoo fell silent.

"So, you met Jeannie—"

"Yeah, I know, I'm thinking, Jesus, I'm old, brain don't work so good anymore. Fuck. Jeannie, right, she was Danny's lady, or at least he brung her down, and they got in some of the acid wine, and a bunch of us was around in this room, playing some game one of the naked chicks was doing, maybe we was bangin'er I don't know, hard to bang a bitch when your face is melting and the sky is purple, ha, and then, and I don't know what happened, but we heard someone screaming, then calling for us, calling for me and Cheater and Sonny and PJ and we run out and Danny's got Jeannie on the ground, got his foot on her neck, got a fucking pistol from somewhere, was supposed to be no guns at this thing, just pussy and acid and lots of dope. So he's waving this gun at her, foaming at the mouth, no one knows what he's saying, Sonny tells me go calm him down, I was always good like that, I could talk brothers out of stupid shit every time, so I started talking really quiet next to Danny, real quiet, shit like, 'you the king, man, you don't need to prove it, feel that breath, man, feel it goin' in and comin' out…" Cam felt his own breathing matching the rhythm of his words. "Then he just, runs. Drop the gun, shrieks like a fucking girl, and runs off into the woods. We didn't see him for three months, he was kinda retarded after that, couldn't do shit like remember how to start his hog all the time, or anybody's' name. We kept him around 'cause, who else wanted him? Sonny had him do errands and shit, then after a year or two he just took off again. I saw him maybe fifteen, twenty years later, just got out of the pen, he was standing on a corner in Haight with a whole bunch of jackets on, no shoes, just rocking back and forth on the corner. Part of why I took Jeannie and said let's get the fuck out of here, go back East."

"That's when you got together with her? I thought—"

"No, no, we already was together, she waited for me while I did my stretch. Well, she fucked around a little, but mostly she waited. She was a good woman."

"Did you—what happened after Danny ran off? At the party, I mean," Cam said, trying not to sound impatient. Magoo looked puzzled, then a gear clicked.

"Right, so, he took off, and I picked her up and damn, if she wasn't about as fine a piece of ass as I'd ever seen.

Hadn't noticed when we was riding down, I mean, you don't look at a brother's bitch less you want trouble from every angle. I picked her up and brushed her off and asked if she was ok and she said 'yeah' and then she was gone, just disappeared somewhere. Acid'll do that, you know. I was just staring at the piece of ground where she been standin'. So, yep, had some pussy hankering bad, now, she was gone, went and found me a skinny, crazy-eyed little bitch, started making it with her, she climbs up on me and pulls out the gun, same fucking gun, don't know where she got it, where she hid it, there it was, and she says, 'oh baby, you make me feel so good, I'm gonna cum,' waving this pistol, rubbing it on her face and shit, I'm getting a little nervous, don't want my noodle to go soft with this crazy bitch on me, then she says, 'take it baby, take this gun and you put it to my head, and when I cum, I want you to blow my fucking brains out, I wanna cum and die all at once, up into the cosmic rain, baby', some shit like that, so I grab the gun and flip us both over and fuck her good and hard and she comes and I put the gun to her head and yell 'BANG'!" Cam and everyone else in the day room jumped, and Angela poked her head out from the nurse's station: "Everything ok, Cam?"

"Uh, yeah, fine, just some stories," he answered. Magoo was clucking softly to himself. He lifted his head and went on: "Bang, baby, bang, I yelled it and you know what? She shit. She came and shit at the same time, this scary little albino looking turd fell out of her ass, I know 'cause I rolled in it getting off her. Psycho pussy, man, keep away, keep away."

"Wow, that's, that's pretty messed up."

"Yeah, it was pretty fucking weird."

"So, then later you found Jeannie again?"

"Fuck later, I found her that morning. I was about off pussy totally, wandering around drinking wine, smoking, eating more acid, and there comes the sun across the mountains and there comes Jeannie, walking down toward me, an angel. And she took me right in her arms and off into the field we went and she lay me down and lifted her dress and you know, she had these two little legs, tiny little dwarf baby legs growing out the inside of her, uh, her left thigh, said they was her twin sister that died in her momma. She started stroking my joint with those little toes, boy, I tell you what, I never looked at another woman again. I fucked a bunch, but never looked at'em, ha!" He started cooing again. Cam reached over and pressed the "record" button, sat back, and shook his head.

"Can I get some dope now?" Magoo asked after a long pause.

"Absolutely," Cam answered. "I'll bring it tomorrow."

****

That evening, Cam stuffed Kubrick, his bong, with some of the weed he'd gotten for Magoo and marveled at his luck. Magoo seemed like the real deal, a Hell's Angel from the days when that meant something, gadfly to hippie ground zero, surely his stories would only get better and better. He'd played it dumb, of course, he'd figured out as much when he did his first interview with Mr. Highsmith, a nuclear bomber pilot whose recall of events was more impressionistic than factual, and when Cam pointed out some inconsistencies, Highsmith got huffy and refused to do another recording, then died before Cam could convince him otherwise. Playing dumb came naturally to Cam, as it did many of his friends, male and female alike, who'd learned that revealing knowledge meant people judged you differently, often trying to make you bear some new responsibility. Ambition, passion, curiosity: these were the traits that made people stand out, that made the great sifting mechanism of school and church and club mark a life "special," and special meant pain and struggle and stress and a teenage Xanax addiction. Better to seem clueless and stay happy.

He put on his headphones and found some threesome porn on the internet, did another bong hit, and masturbated, Magoo's voice coughing in his ears, the girls on the screen red-lipped and awkward, bandying an anonymous cock back and forth between their mouths. Once he had finished and cleaned himself up, he started the recording again, this time in front of a story board, sketching ideas for the animation. This could be the one, he told himself, the one that goes viral and gets me the fuck out of Candler City for good, out to L.A or somewhere interesting, somewhere he could have a job that made two girls want to fuck him. Or one, at least, that would be a good start. Treadwell's stuff was too made up, too obviously straining for weirdness, and she was the best he'd found, the clown guy was promising but he kept getting lost in dirty jokes, Highsmith died, and his war stories were just too corny anyway, everyone else was just... old, just boring and old and regretful, wondering how they'd gotten so old and amazed at the meaninglessness of their lives. I don't want to be them, Cam told himself again, it was a mantra, I don't want to die wishing I'd done different, and this Magoo guy, wow. A few more stories like this and I might have enough for a feature short. His phone buzzed and he ignored it, too stoned and too far into the story board to care, and if they didn't text, it was his Mom or Boss Dickhead anyway. He sat back, fingers stinging from the flurry of sketching. Yes, this is good, good shit, he thought, and turned back to the computer, fresh tissues drawn and placed beside the bottle of lotion, purposeful and delicate as a shroud.

Chapter 4

Angela was pissed. For the second day in a row, she had "welcome duty," as Nurse DeFazio called it, sitting at the front desk while the new aide, some skinny little puta who looked like she knew her way around a crack pipe, got her training checklist done and signed off. Chris could sit here and answer the phone, he was off at four anyway, but DeFazio said Angela was more "palatable" for visitors, whatever that meant. It wasn't like Chris was going to rap at people coming through the door, or practice his gangster glare on them, and it wouldn't be that hard to cover the neck tattoo, let him wear a scarf. So, despite her insistence that wiping bottoms was preferable to greeting visitors and answering the phone, there she was, a licensed Patient Care Assistant, greeting visitors and answering the phone. Coupled with the fact that no one, other than the small group of residents who'd taken the shuttle to the grocery store, had come through the front door all morning, and that no one, other than Doctor Small, announcing he would, as usual, be late for his weekly walkthrough—she doubted he would show up at all—had, to judge by the call log, phoned ElderGrove since yesterday afternoon, Angela was nearly ready to quit. There were other jobs, didn't DeFazio know that? Other facilities without strange rules, like asking people who needed sponge baths which hand they preferred you use, or the weekly reflective reports all the aides had to write. Not that she didn't find the reports weirdly fun and useful, she did, despite a feeling of apprehension that grew as the Sunday evening due date approached, but it was the nature of the thing, the fact that DeFazio had all these weird rules, rules like nowhere else Angela worked, rules that seemed stupid and were sometimes stupid but other times were really helpful, and it was the latter occasions that were more disconcerting, since she couldn't tell why they worked, exactly. Welcome duty was another example, why not just hire a receptionist? There was plenty enough office work that needed doing to justify the expense, but DeFazio made all the aides work the front desk at least a few hours a week, and did nearly all the paperwork herself, which was insane, and explained why she was in ElderGrove seventy or more hours a week. Angela knew she meant well, or hoped she did; she understood that welcome duty might seem like a break from harder, yuckier work, but not everyone wanted a break from harder work, some people liked to feel needed. If only she was brave enough, and comfortable enough with DeFazio, to voice her concerns in those weekly reflection emails... but she wasn't, and probably never would be, she was a good Catholic girl who kept her mouth shut rather than criticize others and besides, DeFazio was kind of scary, obsessive and sharp like Angela's Aunt Isabel, who'd hounded her husband to an early death and spent the rest of her life collecting orisha dolls and making sure nothing in her living room moved, and then when she died they found her stomach full of tacks, thimbles, and at least one spoon. So said Angela's Mami, in any case, who had her own problem with compulsive lying.

And now her Mami, too, was gone, and so she was all alone, both her blood uncles had never left New York so all her extended family was still in the Bronx, which was not so far geographically, but they'd never been close, the two halves of la familia Padilla. Mami and Papi and Isabel and Jorge fled for good reason, and even after abuelo Padilla was found with his tongue pulled through the gash in his neck, his shadow remained, and that, as Mami told Angela, was plenty enough darkness to avoid. Jorge died when Angela was seven, Papi when she was eleven, and Isabel when she was fifteen, and when Angela made it more than four years without a death and reached the wizened age of twenty, she figured she was home free and Mami would live forever, so she went and married an idiot with a nice car, had her daughters, and divorced his lazy ass. Mami lived long enough to help get the girls past diapers and for Angela to get her PCA before breast cancer took both her breasts and metastasized anyway, so that Rosie, the eldest, would forever remember Mami as bald, thin, and sexless, instead of the loud, curvy Mami with the blood-red dye job that Angela knew, the one who she swore slept in a pair of vinyl leopard pumps.

So why was she here, putting up with this receptionist shit when she could make more money in one of the ritzy places in Ottawa Hills, or even the new one down in Toledo, GentleLake or something, she knew they paid at least a dollar and half an hour more, and she had two girls and no family, what the hell? She picked at a fringe of veneer that was starting to come off the back of the reception desk and thought, that's why, because these people deserve care as much as anyone else, just because they don't have money don't mean they got to be stuck with crack heads like the new girl, fucking with them and letting them rot in front if the TV. "Angela?" she turned and saw DeFazio standing in the doorway, smiling like she always did, like she was trying to remember how to smile, not faking it, exactly, more like it was something she'd never quite gotten the hang of, but had convinced herself she once was good at.

"Uh-huh?" she answered, more petulantly than she'd meant to.

"I'm going to have Mary take over the front now, thanks so much for covering it. You can go back and get ready for afternoon medicine, but take a break if you need to first, I know front desk can really wear you down." Mary peeked from behind DeFazio's arm and gave a meek wave, she was so skinny Angela hadn't even seen her standing there.

"Ok, great. Have fun, Mary," Angela said, pushing past both women with as much grace as her hips would allow. She'd never developed the talent for enjoying her body the way her mother seemed to, and as she grabbed her scrub top and headed for the supply closet—the best ElderGrove could provide for an employee changing room—she caught a glimpse of herself in the small mirror beside the door and saw she was grinning, and chastised herself. She'd worn too much lip gloss again, she saw, but her mouth was just so weird looking, like she had two kewpie bows in it, or she was some species of fish, so she always forgot and tried to smear it's shape with reds and purples. The rest of her face she didn't mind so much, Kevin always said her eyes were big enough to fall into and they were her best feature, balanced and dark and just turned up enough in the corners to be a little sexy. Her nose was there, nothing to see, move along. Why did she care? It really sucked being a woman sometimes, always catching herself looking at herself in windows and mirrors and worrying, checking other girls out. She didn't need a man, anyhow, she was doing just fine, but that fucking pendejo better pay up the child support or—or what, or nothing, what could she do but keep filing with the agency.

She pulled her shirt over her head and had a flash of memory, Kevin's smell as she lay on his chest after making love, and she sighed, angry at herself but also keenly aware it had been a very long time since she had a man in her bed. She left the closet and picked up the medication chart, scanning it quickly for anything different. DeFazio or Nurse Clemens, or the night nurse (whoever that was this week) and very occasionally Dr. Small or Dr. Pfluke, dispensed the medication, and Angela or whoever was in charge of delivering it to the residents checked again to be sure it was correct. That was one of DeFazio's rules too, but Angela thought it was right, they were short staffed enough, and she knew sometimes DeFazio let some of the aides who'd been here a while measure out meds when she was too busy, but she always went back and double checked before dispensation. One of the old-timers, Jennifer something or other, she moved on a few weeks after Angela arrived, had told a story about a temp nurse who filled in when DeFazio was out getting an operation on her knee, a rich white lady who said her husband was a surgeon and she gave the wrong meds to someone and nearly killed them, then they found out she was stealing all kinds of drugs and even drinking on the job. DeFazio had never even called in sick since that happened, Jennifer claimed. You have to trust people sometimes, Angela thought, and hung the clipboard back on the wall, ready for after-dinner dispensation.

In the day room, Mr. Zimmerman and Dorothy were both zonked out in front of a TV turned down low, her wheelchair beside his rocker, both their heads slumped to the same side of the their chests like doves asleep in the eaves. Eustace Stueffher was knitting and chatting with Constance Zubovsky, which was normal, as they comprised ElderGrove's God Squad, and Dick Klickinoi was sitting in a chair beside them, reading a magazine, which was not normal at all, Angela couldn't remember the last time he'd left his room, it was right when she started working here, he'd had a hip replacement, she thought. Somewhat apart from this group sat Tom Kinney and Mrs. Treadwell, playing cards. Angela smiled and greeted them quietly as she moved toward Mr. Klickinoi. "Why hello, Mister—"

"Dick," he barked, not looking up, "just Dick." He turned the page.

"Ok, good, hello, Dick, how are you?" she persisted.

"I'm lousy, lousy with noise and carrying on. Can't a man die in peace?" He raised his head and his eyes were watery and unfocused, his eyebrows still miraculously black under a shock of white hair.

"Oh come on, it's not loud out here, and you're not dying!"

"Of course I'm dying, that's what we're all doing here for god's sake, and no, it's not loud out here, that's why I'm out here, not back in room next to Mister up all night yelling and playing the radio and god knows what else—"

"Mr. Magoo is in the room next to Dick's," Constance interjected. As if on cue, a muffled whoop, followed by gargling laughter, could be heard from down the hall.

"Ah," Angela said. Dick continued flipping the pages of the magazine. Angela wondered if he knew he was reading *Vogue*. "Well, maybe if you asked him very nicely—" Dick glared at her, his hair gently twitching as his head quavered. "No, no, that wouldn't work, would it."

"Angela?" Tom called from behind her. She turned as he placed a peg in a small wooden board and gathered the cards together.

"Tom?"

"Magoo is a troubled man. I'm not sure his kind of trouble can be assuaged or mollified. Perhaps a different tack is necessary," he said, and shuffled the cards clumsily, before handing them to Mrs. Treadwell, who handled them gracefully while agreeing with his assessment: "Indeed."

Angela went and stood by their table, grateful not to have Dick's eyes boring into hers, though she could feel them still at the back of her skull. "And what kind of tack do you have in mind?"

"Why none, specifically, except that he seems to be a man who responds to force, to threats, shows of power, that kind of thing. Do you agree?" he asked Mrs. Treadwell.

"Why bother?" she replied noncommittally.

"I don't think Nurse DeFazio would like that idea," Angela answered, "you know she always want to encourage a positive atmosphere around here." Another whoop sounded from the hallway.

"And how can a positive atmosphere be created when one element is working so hard to prevent exactly that?"

"Indeed," Mrs. Treadwell added. Down the hall, a door opened, followed by a series of thuds as Magoo tried to steer his wheelchair through his door. "Hey!" he bellowed, half-in, half-out of his room. No one replied, and only Angela looked at him. "You! Chicky! Senorita!" he yelled at her.

"I'm sorry, are you talkin' to me?" Angela felt her blood rise and pulled it back down into her heart. He's an old man, a scared old man, she thought.

"Yeah, you, come give me a hand! Isn't it your fucking job? And a hand job would be nice, come to think of it!" he laughed and started to wheeze, and then his whole body began to convulse. Angela walked hurriedly to him, worried he was having a seizure. As she reached his side, his head popped up like a stubborn cowlick: "Ha! Tricked ya!" he fell to laughing again.

"That is NOT funny, Mr. Magoo!" Angela felt herself yelling, but could no longer suppress it. "And you know my name is Angela, let me spell it for you, A-N-G—"

"Oh shut your piehole, I know your name, don't get sassy with me, senorita, I'll tell your boss you been taking siestas in the broom closet. Wheel me over there, next to the faggot." he tried to cross his arms and succeeded, barely, in piling them on his lap.

"Excuse me?" Angela and Tom said on chorus.

"You're a faggot, Dick told me, right tricky Dick?" Dick's face went cloudy and he buried his gaze in the back cover of the magazine, an ad for Dior perfume.

"That is rude and just, just not nice, and I'm taking you back to your room!" Angela exploded.

"Oh no you ain't, you work for me, chiquita."

"It's alright, Angela, this troglodyte is obviously scared out of his wits and clamoring for a bit of attention, which is totally understandable, since most people would rather not look at such a mess," Tom interjected, and dealt the cards.

"Hey now, no offense, I like faggots just fine, ok, queer, is that better? Nobody sucks cock like a faggot, I mean, like a queer."

"Nice to know on which side one's bread is buttered," Tom replied.

"Oh sure, I used to let some of the swishes hung around the Marine base suck me, got right into it, yessir, but you sure do talk funny for a colored boy."

Tom stopped looking at his cars and peered instead over his glasses at Magoo. "If you weren't already a hair's breadth away from the grave, I would have to kill you, you strange dog. As it is, I think I'll just sit back and watch you writhe in pain like a carp on a dock in the bright summer sun, at least for the brief, foolish sliver of time you have left. Don't go dying too quickly now, darling."

Magoo laughed and coughed up something into his lap. "I like you, funny man. You don't talk like a negro, and you don't wave your hands around like a fag, you got—personality, you do." His head lolled back on his neck and he had trouble bringing it forward again.

"Well, that makes one of us," Tom answered, "oh, I'm sorry, two of us," he finished, smiling at Mrs. Treadwell.

"Indeed," Mrs. Treadwell agreed.

****

Carol Ann thumbed through the filing cabinet and brought out Magoo's file. "Yes, here it is, he signed the Rules of Etiquette form just like all our residents do, well, his daughter signed for him, but she is authorized on all this paperwork. I called and left her a message making it clear he was being problematic, but I can't just throw him out on the street."

"No, course not, I don't want him to leave, but he's got to stop messing with everybody," Angela replied. "Not the staff, we can handle it—" Gary, the janitor and recipient of a flung bedpan from Magoo early this morning, nodded and looked at the floor— "but the residents are really upset. The things he says to them...."

Carol Ann sighed. Her afternoon meeting with Dr. Small went as well as could be expected—he failed to show up, as he had for the last three meetings, instead emailing her a report for her to fill out and he to sign—and now this impromptu meeting, or minor insurgency, was taking place in the lobby, behind the reception desk, one of the few places employees of ElderGrove could talk out of earshot of the day room, and even then their discussions were apt to be fractured by visitors, deliveries, and so forth. So they talked quickly, in loud, barking whispers.

"Can we change his meds?" Angela asked, assuming Carol Ann would give her a nasty look in response. Instead, she sighed again.

"I thought about that, actually. Something to change his mood. But it's totally unethical, no deal, unless we can get Dr. Small to agree," she finished, knowing any help from Dr. Small, or Dr. Pfluke, for that matter, was unlikely.

"So we wait for his daughter to call, and then what?" Chris asked, bouncing on his heels. He had twenty-five minutes to get to his night job, and didn't want to spend more of it here than he had to.

"Then we tell her that her father is being problematic, and that we have the right to ask him to leave if he refuses to behave according to the terms of the contract they both signed." Everyone was quiet, each calculating how much time they would have to spend managing or avoiding Magoo before something gave way. The sound of their breathing grew louder, and Mary, the new aide, popped her head through the reception door: "Nurse DeFazio?"

"Yes, Mary?"

"I need to use the rest room," she whined.

"Ok, so use it," Carol Ann said.

"Um, but the dinner's just about done." The meals were prepared in the small kitchen and stacked on carts, for disbursement to those residents who chose to eat in the day room or in apartments. They all got the same meal, more or less, tweaked for each resident's dietary needs, and were tagged with their names. Eddie, the cook, learned his trade in prison, which served him well at ElderGrove, since both establishments got their ingredients from the same supplier. Once Carol Ann threatened to fire him if he didn't stop salting everything, they got along swimmingly.

"Oh, ok, is it that late?" Carol Ann looked at her watch. ""So that's that, there's really nothing else we can do until Mr. Magoo's daughter returns my calls. We'll just do our best, just like we always do," she said, and nodded, waiting for assent. Angela, Gary, and Chris all nodded, and all three moved in separate directions. "Peace," Chris called over his shoulder, and Angela waved. Carol Ann and Gary were already through the door into the facility.

After dinner, which, for the first time in recent memory, every single resident, except for Mrs. Treadwell, chose to take in their room, Carol Ann wheeled the meds out into the day room while Angela followed with the clipboard, ready for a final check before dispensation. The sounds of muffled TVs mingled in the hallway, the lights in the hall ceiling a pallid yellow. "Will you be alright by yourself? I have so much paperwork to finish," Carol Ann asked Angela, as she did almost every time she left Angela to do the meds herself. "Yes, I'm fine, you ask me every time, I know what to do."

"Ok, great, thanks so much, Angela. You really are an excellent care-giver, you know? I just want you to know how much I appreciate all your help."

"Thanks, I really try," Angela smiled.

"And you succeed," Carol Ann said, letting her hand drift to Angela's shoulder briefly then yanking it off and stiffening. "Very good, after meds there's the end-of-shift checklist and then you go home, right?"

"Right, well, to pick up my girls, then home."

"Good, well, don't forget to punch out."

"Ok." Don't forget? What a bitch, what did she think, I come here for fun? It was always the same, Angela thought, DeFazio would seem almost human and then ruin it with some stupid order, some rule, some way of reminding you who you worked for. Now who's the bitch, why am I getting so mad at her? "Whatever," she whispered to herself as she pulled the clipboard down and wheeled the med cart out to the day room.

Mr. Zimmerman and Dorothy had returned to their chairs after dinner and were bickering with Frank over the television choices for the evening, and Mrs. Treadwell was knitting. Otherwise, the day room was empty, which was typical for the hours following the day's final meal. It was Angela's favorite time, when most of the residents were drowsy and, usually, agreeable, or at least too logy to argue strenuously. She smiled at Mrs. Treadwell and went down the checklist, initialing beside each name and the prescribed meds as she checked the contents of their pill cups. "Fuck me!" came a strangled cry from the hallway, and she nearly dropped the clipboard. "Fuck me, I'm dying!" Now she darted down the hallway, listening for the source of the cries. "Oh Jesus I'm fucking dying!" She grabbed the door handle and shoved hard, crashing into the room to see Magoo laying on his bed, his robe open and his penis laying grey in his hand like a slug on a baseball mitt. "Would you look at this? I haven't had a boner in three fucking years! I'm fucking dying!"

"No, Mr. Magoo, you not dying. You gonna take you medication and go to sleep, and then you gonna wake up and make everybody hate you just a little bit more. But you not dying, sorry." She slapped his robe down and tried her best to make it snap his tiny cock. She hated slipping back into her barrio voice, the one she worked so hard to bury, but enough was enough, and when she looked up, he was grinning crookedly. Oh won't you just die, she wanted so badly to say it... "I'll be back with your medication in a minute, and that robe better be down where I left it."

"You bet, chica," he replied.

Mr. Zimmerman was outside the door. "He alright?"

"Honestly, Mr. Zimmerman, no. He's an asshole," she answered, and Mr. Zimmerman snickered.

She clacked her heels on the way back to the day room. Mrs. Treadwell was rooting among the pill cups, one hand still clutching her knitting.

"Mrs. Treadwell, I'll get your medication, please," she said, and pushed the old woman gently to one side.

"Oh, sorry dear, I thought it was serve yourself tonight," Mrs. Treadwell replied, and sat again to her knitting. Dorothy was asleep again, farting up a small dust devil around her chair. Two more days, Angela told herself, two more days and I get a day off, a whole twenty-four hours away from this crazy place. I need some wine, a little mota, something—I just need to go home. "And no, I won't forget to punch out, you tight ass," she whispered in the general direction of

DeFazio, hunched somewhere in the glow of the computer monitor, deep in the bunker of the nurse's station.

Chapter 5

The couch groaned as Cam rolled off it and flicked his phone on to check the time. He'd laid down for a moment, just, and now it was the next day, of course, he wondered why he tried to fool himself, swearing it would only be a nap. His brain was a liar, too focused on simple self-preservation. The neural net couldn't take much more after seven hours staring and clicking and trying to flesh out the piece he'd storyboarded earlier, seven hours of sitting on his ass, wondering if he'd be called in again for an afternoon shift when Andy and Michelle were already there. Stupid boss. Stupid work. Stupid brain, his face felt covered with mud, his joints filled with cement. But, he had finished the backbone of the Magoo animation, and he knew enough to not watch it now, when he would surely hate it and every flaw would leap out at him, talons drawn. No, now he would go and fetch the weed Magoo wanted, only a day late, and thereby return the favor Magoo had slurred into his recorder. And if stupid boss called, well, fuck him. No one says just because a phone rings you have to answer it.

He brushed himself off and changed and went down the hall to Cookie's, but Cookie was dry, and so he texted Sam, but Sam was dry, so he had to drive over to Mad Mike's, something he avoided if at all possible, since Mike was indeed mad and his wife Lacie was plain fucking crazy, and he'd watched their dog, Lola, give birth to a litter of puppies and then eat them all, one by one, the last time he tried to score there, they were just the kind of folks who liked to make you wait and watch things like that. But luck was on his side and Mike was on the way out, was in a hurry, even, and so he grabbed a pre-weighed bag out of a larger sack and that was it, Cam didn't have to watch puppy murder or listen to Lacie talk about flying saucers.

As he drove to ElderGrove, he found his thoughts drifting toward Angela again, as they did ever since she started working there. She had kids, he wasn't sure he was ready for that, but then again they might help motivate him, they probably liked cartoons, and he could definitely be more active—he pinched the fold of fat that hung over his belt—and kids made you more active, right? Getting up early, taking them to the park, that kind of thing. He looked in the rear view mirror and caught a glimpse of his wispy eyebrows, his piggy green eyes, and felt a sudden weight drop in his chest. A woman like Angela won't fall for a nerd like me, he heard a voice in his head say; he tried to keep it away, but it kept coming back, his reality voice: you're an overweight, pothead nerd living in a small city near Toledo, Ohio, your animation skills are barely competent, your social skills less so, and the only women who pay any kind of positive attention to you are at least eighty years old. Shut up, shut up. He thought about pulling behind the WalGreens to get high, and thought better of it. Go forward, stop sniveling, be a man for once in your life.

The lobby of ElderGrove was empty, there wasn't even a receptionist at the desk, which was odd. A small sign propped against a hotel-style bell indicated all visitors should ring for entrance. That's new, Cam thought. DeFazio was always adamant about having a live body at the front to greet people. He puzzled over whether to ring it or not, considering what category of visitor he was, decided he wanted to hear the noise the bell made, and tapped the plunger. The bell made an ill sounding "plink," and Cam was sure no one would hear it, so he headed for the door. "Can I help you?" a voice called just as he put his hand on the door, and he backed up a bit to see a very skinny, somewhat greasy looking woman smiling nervously at him from behind the reception desk. Was she there all the time and he somehow hadn't seen her? Her eyes were focused somewhere to the left of his head, he noticed. Few tics made him more nervous, and he felt his face redden.

"Ah, uh, yeah, hi, I'm Cam, I used to work here, and—" she kept smiling, but the rest of her face had started to quiver. "I come to visit folks and record them. Like, Mrs. Treadwell, and Mr. Magoo, I'm here to see Magoo today." He knew he was speaking too fast but damn did she make him nervous.

"Oh but he's, um—" she brushed her hands down the front of her stained scrubs. "Let me go get Nurse DeFazio," she squeaked, and vanished through the door to the nurses' station. Cam felt like he was suspended from a wire running through his shoulders, holding him upright but preventing him from moving laterally. The main door swung open and Nurse DeFazio pushed her head through like a tortoise, looking around the lobby before focusing on Cam. "Cam, yes, hello. Ah, you had an appointment with Mr. Magoo?"

"Yeah, I did, I thought."

"Well, ok, come in." Her head snuck back behind the door, but she didn't open it, so Cam pushed through. The day room looked the same, a few residents slumped about, the TV down low, why was everyone acting so weird?

"Cam—come over here please, sit" Nurse DeFazio called in a loud whisper. He went to where she sat, behind the nurses' station counter, partially hidden by a vase full of flowers that looked like they'd been spray painted. "Sit, please, sit down." He sat.

She stared at him, pointedly, and he realized for the first time that her eyes were slightly crossed.

"Cam, Mr. Magoo has left us." She smoothed her lap with both hands, wiping away from herself.

"Left? Like, he moved out?"

"No, as in 'passed away'."

"What? Already?"

"Yes," she said more quietly, "but please don't upset anyone, he's passed on and no one needs to be reminded of that right now, so—"

"Wow, shit, that was fast. I mean, he looked like he was kind of a mess—"

"He had several serious health problems, yes, but, well... yes. He was not in good health, and, so, we need to move on."

"Right. Wow. I said that already, sorry. It's just that I just met him, I mean. I don't know what I mean." He lifted his bag from the ground and put it in his lap, unsure if he should stay or go. He could smell the weed in through the bag.

"We all are a little in shock, it was very sudden. It's ok." She tried to smile. It looked like carp shuddering on a bedspread.

"Yeah. So. I guess I should go."

"You're welcome to stay and talk with some of the residents, I know you give some of them great comfort. I really appreciate what you do. Do you ever think of getting your certification to be an aide? You'd be really good at it. Or even a nurse!" She tried to laugh, but it worked about as well as the smile had.

"Ah, yeah, thanks. Ok, well, I—" Cam looked around, looked the filing cabinets, the computer, the tchotchkes, the flowers in the cheap plastic vase, DeFazio's messenger bag shoved under the counter. Why was he here? It was all so sad. He felt his lungs swell, a rippling pressure that surged up into his cheeks, his eyes suddenly full. He smiled crookedly at the nurse. "I gotta go."

"Of course," she said. Cam stood and walked out of the nurse's station and nearly knocked over Mrs. Treadwell. Boy she had ninja skills, he thought. "Hello, young man," she said, staring at him milkily.

"Hi Mrs. Treadwell."

"Do I know you?" He noticed she was wobbling slightly.

"It's me, Mrs. Treadwell, Cam. Remember, all the stories you told me? I recorded them?"

Her eyes narrowed. "That awful man seems to have left." Cam felt his lungs swelling again. "Yes, I need to go, Mrs. Treadwell," he said, pushing past her as gently as he could.

"Will you come back next week, Cam?" she called as he moved slowly toward the door. He stopped and looked down at the floor. The same cheap, flecked vinyl tile he'd tried to make clean so many nights, pushing to grime and dust around, down into the cracks where the tiles had split, fusing with them, until there was more compressed dirt than there was vinyl.

"Sure. I promise." He pushed the door open and went out through the lobby. The skinny girl waved shyly from the front desk. He waved back. "Was he a friend of yours?" she asked.

"Not really, I mean—" he stopped, confused. "I thought he was cool. He had good stories."

She nodded. "Everyone here thought he was a pain in the ass, but, like, tons of people have been calling today," and the front desk phone rang, on cue.

"Hello, ElderGrove Residential Living Facility," she said, smiling up at him, then rolling her eyes. "Yes, visiting hours for Mr. Magoo will be held on Monday at five p.m. at the Werdigo Funeral Home on Grant St., Candler

City." Cam saw she was reading from an index card. He returned her smile and walked out the front door. It had started to snow again, but the sky before him was clear, blue and glowing. He stuck out his tongue and waited to catch a flake, then let the tears come slowly down his face, tracing cold lines into his cheeks.

****

Maggie lifted the lid off the pot and poked the contents with a wooden spoon. "Leave it alone!" Carol Ann barked from her seat at the kitchen table, much louder than she'd intended to. Maggie stirred the quinoa anyway, then replaced the lid. Her face said she'd had enough of Carol Ann's shit for today, flat and emotionless except for her right eyebrow, fixed in a wry arch. She lit the half joint in the ashtray and took a long drag.

"I'm sorry, I didn't mean to bark like that. But really, you aren't supposed to lift the lid while it's steaming—"

"For the last time, that's rice, not quinoa, and I really don't feel like having this fucking argument again." She took a sip of wine and stared down at the book propped open on the table. Carol Ann fidgeted with her own glass of wine, with the hem of her untucked shirt, then trapped her hands, one on the other, in her lap.

"What?" Maggie said, hand on her hip.

"What what?"

"Come one, something's eating you, what's the four-one-one." She picked up the smoldering joint, looked at the tip, then stubbed it out.

"We, ah, I lost one of the residents."

"Ok, sorry, what else? I mean, did they die some terrible way?"

"Yes and no." Carol Ann got up from her chair and went behind Maggie, wrapping her arms around her midsection.

Maggie didn't stiffen, but she didn't relax. She always gets weird when I touch her lately, Carol Ann thought, at least once she's stoned, anyway, like she leaves her body the minute I come in contact with her. "It was an accident. He got the wrong meds, one of the aides gave him the wrong meds and he was allergic and he died." She felt Maggie's body sag slightly, before turning to face Carol Ann.

"Shit."

"Yeah. Shit."

Maggie looked at the floor, then back up at Carol Ann, eyes glistening.

"I'm so sorry, babe."

They held each other, listening as Mr. Slack next door wheeled his garbage can back into the garage.

"And you know what makes it even worse?" Carol Ann said, pulling away and filling a glass of water.

"What?"

"He was a total prick." Maggie's mouth dropped. "No, really, he was rude, crude, and socially unacceptable. He'd masturbate every time anyone tried to give him a bath, well, he'd try to masturbate, then laugh and call them names. Like it was their fault his junk was useless for anything but a piss." Maggie's frozen expression shattered and she laughed, a dark rumble that rose from her belly and blasted forth like birds from a church tower. She even laughs better than me, Carol Ann noticed; she's the pretty, athletic, graceful one, the one with the trim ankles, the one people are drawn to and I'm the shlump, the fat-legged, narrow-shouldered, bad haircut-wearing, boring little drudge who works too much at a thankless job and has nothing interesting to say. A certainty clicked in her heart like tumblers settling: she's going to leave me, and there's nothing I can do about it.

* * * * * * * * * *

Tom was chagrined to wake, for the third time in a week, in front of the television, where a man in a yellow shirt was yelling at a vacuum cleaner, or maybe he was yelling at the pile of dirt he was vacuuming off a square of carpet. Garbage in, garbage out, and it's garbage I'll be if I keep falling asleep in front of the idiot box, he told himself, hooking his hands around the chair arms to hoist himself upright. Mrs. Treadwell snored thinly beside him. She had taken to following Tom around the day room like a silent and somewhat reproachful pet, saying little more than "indeed" and "oh now stop," peering at him from under her wispy brows accusingly when he spoke to other people. Well wouldn't they be surprised back in Sanford, Mississippi to see Thomas Kinney consorting with a white lady so brazenly, he chuckled to himself, and began easing his wheelchair back as quietly as he could, trying not to wake her. He didn't really need the chair, or at least he told himself he didn't need it, he could walk fine, it just took a long time and hurt far more than he really needed to think about, most days. He heard a yelp from behind the chair and twisted his neck to see Dorothy behind him, also snoring, and where he had hit her knee gently with a wheel. She hadn't woken, but he felt eyes upon him and knew the small rodent cry was enough to wake Mrs. Treadwell. He wondered if she really slept, or just closed her eyes and pretended so she could watch him more closely. He smiled at her, and she peered up from under her brows. He sighed, and settled back into his chair, fumbling with the crossword puzzle he'd left on his thigh. Was this really the woman they all swore talked a blue streak on command, made up bizarre stories for that pudgy young man to record? He couldn't believe it, though he definitely could believe the fat boy went around recording people's private stories, he surely did something nefarious with them, sold them to the tribe of Oneiroi, demons gone to seed from neglect, abandoned, starved for dreams and stories. Not that he wanted her to suddenly start talking, the quiet was very welcome, no one missed that sad old redneck one bit. He looked over at Mrs. Treadwell, who was snoring once more, or pretending to snore, and he felt the same nagging scene poking at him, coiling his thoughts around it: Mr. Magoo, wild eyed and covered in spittle, palming and swallowing the wrong medication, they were all in danger, trapped in a yellow shoebox with oxycontin-addled monsters who could barely read, let alone help if real danger appeared. Maybe it wasn't the wrong medication at all, maybe he was just old and he died, it happened, and the whole wrong meds rumor was just a bedtime story to make it seem like they were all still a part of a story, any story. It's better to have someone want you dead than for no one to care if you're alive, he decided, and looked back at the TV. He couldn't understand a damn thing that was happening on the screen, and he was glad.

Chapter 6

Werdigo Funeral Home occupied the former home of Judge Reynolds V. Hendricks, a towering, hirsute Scot who, in 1832, moved to Fairfield, Ohio with his wife and four sons, grabbed the little farming village by the scruff of its neck, and dragged it into modernity by transforming it into a thriving den of vice, bankrolling the transformation, rumor held, with a trunk full of gold stolen from weapons traders returning home after supplying both militias during the Toledo War. In 1893, Fairfield became Candler City, named for Enos Candler, Anti-Saloon League stalwart and local dentist, and regular customer of the Diamond Hotel, a high-end brothel run by Ms. Ruby, who appeared in Candler City just as William Hendricks, the youngest Hendricks boy, died without an heir. The building remained a brothel until 1952, when Rufus Werdigo, recent immigrant from Trinidad, convinced Chuck Waverly, the Chief of Police, to raid the Diamond regularly until "all the doves had been flushed from the eaves." Werdigo opened his funeral home in the building, while Waverly's cousin Tom enjoyed increased traffic at his own brothel, the ostentatiously named Green Dragon. The Werdigo Funeral Home outlasted both the Werdigo family (Rufus failed to produce children with any of his three wives) and the Waverly clan (the last members of the family moved to California in the 1990s) in Candler City, despite it's comparatively high prices, perhaps due to the stubborn presence of risque murals on the walls of many of the rooms, which several layers of paint had failed to entirely conceal, if you knew where to look, and knowing where to look was one of the first pieces of lore children learned on the playground of Hendricks Elementary. Cam had learned it from Laser Edwards, whose given name really was Laser, and who knew all the lore before anyone else, as if he learned from some secret source outside the playground, and so Cam found himself staring at the faint outline of a reclining, Rubenesque nude while waiting in a very long line to pay his respects to Magoo, whose name, as the sign board in the lobby announced, was in fact spelled Mageaux. This last fact puzzled Cam, as did the long line of well-wishers, since his admittedly brief impression of Mageaux was not one of a person who made friends easily, let alone hundreds of sobbing friends of all ages.

He stood stiffly, inching forward as the line crept along, peeking at mourners he thought he recognized, only to decide, each time, it was not the person he thought it was. The line wound up the long central hallway and back down again, then curled around into the viewing room. The doors to the chapel were open, Cam noted, and every so often someone drifted in or out. When his Great-Grandfather had died fifteen years prior, he'd made a beeline for the chapel where, rumor had it, the most lascivious mural took up the whole back wall, but it had been covered with a heavy peach-colored curtain. The line shuffled along, and Cam forced a smile of sympathy at the mourners emerging from the viewing room. Who were all these people? They certainly didn't look like bikers. He squeezed the USB drive in his pocket, feeling foolish that he'd brought it along, as if there would be anywhere to play the animation he'd worked up for Mageaux's story, but it was great, a real breakthrough, he thought. *I can't imagine how this crowd would react, except maybe they'd* freak out, what did they know about the man's life? Were they friends of his children, or his wife? Did they know about all the drugs and prison and violence and... and what might they think of Cam's rant, tacked on the end of the video, a spume of invective lobbied at the system that produced ElderGrove, that shunted away old folks of little means into dirty old closets where distracted, uneducated employees like Angela could kill someone like Mageaux, yes, kill him, with negligence? Why did he bring it? It was already on YouTube, did he think they would have a screen and projector here for him?

At last he rounded the corner into the viewing room and gasped: there, beside the poster board collage of photographs, was a portable movie screen, playing a slide show from a laptop! He stared until the person behind him coughed to move him forward, and he began to register some of the images that were flashing by him: Mageaux at the Grand Canyon, clean cut, dressed in plaid shirt and shorts, with a small, trim woman and two young children; Mageaux in a Christmas sweater, laughing at something off camera; Mageaux with safety goggles on, cowlick sticking up from his crown, demonstrating the operation of what looked like a band saw to a group of young men with dangerously wide lapels. Cam bent to look at the poster board, at more examples of what seemed a perfectly conventional life, a wedding, a birthday, Mageaux as a child, dressed as a cowboy. This is not right, he thought, this is not the same man, did he have a brother? A twin, perhaps, since the man in the photos was certainly the one Cam had interviewed.

The person behind him coughed again, and Cam turned to face a puffy-eyed woman in a dark plum pantsuit, hand extended to him, head bent slightly forward. He took her hand, warm and moist, and shook it. She smiled painfully and let his hand drop. He knew he was supposed to say something, but his throat was clenched tight. "Thanks so much for coming," she said.

"O-oh sure, great, he was a great guy," he stammered. She looked at him oddly, then turned her attention to the coughing person behind him.

He shook more hands, moved down the line, and found himself in front of the coffin. It almost seemed to match the woman's pantsuit, a dark red wood with shining handles, the top half propped open to reveal Mageaux, shaved and buffed with makeup, face frozen in a half smile. Cam had never seen him without a beard. His face looked like it was made of frosting. Cam felt himself starting to cry, so he put his hand on the edge of the coffin, brushing the stiff satin interior wall with his fingertips, and turned away. He had already decided he wanted to be cremated, and every time he saw another body lying in state, his conviction was renewed. None of this being tucked away like a mouse in a shoebox full of tissue paper, dropped down into the skin of the earth, left to rot while centuries ground along above. He felt sick. Two empty chairs, worn at the arms, flanked a small table set with a lamp and a box of tissues. He let himself down into one of the chairs and blew his nose with a tissue. He looked around for a trash can but saw none, so he stuffed the tissue in his back pocket.

"Hey," a voice said, and he turned to see one of his regulars from the bar, one of the doughy middle-aged sales dorks who came for the free happy hour food, Jim or John or something like that. His hair was spiky, just as must have been twenty years ago, when he first discovered there were women stupid enough to have sex with him.

"Hey," Cam answered.

"Sucks, huh?" Jim or John took out a mint from a metal container in his coat pocket and sucked on it.

"Yeah, sucks," Cam answered.

"You look kinda young to be in one of his classes, right?"

"Yeah, I guess I do."

"Were you?"

Cam looked at his suit, dark blue and shiny, and his yellow socks. He felt a strong urge to do the man harm, and then felt a great in rushing of guilt for feeling the urge in the first place.

"No, man, I didn't even know him that well. Just met him at ElderGrove. But I liked him."

"ElderGrove? That's where Sheila put him? What a cunt."

"I'm sorry, I don't know Sheila, and I didn't even know Mageaux was a teacher until about five minutes ago. What did he teach?"

Jim or John settled in, crossing one leg over the other. "Well, lemme tell ya. Mags was my Wood Shop teacher, I know he also taught Machine Shop. And I had him for History class one year, he was filling in, I think. He was always doing stuff like that. He was my cub scout leader too, but I didn't stay that long. He was just an awesome guy, always helping people out. Sheila over there, Miss Ice Queen, is his daughter. He had a son, too, a retard, sorry, uh, what is it called? Where you have a slope face."

"Down's Syndrome?" Cam offered.

"Yeah, that's it. Matt. Great kid, used to worship the Indians, poor bastard. Well, they had some good years with Belle and Baerga and Candyman, right? Who played first base on those teams?"

"Never really paid much attention to baseball," Cam admitted. John or Jim squinted, then continued holding court.

"Yeah, Matt was a great kid, and Sheila was always a bitch. I made out with her once, some party in high school, she was stiff as a board. She left for college and never came back much, good riddance. Couple years ago, Matt died, got hit by a car, I think, and that just killed Mags, and his wife, they both loved the kid so much, she died pretty soon after, like a year or something. She might have, you know, there was rumors, she did it herself." He sighed softly, and Cam could tell suicide was an option John or Jim had entertained himself, fairly recently. "That was all, what, ten years ago? Nine or ten, maybe fifteen, I don't know. Didn't really hear much about Mags until this. Really sucks."

Cam looked at his fingers. His head felt very heavy and, paradoxically, entirely hollow. This was wrong, all wrong. The video he'd done, the stories he'd recorded... "Yep, sucks," he said to John or Jim, rising from his chair unsteadily.

"Yeah, Hey, you working tonight? I'll buy you a shot," Jim or John said, offering his hand.

"No, not tonight. All weekend, though," Cam answered, shaking the man's hand with the same enthusiasm he felt when flushing a urinal.

"Alright, well, cool, take care."

Cam muttered something and stumbled past the little clots of mourners, past the puzzled children, past the professionally sympathetic morticians in their expressionless suits, past the ghosts of ribald murals hiding in the walls, and emerged in the now-dark parking lot. Most of the snow had melted, but it was still bitter, and the streetlights had a sickly yellow tint. I keep ending up in dark, cold parking lots, he thought. I keep misreading people and misunderstanding what they are trying to tell me. I need to get the fuck out of this town, go somewhere sunny, somewhere sunny and stupid, where everyone says what they mean, there's nothing secret, nothing below the surface. Probably L.A. At least California. His parents would be sad. He needed to go see them. Tomorrow, for sure, after work. Or the next day.

* * * * * * * * * *

Carol Ann drove home worrying out loud about how the new night nurse, Chanelle Tshoke, was getting her keyboard all sticky, and about the new regulations her friend Dex had told her were coming—how the hell were they supposed to pay for six new PCAs? Where was the money going to come from, did the politicians think of that before making their high and mighty pronouncements?—and about Maggie's cheating and drug use and about whatever other worries she could dredge up, since driving home with a serious fret on and the radio up very loud (bad classic rock was best) was one of her primary coping strategies. Some days she just drove around Candler City, a few times she'd been to Toledo and back, and after one particularly stressful day, she'd crossed the state line into Pennsylvania and kept on going. She did turn around eventually, of course. And Chanelle came well recommended, she'd been laid off from her last job and seemed perfectly competent, but she kept fingering the little cross around her neck like she was trying to ward off Carol Ann's dyke rays or something. And one of her eyes was more closed than the other. And she smelled like bologna dipped in baby powder.

Pulling into her driveway, Carol Ann flipped off the radio. She and Maggie lived in the left side of a duplex, renting from Mr. Slack, who lived on the right. They had argued enough times about buying their own place that they no longer argued about it, it was a level of commitment Carol Ann knew they would never reach. Maggie swore it had nothing to do with commitment, she just hated the "capitalist noose" of a mortgage, but Carol Ann knew that was just code, the noose was her. Still, it was a nicely laid out apartment, and had a great back yard and deck that Mr. Slack graciously allowed them full use of, while maintaining full control of the front porch, the better to spy on his other neighbors.

She heard laughter as she climbed the side steps. They

were icy, scattered with fresh pellets of ice melt but still slick, and an image of herself slipping backwards and cracking her skull on the driveway flashed across her mind. Her heart sped and she felt a flush rise in her chest, but the fear quickly turned into a kind of possessiveness, a reluctance to let go of the idea of a tragic accident laying her low as Maggie guffawed inside. She slid her key into the lock and turned it the wrong way, as she did most of the time, then turned it back the right away and pushed her shoulder against the door. Maggie sat across the kitchen table from a butch looking woman Carol Ann thought she recognized from Rose's, a short and stocky woman with a greying buzz cut, baggy jeans, timberland boots, and a nose ring. They both stopped laughing, and seemed to be holding their breath before bursting again into loud laughter. Carol Ann reddened, though she knew they weren't laughing at her, though they might be, and the tang of pot smoke huffed to her nose, heavy and fresh. She offered a perfunctory smile and went to hang her keys on wall, then slid off her winter boots. The laughter settled, and finally Maggie spoke, as Carol Ann walked around them toward the sink. "Hey babe," she said, trying too hard to sound sunny. Carol Ann dodged Maggie's outstretched hand, mumbled hello, and snuck a horse-eyed glance at the other woman. She got a glass from the cupboard and filled it with water.

"Babe, you remember Nola?" Maggie offered, as Carol Ann turned to face them. Nola gave her head bob and shifted in her seat.

"No, I don't think so, is this who you're fucking tonight?"

There was a very brief silence, the kind found just past the edge of a cliff. Nola let out a loud "Whoah, ok," stood, took her down vest from the back of the chair, and started putting her arms through it. "I'm outta here. Thanks, Mags. Nice to see you again, Carol." Carol Ann bit her lip at the obvious snicker in Nola's voice. Fucking bitch.

"No, it's cool, stay Nola," Maggie said, also rising.

"Nah, you kids have fun," she said, and was gone, moving faster than Carol Ann suspected she could in those stupid boots. Maggie fell into her chair and hung her head. Carol Ann felt unable to move, to bring the glass of water to lips or set it down. They stayed that way for a while before Maggie lifted her head and spoke, toward the table, away from Carol Ann.

"I can't fucking take this any more, babe. I just can't. What they fuck, she came over to watch American Horror, can't I have friends? What is it with you?" Carol Ann stayed frozen, and Maggie sighed, then fished a joint off the lip of the ashtray. She lit it, took a long drag, and held it. Carol Ann came unstuck and watched herself put the glass down sharply, walk quickly around the counter, and slap the joint out of Maggie's hand. "Jesus!" Maggie yelled.

"Just stop being such a slut. *American Horror Story*? Seriously? Do I look that stupid? You're a slut, don't pretend, and don't try to bullshit me."

"Fuck you, Annie dear," Maggie answered, glaring at Carol Ann. "Yes, I fucked around on you, yes, we had problems, I thought we got over all that! You're fucking slipping, baby. Losing your shit. You're like a prissy old breeder, what happened to the dyke who danced in the gutter and laughed at the fucking guidos who were yelling at her from the bar, remember that? You drank them under the table, remember? Remember telling my mother to eat shit? Would you do that now, or would you trade needlepoint tips with her? God, Annie. I just can't do it any more."

Carol Ann watched Maggie slip past her to bedroom. She stood, staring at the surface of the water in her glass while Maggie clattered around behind the door. The water had a skin, a boundary where it stopped trying to fill the space allotted it, where gravity pushed it down and settled it into the shape of the glass. It was full of things, millions of tiny, living, swimming creatures, full of fragments of rust from the pipes, full of bits of shit from the sewers. She wound her fingers around the glass, it sweated slightly in her hand, pulsated oh so gently. She lifted the glass over her head and poured the water on her crown, shuddering as it ran down her neck, her collar, her chest, her shirt clinging to her in patches. She put the glass down and stayed standing, not moving save for a quivering that started in her knees and soon spread to both her legs. She stayed that way as Maggie came out of the room, eyes rimmed red, lugging a suitcase. She stopped and looked at Carol Ann, who stared past her. "Oh Annie," she whispered, backed toward the door, then turned and left, pulling gently enough that click of the bolt sliding into place seemed terribly loud.

Chapter 7

The reason Mrs. Treadwell slept so quietly, Tom discovered, was that she wasn't really sleeping at all, as he had suspected. The other residents slept like most people did, though much more often: they farted, moaned, burped, twitched, shifted their bodies, drooled.... Mr. Zimmerman, in particular, was known for slumberous, room-clearing gas, as was Dorothy, and since they so often fell asleep together, it was easy to wake with one's eyes stinging if you happened to also drift off near them. But Mrs. Treadwell, she barely moved, and certainly never made a noise or a smell or even a rivulet of spit, not an eye flutter. Tom faked sleep himself one day and caught her peeping, he thought, at one of the new aides, Mary, her name was, the spindly little white girl who had very quickly learned to avoid each resident with gusto. If he hadn't propped his door open one night, while suffering a regular bout of insomnia brought on by indigestion from the disgusting food they served at ElderGrove, he wouldn't have thought to pay attention Treadwell's sleep pattern in the first place, as he spent a fair portion of his time trying to dodge her, since she persisted in following him around, doting clumsily, trying to feed him brownies and cakes and herbal tea. He had lain awake, groaning quietly, when he saw a flutter outside his door, and just as he had convinced himself it was his imagination, there it was again, then a pause, then a flutter, clockwork. He managed to get himself to door again and propped it open a bit further, replacing the shoe he'd shoved in the gap with a waste basket. He felt the fluttering behind him as he made his way back to bed, then put his glasses on and lay in bed, facing the door. He knew Mrs. Treadwell's figure well by now, and her peculiar, drifting gait; she went by again a few minutes later, the other direction, then returned, then back, with a bizarre precision. When he woke the next morning, his glass were bent slightly where his head had fallen to the pillow. He allowed as how her behavior was very odd indeed, and resolved to pay much closer, and much more surreptitious, attention to this queer little white lady.

This newfound attention to Mrs. Treadwell's comings and goings was, he knew, at least partly to give himself something to do, for ElderGrove was a very dull place. One did not engage in debates of high intellectual caliber in the day room, no one cared if Twisted Arc deserved to be destroyed, or what a middle-brow elitist E.D. Hirsch was, let alone why Luther Vandross should just get his fat ass out of the closet. He was certain he was absolutely the loneliest person in the facility. Even the ones who never voluntarily came out of their rooms had their dementia to keep them company. He spoke to Hector's duende regularly, of course, but he knew Hector wasn't really there, except inasmuch as the dead are always present, rhythms that persisted even when the bodies no longer danced. So he fancied himself a bit of a detective, Coffin Ed and Gravedigger Jones for the soft-food set. And she didn't disappoint, as an object of surveillance, since she was, as they say, shady. Such as her ability to disappear for long spells, then reappear with enough presence to make you wonder if she'd really gone away, like a bad song that gets stuck in your head for years and years and years. He also knew he could be imagining it all, making connections that weren't there; just because there was no answer when he knocked on her door didn't mean she wasn't in there, for instance, and he hadn't mustered the courage to try and pick the lock to her room yet. He did wonder why her door was often locked, when none of the others ever were, that he could tell.

Hector had chided Tom for his conspiracies, his visions of coincidence and synchronicity, even as he indulged them, like when Tom became obsessed with the fact that the Jonestown massacre happened November eighteenth, his dead sister's birthday, which so convinced him that the number 111874 would win the Buckeye 300 that he bought everyone at the Grotto a mai tai in anticipation of his windfall. He woke with a hangover and an undiminished passion for amateur numerology, "as if there is any other kind," Hector would say. Lord, if anyone in the Grotto that night knew they were tippling presumptive proceeds from Jonestown, he would have been barred. So what, he had a dark sense of humor, as did Hector, as befitting a professor of classics. But that was then, as they say, and the now was a papery little woman who spoke little, walked like she was being blown by a stiff breeze, and slept not at all, from what he could tell.

He watched her now, delivering little plastic shooters of medication to the sparse population of the day room. Once Mary discovered Mrs. Treadwell liked handing out the cups, well, Mrs. Treadwell got to hand out the cups, unless DeFazio was there, of course, as she was more often than not. She'd gone home early this evening, Tom noticed, and she'd spent most of her time here hunkered in the office, rather than getting her butchy little nose in everyone's business, trying to make us all play Parcheesi or sign up to go to Water Aerobics at the Y. She wasn't that butchy, really, now that he thought about it, she was too squirrelly, nervous and controlling and so dull—he would have pegged her as bi, had she not so quickly come out to him about her "partner." What a terrible word for a lover. The younger generation had no class, no struggle to make them realize style was the great defense against those that would degrade and dehumanize you... that sounds like Hector again, his voice and mine are so entwined I can't tell which is which. Tom had a flash of waking up on his floor, unable to rise, feeling like his head had been turned inside out and left to dry on a beach somewhere, Hector standing over him, hand outstretched, then guiding him to the phone, to the buttons marked 9-1-1. He'd been dead nine years then, when he helped rescue Tom from the aftershocks of his first stroke. Not bad for a ghost.

He must have really dozed off, while pretending and spying on Mrs. Treadwell, since he woke with a start when he felt a hand shaking his shoulder. It was Mary, and she had his cup of meds. He took them and swallowed them down, the pain killers were really quite dreamy. Mrs. Treadwell had vanished again. A small group of residents huddled around the television, waiting to be told they could go to bed. Clearly these were the golden years, Tom thought. And then he felt her sitting behind him, staring at the back of his head. He knew she only wanted him to turn around, could feel it like a finger stroking his neck. Well. He wasn't her boy. She could just wait.

****

After she put Rosie and Alison on the bus, Angela went back up the stairs to her kitchen and poured another coffee. She sat and stared at the manila folder on the table. The résumés were beyond stale, they were laughing at her. Why had she spent those years being scared of fat old nursing professors? Her Mami wouldn't let this stop her, she'd be charming some bow-tied little man into giving her a job, never you mind checking my last employer, you don't want to call them, sure they were the only job I've ever had as a PCA but come now, chico, let's think of the future. She sighed. I'm not my Mami, I'm not even a shade of my Mami, I'm just a girl who eats too much and thinks too slow. She felt like smoking some weed. She felt like crying. A sharp noise made her jump, her door buzzer, she realized. It had been a while since anyone used it. She went to the wall and pressed the intercom button.

"Hello?"

"Ah, hello?" The voice on the other end was male, and kind of shaky.

"Yes?"

"Angela? It's Cam. Cameron, from ElderGrove. I mean, I used to work there..."

She looked down at her pants, touched her hair. What? I mean, why is he here? What could he want?

"Ok, what—why are you at my house, Cam?"

"I—I just wanted to talk. About what happened. About Mr. Mageaux."

She pressed the buzzer and immediately wished she could take it back, untouch it, lock the door and never let him or anyone she knew from that place anywhere near her life. But, too late Angela, you stepped in it again. She checked herself in the mirror once more, she didn't know why, he was a nice guy, a little bit fat and sloppy, but he seemed kind and funny. And what else did she have to do today anyway? What did she ever have to do? She thought of Rosie and Alison, her rudders, steering her away from all the bad water she so often wanted to float away on. There was a knock on the door. She pulled the knob, leaving the sliding chain engaged. Sure enough, Cam stood on the other side. He was looking at his shoes, lifting his head only after he heard the door thunk as the chain went taut.

"How you got my address, Cam?" Angela asked, suddenly very afraid.

"Oh, yeah, this is kinda weird, I know. I went to Elder-Grove and asked, I told Mary I wanted to interview you." He shuffled his feet on the hall carpeting.

"You want to interview me? Who's Mary?"

"Mary is a new aide, and yeah, I would like to interview you, if you think you want to. Or if you just want to talk, that'd be cool too." He smiled. He was actually pretty cute, she thought. A nice smile.

"Ok, well—ok." She closed the door, undid the chain, and let him in. He stood in the middle of the kitchen, looking confused, like an animal freed from a cage, but unsure what to do without walls.

"Come, sit," she said, pulling a chair out from the table. He lay a knapsack on the ground beside the chair and slumped into it. "You want some coffee?"

"Sure, great," he said. She poured coffee. "Milk?"

"No, black is good."

They sat and sipped their coffee, peeking at each other. Angela again felt a rush of panic and stood up. "I don't know, I don't know I really want to talk about this, I don't want you to record nothing, please, please," she stammered, starting to pace.

"No, that's ok, I just thought—well, I went to his funeral, and it got me thinking. I'm sorry, I'll go," Cam replied, standing and hefting his bag. Angela sat again, and laughed nervously. They were like pieces of hair that wouldn't stay down. "I'm—go ahead, sit. Tell me about it, just no recording, ok?"

"Sure," he gushed with relief. He sat. "So. So yeah, I went, and it turns out, Mageaux, spelled M-A-G-E-A-U-X—did you know that?"

"Yes, I think," she said.

"I always thought it was M-A-G-O-O, like that cartoon."

He laughed. "But anyway, I went, and turns out he was, like, a saint. I mean, he wasn't some wild man at all, he made all that stuff up, like he made up a whole new persona. I'm still kind of freaked out about it."

Angela furrowed her brow, then relaxed and put both hands around her coffee cup. "I know this happens sometimes, maybe he had brain damage, or sometimes Alzheimer's, it can make people, um, invent stuff, like, whole other people. Or maybe he was acting like someone he knew, someone he thought about a lot of the time."

"Really? That's so weird. I mean, really interesting, and sad, but man, weird. That would explain Treadwell, I guess." Angela stiffened.

"No. She is bad, just bad. She change the meds, not me. She know I saw her, she know I tell DeFazio I saw her but so what, no. Treadwell is bad, muy malo."

Cam's mouth fell half-open as the rest of him froze. After along pause, staring at Angela, who stared only at the cup she was now squeezing too tight, he finally said" "Huh?"

She raised her head, her eyes wet and furious. "She killed him."

"You think—what? She switched his meds?"

"Yes. On purpose. She take Zubovsky, Z, put them in Mageaux, M. When I come in she be playing with pills, always she plays with the pill tray, I don't think about it. Later, I think about it. When I go back to work, I tell DeFazio, DeFazio get Treadwell in to the office, ask what happened, Treadwell pretends she senile, don't remember nothing." Angela felt her words decaying, melting as she started to cry. "Then when she walk out, old bitch, she know Defazio not looking, she stick her tongue out like this—" Angela stuck her tongue out as grotesquely as she could, trying to remember the scene without remembering how creepy it was, her tongue, dry and grey. "She did it."

Cam was dumbfounded. He certainly could believe

Mrs. Treadwell had been messing with the meds, he'd seen her get caught doing that himself. He could even believe she had accidentally switched cups, or picked up one and spilled it into another, but intentionally giving Mageaux the wrong pills, killing him? Well, she'd have to know what he was allergic to, first of all, then what all the different pills were—that was a bit much. But if Angela really hadn't done anything wrong, then it wasn't fair, it wasn't right that she got fired. Everyone knew Mrs. Treadwell fussed with the med cart, DeFazio included. DeFazio especially, for shit's sake.

"Wow. I don't know what to say," he said. He put his hand over hers. It was warm and bit too moist, but it still made Angela relax, something in her belly loosening. She sighed.

"Did you tell DeFazio?" Cam asked, "about sticking out her tongue, I mean?"

"Oh sure, I told her, she said it don't even matter, it's my shift, my responsibility. Me saca, thinking about her, she just want somebody to blame so corporate lave her alone."

"That sucks." They sat for a while, his hand resting on hers, listening to the snow melt. He lifted his hand, smiled, and sipped his coffee. "Maybe if you could get someone else to say they saw her messing with the pills, DeFazio would let you back."

"No, no, I don't want to go back there." Angela looked out the window. There weren't many jobs out there for a PCA laid off for letting an old man die. Word got around, everybody who did the hiring around here had to know her name by now. "But I got to get her to see it wasn't me. Maybe get her to hire me back, so I can quit, so not everyone in this shit town thinks I'm..." she dropped her eyes to the folder on the table, all the resumes on their stupidly expensive cream paper, the empty space on those pages threatening to swallow her.

"Let me try," Cam said. She looked up, feeling suddenly threatened.

"Try what?"

"Try to get her, Mrs. Treadwell, to admit she likes to fuss with medicines, uh, get some of the other people there to say they seen her do it too. I can record them, you know? I've had good luck getting a lot of them to talk, especially Treadwell."

Angela nodded. "Yeah, how did you do that? She don't like to talk to nobody."

"I don't know, I just told her I wanted to record her telling her story, just like the first one, Mrs. Gunderson, do you remember her?"

"No, before I got there."

"Yeah, no doubt. I wanted to record some stories for school, and Mrs. Gunderson had been a stripper way back when, I figured she had some cool stories—" Angela reddened and looked down at her coffee. "And so while I was recording her, Treadwell comes over and just sits there staring, makes Gunderson all nervous, then tells me she has some stories too, and boy did she. She made them all up, of course, they were too crazy, but that's why they were cool. So I started recording her, too. Gunderson died a little while later, you know, she was old. So yeah, maybe I can try, to get her to talk, I mean, then DeFazio would have to take you back, and some other people had to see her, she's known for getting into shit she's not supposed to"

Angela lifted her head once more. "Why?"

"Why what?"

"Why you want to help me?" Now it was Cam's turn to redden.

"Because I like you. And it's not right, it wasn't your fault." He nodded, a bit too hard, and noticed he was nodding and felt the world staring at him, like there were cameras in the corners, broadcasting to the world.

"I like you too, Cam." She put her hand on his, this time, smiled, and drew it back again, sipping her coffee, lukewarm though it was. "What do you do with them again, the recordings?"

"Oh, I make animations of them and put them on YouTube."

"Animations? Right, you told me, I think, like cartoons?"

"Yeah, kinda, but not like, you know, Mickey Mouse, kinda more, edgy, I guess. I'm building a portfolio, I guess."

"Ok, so like what?" Angela said, rising to fetch the coffee pot to warm their cups. "Like *Spirited Away*?"

Cam lowered his head and raised his eyebrows. "You've seen *Spirited Away*?"

"Sure, I like that one, that guy, ah, *Princess Mononoke*, and the one with the kids whose mama is sick—"

"*Totoro*? I love *Totoro*," Cam interjected, "wow, Miyazaki is one of my influences, for sure, he's kinda why I got into film in the first place."

"I always tell my girls be good or they never get a ride on the catbus."

"Catbus!" They laughed together, then looked across the table shyly, full of fresh, raw, tender feelings for another's presence, for the rhythms of breath and blood and self that we guard ourselves from knowing, from syncopating with our own, until we can no longer ignore our own isolation—or because the rhythm of another is so compelling our hearts cannot help but start to sway, to dance.

On the front stoop, as Cam left for work, Angela grabbed his sleeve and kissed him, quickly and with great force, then slipped behind the door and ran up the stairs. Mami would be proud, she told herself, proud because she was going to try and get her job back from that bitch nurse and because she was brazen, grabbed the man she was interested in and, well, gave him a kiss, but that was a start. On the other side of the door, Cam grabbed the railing. He thought he might faint, and surely did swoon—she was a little pudgy, but then so was he, and she had kids, where was Mr. Angela, anyway? Maybe he was a gangbanger, shit, he needed to be careful, but he could still feel her lips on his, could smell her, coffee and something like lilacs, and maybe baby powder, let the gangbanger come, he would be cool. He would be so cool there wouldn't even be a fight, he'd just walk in and Paco or whatever would squint, and flex all his face tattoos, and just decide it wasn't worth it, Cam was here and he was in charge now. Sure. He was scared shitless, even if there was no baby daddy lurking, even if he wasn't a Latin King. He was so scared, the sun was brighter, the air cleaner, and he felt like singing.

Chapter 8

Constance watched Mrs. Treadwell staring at Tom as he tried to turn the page of the book he'd been reading since breakfast, then turned to stare at him herself. He must have been a very handsome young man, she thought, before age began dragging his face down, so much like a tent left out in the rain and wind, slackening. And moreso on the left side, a distinct droop to the eye and lip on that side, but that's what you get when you live a life of sin, the way he has. She shuddered, thinking of men doing things with other men, women with other women, it was the devil, plain and simple. So much sin, everywhere, in the young ones and the old ones alike, even her friend Eustace had wandered from the path, refusing the simple gift of charity Constance knew she could afford, it wasn't that much money and, well, she needed a dehumidifier badly, bear ye one another's burdens, the good book said, but Eustace had called her names and—sometimes she felt a disgust rising in her soul, not a Christian feeling, she had to remind herself how much work there was to do, so many lost souls, so many who needed saving. "Can I help you?" Tom asked, and she knew she had been staring at him, lost in reverie. She shook her head "no" and stared instead at Dick Klickinoi, who was, in turn, staring at Dorothy, who was wobbling in her wheelchair, subtly at first, then with greater violence, her hands beating themselves against the arms. Tom peered at them both over his glasses

"Nurse! Help! Nurse!" Dick suddenly shouted, causing Tom to let go of his book, which slid off his lap to the floor. Nurse DeFazio and Chris appeared quickly, barking quietly to one another, prodding and rubbing Dorothy, affixing devices to her, measuring, squinting, and just as quickly, wheeling her through the doors to the front lobby. Why don't they just let her go? Tom wondered. Why doesn't she just let go herself?

Tom watched Dick Klickinoi try to hide his tears in his arm. It was good that Mr. Zimmerman was on a trip to the grocery store, Tom thought, the scene would have been so much uglier. Is that what I looked like when I had my last episode, at Christmas? When I apparently couldn't recognize the tree, or my daughter or her boyfriend, and my brain had felt like a box full of unconnected wires? No, I hadn't thrashed about, Helen said she wouldn't have noticed anything was wrong except I'd stopped insulting whatever his name was, the stupid white boyfriend who still thought he was a hippy in his late forties. Whatever happened to Dorothy, it looked pretty bad. We all hoped she wouldn't have to go the West Wing now, but she had been unable to control her bowels for the last two weeks, and her night screams had woken all the residents every night for the last few days. He looked at Mrs. Treadwell, who was doing her level best to pretend she wasn't paying him any mind.

"Backgammon?" he asked. She lifted her head and did the thing he took for a smile, then rose to get the backgammon set. He watched her carefully unlatch the set, investing her actions with a certain reverence, trying to fill, he thought, the space beside the TV where Dorothy's chair had sat. She shook out two dice, placing one in his hand. She would shake the cup and roll the dice for him, as it was too difficult to curl his fingers around them: a direct part in half the roll to see who played first was enough for him "What are... you..." they heard Dick spluttering. He was crying openly now, his face speckled with spidery red patches.

"I'm sorry, do you want to play?" Tom asked.

"What? How can you, just, just—"

"Just what?"

"She's gone, don't you know that! You sat here and watched her, watched the whole thing happen and now, now, you play a game? How can you do that?" He dropped his head and held it in his hands. Tom looked at Mrs. Treadwell, who stared back implacably, then blurted:

"She's not dead, she will be soon, but not yet."

"We'll all be dead soon, and there is nothing we can do to stop it, not a damn thing. But we can keep on going until then, we can continue being alive. Come join us, we'll play Parcheesi, if you like," Tom said. Dick remained hunched over, shaking gently.

"Why do we keep going?" Mrs. Treadwell asked, her voice suddenly dense, almost loud. Tom felt his mouth twitch. The woman spoke once or twice a day, if that, usually only in response to a direct question, but when she did, good lord.

"That's a fine question, my dear. Perhaps because the road up and the road down are the same, as the philosopher said. Perhaps because I want to see if any surprises will happen tomorrow. Perhaps because it is a habit, an addiction. In any case, eternity is a child playing a game, and so the kingdom belongs to the child. A friend of mine told me once that it was hard, that it was too hard for him to go on, and I told him, if that's true, if you aren't just complaining, then you will stop of your own accord. He lived fifteen more years, complaining all the while." Mrs. Treadwell pinched her lips together, then nodded and rolled her die on the table top. Tom dropped his beside it, beating her roll six to three as Dick stood, trembling, refusing to look at either of them, before turning to walk slowly back to his room.

Mrs. Treadwell led, three games to one, when the shuttle came back with the afternoon shoppers. Mary Rose and Eustace came first through the lobby doors into the day room, looking exhausted but happy, followed by Mr. Zimmerman, clutching a small bag to his chest, grinning broadly. Each exchanged quiet hellos with Tom and Mrs. Treadwell, trying not to waken the three residents who had recently settled in for a snooze in front of *Wheel of Fortune*, and proceeded down the hall to their apartments. Tom squinted at the last person through the door, trying to remember his name until Mrs. Treadwell blurted, "Cameron" and reminded him of the young man's name.

"Hi Mrs. Treadwell," he answered, sitting at the table across from her and from Tom, who frowned. Mr. Zimmerman appeared beside them, still clutching the bag to his chest.

"Has anyone seen Dorothy?" he asked, shifting from foot to foot. Across the room, Chris, the aide, looked up from his chart and began moving toward the table.

"Ah, she had an episode, Mr. Zimmerman," Tom said evenly.

"An episode? What the hell kind of episode?" He ended his sentence with a shout, and Chris arrived to take his elbow and lead him toward the nurses' station, speaking softly to him. Tom went back to frowning at Cam, while Mrs. Treadwell beamed. "Are you here to record me again?"

"Um, yes, maybe I am," he answered. Maybe? Tom frowned harder, then realized his frown wasn't nearly as effective now that his lip hung down to one side.

"Oh good, I've remembered some very good ones," Mrs. Treadwell said, folding her hands in her lap expectantly. Cam smiled at Tom, who gave up trying to frown and simply looked away. They heard a shout, then the sound of loud sobbing as Mr. Zimmerman walked past them, returning from the nurses' station, still clutching the bag. His sobs echoed down the hall, then tailed off as his door slid shut. "You have your recording machine, then?" Mrs. Treadwell continued.

"Yes, yes, just a minute," Cam replied. He put the recorder on its stand and smiled again, but his brow was creased with worry. "Can I, instead of just telling a story, can I ask you a few questions first?"

"Of course, of course."

Cam nodded, then looked at Tom, raised his eyebrows. "It's ok if he stays? You don't mind?"

Tom narrowed his eyes. Is she going to leak state secrets, dough boy?

"Indeed. Tom is my friend, maybe he'd like to hear some of my stories as well." Tom nodded. He'd heard her speak this much, this animatedly, exactly once, when the boy had come to record the foul-mouthed old hippy.

"Good, great. Maybe we can record you when we're done, Tom."

"Most likely not," Tom replied saltily.

"Yeah, ok, or not," Cam answered, after a pause. He pushed a button on the recorder, and a red light blinked. "Ok, ok then—" Cam stammered. As they stared at him, he felt something shift in his bowels. Oh boy, what a perfect time for his IBS to act up. Just stay clenched, Cam. "Ok, Mrs. Treadwell. Do you remember Angela?"

"Angela? Angela whom?"

"Angela, the aide who worked here. She was pretty, plump, dark hair, Puerto Rican, I think she helped you bake once or twice?"

"Angela, no, I'm sorry, that doesn't sound familiar."

"Ms. Padilla," Tom offered.

"Oh yes, Ms. Padilla, of course, I remember her."

"Good, ok, now do you remember Mr. Magueax?"

Her face hardened. "Yes. I remember him. Awful man."
Tom nodded his agreement.

"Yes, well, in any case—now, I'm going to ask you a very hard question, but please, try hard to remember: do you remember, when Ang—when Ms. Padilla was here, did you ever, um, did you ever try to get your medicine from the cart yourself? Instead of letting her give it to you, I mean?" He was breathing hard, his bowels ached. Mrs. Treadwell stared at him, eyes wide.

"I sometimes get my own medicine, yes, of course, everyone knows that. Why are you asking me this?"

"Well, because Angela—Ms. Padilla—lost her job and her license, after Mr. Mageaux got the wrong medication, and if it wasn't her fault—"

"I'm afraid I don't know if my father is in a position to help her get it back, but I can ask him, of course." She pulled back from the table, palms in front of her as though directing traffic to stop and wait.

"Well, I don't know about that, I just remember sometimes you liked to hand out meds when I worked here, and Nurse DeFazio got so mad at you, but you liked handing them out—I mean, I covered for you a few times myself—"

"Covered for me? What are you saying? I don't know what you are saying."

"I'm just—ah. I'm just trying to figure out what happened, see if I can help get this cleared up and get Angela her license back, if it was just a mistake."

"If what was a mistake? I don't think this is a conversation I want to have any longer. And you can tell that fat, lazy bunter that if she lost her license, she deserved it. Sloppy architecture, no wonder it fell down."

"Ok, ok, sorry, I just—"

"Excuse me," Tom interjected. Cam and Mrs. Treadwell both looked to him expectantly.

"It seems like this young man is making innocent inquiries

on behalf of his friend—more than a friend, perhaps?—and meant nothing by it, we all are capable of missteps when we care about someone else's welfare." Mrs. Treadwell put her hands down. "I was only here a short time, but I seem to remember you liked Angela," he said to her. "I even think you made cookies with her, as the young man mentioned."

"I don't remember," Mrs. Treadwell offered.

"Perhaps not, but I do. It's easy to forget things at our age, even convenient. Perhaps a peace offering is in order, in any case, to show the magnanimity of your august person, your wisdom."

"Indeed," she replied.

"Then, if I might suggest, perhaps you could make her some cookies, while this young man and I chat."

"Make who some cookies?" She stared at Cam.

"Ms. Padilla," Tom reminded her.

"Oh. What kind?"

"Whatever kind you think she would like." Mrs. Treadwell thought for a moment.

"Alright, but he has to help. You made cookies with me before!" She beamed again, suddenly.

"Yeah, I definitely did," Cam answered. "I put salt in the first batch instead of sugar, you caught me before I put them in the oven."

"Yes, I remember, you were terrible at cookies." She stood up. "I must go refresh myself, and then you, Cameron, will help me make cookies for Ms. Pasilla, so she can get her job back."

"Padilla," said Cam and Tom at once.

"Indeed," she replied, and set off for her room. Once she disappeared behind her door, Tom turned to face Cam. "Is that machine on or off?"

"The—oh, the recorder? Sorry, I'll turn it off." He reached toward the recorder, but Tom coughed loudly.

"No, leave it on." Cam nodded and sat back. "She was,

of course, fiddling with the medication the evening before Mr., what was his name?"

"Mageaux."

"On the evening before Mr. Mageaux passed on. She always fusses with the medication, you know and I know that she does, and only in the evenings, because she knows Carol Ann would have a fit if she caught her. The night aides just let her hand them out, much of the time, while that dreadful Nurse Clemens spends the evening on the phone shouting at her boyfriend. She could have fumbled a pill, perhaps she got scared, hearing Ms. Padilla coming to scold her, and dropped the cup she was holding. So, yes, it might have been her fault. But it was still Ms. Padilla's responsibility to check that everyone got the correct medication, and because she didn't, someone died." He laid his arms across his stomach much more sloppily than he intended to.

"Ok," Cam replied, nodding. "That's kind of what I thought, and maybe it could help her get her license back, if, like, you were willing to sign something—"

"If you prepare a transcript of what I just said, I will sign that, nothing more." Cam saw Mrs. Treadwell emerge from her room and start down the hallway. "Ok, I'll do that, and here she comes," he said.

"Are we ready to bake?" She asked.

"Ready as I'll ever be," Cam answered. He smiled at Tom as he rose to follow her, and Tom tried, once more, to frown.

****

Despite three emergency bathroom sessions to relieve Cam's upset belly, the smell of cookies baking soon filled the day room. Mrs. Treadwell placed them on racks to cool, slapping Cam's hand as he tried to sneak one. "Those are for your sweetie!" she told him. As they cooled, Cam went and sat again with Tom, who was now reclining again with his book. "Thanks, sir," he said. Tom looked over his glasses at Cam. "What is your name again, young man?"

"Cameron, sir."

"Cameron, call me Tom."

"Ok, Tom, please call me Cam."

"Why?"

"Why—what? What do you mean?"

"Cam is a pitiful diminutive for Cameron, it makes you seem even younger and more foolish than you are. Tom is diminutive for Thomas, of course, but I'm old, so it makes me seem younger. Doesn't it?" He raised his eyebrows.

"Um, sure, if you say so."

"Don't accept what I say without question, just because I said it, you aren't a baby. Where is my cookie?"

"She says we can't have these, they're for Angela and her daughters. When I told Mrs. Treadwell about her daughters, it was like she really remembered, she got all excited and said she had to double the recipe. She's making another batch for the residents, though."

"She'd better," Tom said, laying his book open on his stomach.

"Mr., um, Tom, do you think I could record you sometime? I mean, your story. Or whatever you want to tell me about, you seem like you would have a lot of interesting stories."

"Fine, come back tomorrow," he replied.

"Really?" Cam shook his head. "I mean, yes, I can come tomorrow, I can come, um—" he looked upwards, trying to visualize his work schedule. "Right, I don't work tomorrow, I can drop off the cookies and then come here."

"I will expect you in the late afternoon," Tom said, as Nurse DeFazio emerged from the nurses' station. "Oh doesn't it smell good in here!" She said to Tom and Cam and the other residents who were beginning to gather, drawn by the smell of Mrs. Treadwell's cookies. She smiled and continued on down the hallway, stopping at the door to Mr. Zimmerman's room, where she knocked quietly. She knocked again, more sharply, then turned the knob and pushed slowly. "Mr. Zimmerman?" she called softly, peeking her head through the doorway. Mr. Zimmerman lay on his bed, still wearing his coat and shoes, still holding the plastic shopping bag. Carol Ann let the door glide shut behind her, then sat in the across from his bed. His face was yellow and puffy, and he stared at the ceiling, his large nostrils flaring every so often.

"Mr. Zimmerman, the hospital called. Ms. Newell passed on shortly after her arrival at the ICU. The seizure was just too much for her body to handle. I'm so sorry." Mr. Zimmerman's nostrils flared again, but he made no other motion. Carol Ann put her hand on his bicep, held it for a moment, then rose to leave. "Please let me know if you need anything," she said, glancing at a photo on the dresser of Mr. Zimmerman in his clown makeup, doing a trick for a shrieking child. Beside it was a picture of a beautiful woman in a 1940s burlesque outfit, a cloud of feather boas, which Carol Ann realized was Dorothy Newell. Had she never looked at these pictures, or were they new? What did she really know about her residents, after all her plans and strategies for "empowering" them... She swallowed hard, nearly a gulp, and pulled the door open. "Nurse?" She turned to see Mr. Zimmerman holding the bag out toward her.

"Give this to someone, would you? Maybe you want it, see if it fits." In the bag was a blue jewelry box. She flipped open the box and swallowed again at the sight of the ring, cheap zirconium and silver plate, sitting proudly in a little crevice of face velvet. She nodded, closed the box, and put it back in the bag. Outside the door, Mrs. Treadwell was waiting in the hall, three freshly steaming cookies on a plate.

Chapter 9

Cam pressed Angela's buzzer a second time. He'd had a surprisingly good phone call that morning with his Mom, who had just sold three houses the day before and was up for some realtor's award. His Dad's skin cancer was benign, and his brother was going to get married this summer, to someone Cam had never met but who his Mother assured him was "every bit Dylan's equal," her way of saying the fiance was tough enough to keep Dylan from letting his dick lead him around town. It was all good news, all perfectly manageable drama, and he was excited to see Angela—so excited he'd forgotten to call, and now here he was, ringing the buzzer for the third time. "Yeah, hello," came an unfamiliar voice from the speaker suddenly.

"Hi, um, is Angela there?"

"Oh sorry, no, who is this?" The voice resolved itself into a feminine register, and Cam felt more secure.

"Cam, I'm a friend of hers, dropping off some cookies for her and the girls."

"Oh right, she told me about you." The buzzer rang and Cam pulled open the door. An older woman with bright red hair and matching lips and nails stood in the doorway of Angela's apartment.

"Hi, I'm Betty, Angela had to go get Rosie at school,

she got sick in class. You want to come in and wait? I don't
know how long she'll be, she has to get Rosie, then pick up
Allie, I could text her—"

"No, that's ok, I can come back later, I just wanted to
leave her these, one of the residents at ElderGrove made
them for her." He handed Betty a shirt box filled with
chocolate chip cookies.

"You sure? I mean, I know she'd like to see you," Betty
said, giving Cam such a quick and thorough once over
that he felt intimidated, as though he were being told, not
asked, to stay.

"No thank you very much, I'm very sorry I missed her,
please tell her I will call her tomorrow," he said, stiffly,
then added, "and, that I'm looking forward to seeing her."

"Sure will," Betty said. "Bye now." Cam could have sworn
she winked at him, just barely, just enough to make him
nervous all over again. Oh well, he thought, women are
like that, all friends and alliances and subtle glances and
secret winks. Or so he'd heard.

He sneezed as he climbed in his car, then sneezed half
a dozen more times in quick succession, fumbling behind
his seat for a tissue as he pulled away from the curb. Spring
had come early, he thought, or maybe it wasn't spring at all,
just another feint, another promise soon to be broken by
a freak snowstorm. Except they weren't freaky anymore,
freaky was regular, the oceans were rising and hurricanes
and tornadoes were just common blotches on the weather
map, projected behind some smiling cretin with a bad
haircut, they smiled like reapers, the grinning heralds of
an era of death and starvation. And what of it? What a species we are, what a dirty breed, shitting everywhere in our
own nests. How could he think about loving someone like
Angela, if it came to love, how could he look at her children
and feel anything other than foul, imagining the world they
would inherit? The world he had inherited, and what had

he done to help? What could be done? Somewhere there were greasy, deathless, jowly men with cigars laughing at their piles of money, riding dredges across the earth, killing us all slowly. But surely not, they don't exist, it's us, it was always us, in a million little ways, this car I'm driving, the computer I use to make my stupid little movies, all the shit I throw away and flush away and all the times I kept my mouth shut when I should have said something, we are all turning the same millstone that grinds us to dust, we are riding ourselves to extinction, why not laugh on the way down.

He turned into the parking lot of ElderGrove, slumped down in his seat, and fumbled his vaporizer out of his pocket. That's how I'm making a difference, he laughed, I'm vaping instead of adding more smoke to the air, to my lungs. A few pulls later he was of a more abstract bent, and ready to interview Tom without his angst threatening to "bleed all over his subject," as his documentary film professor had put it. What an asshole that guy was, but it's advice I still remember.

Tom Kinney was waiting for him at one of the tables, sitting with Mrs. Treadwell. Cam smiled and said hello to both, then snuck a second glance to be sure Tom was, in fact, wearing makeup. He was, some light eyeliner and perhaps some blush, and maybe even a hint of lip gloss. Tom nodded in reply. Mrs. Treadwell stared past them, fixated on something outside the window, seemingly unaware of Cam's entrance. Cam opened his backpack and set up the recorder, then asked Tom if he wanted some water or tea, as interviewees often got thirsty.

"I'll get some," Mrs. Treadwell answered, rising. "Did you deliver the cookies?"

"I did."

"Good, I'm sure they'll enjoy them."

As soon as she was out of earshot, Tom offered: "I believe

Mrs. Treadwell has a crush on me."

"Ha, yes, kinda seems that way," Cam said. When she returned, with both tea and water, Cam asked if Tom was ready start.

"Milk me," he answered. Cam stopped, his finger held above the record button, and tilted his head quizzically.

"Milton," Tom said. Cam shook his head. "Never mind," Tom said. "What do you want me to talk about?"

"Well, how about where you are from, what is was like when you were growing up." Mrs. Treadwell cocked her head toward the corner of the room, her ear pointing directly at Tom.

"Ah. It would have to start there, wouldn't it." Tom sighed, and slid back a bit in his chair. "The first thing you should know, I suppose, whoever is listening to this, whatever doyens of posterity chance to eavesdrop on a muttering old man, is that I was born in a far off, mystical place called Mississippi." He chuckled to himself. Cam and Mrs. Treadwell stared blankly.

"The humor will not translate, I suppose," he said, grimacing at Cam.

Cam smiled and sat back. "Don't worry, you don't need to try and perform, just talk, you're charming enough, that will come across on the recording."

Tom raised an eyebrow. "Flirting like that will serve you well in the future. Oh alright, the beginning: I was born in Blount, Mississippi, near Lake Jefferson Davis, in March, 1928. I don't know the exact date and neither did my mother, not because she was a woman ignorant of calendars, but because she was black woman born to sharecropping parents in the ugliest, most backwater, imbecilic state in the country, as was I, and she nearly died while having me, at home, of course, and the doctor who delivered me left to service the next town over and was never heard from again, so, she, my mother, didn't know if I was born on March nineteenth or March twentieth, so I celebrate both. I was the youngest of six, all of whom survived at least into their twenties, largely because my father, a very educated high yella man from Louisiana, was so frightened by the trauma my mother suffered at my birth that he moved us all to Chicago the year I turned four years old. I really do believe that saved us." He stopped, took a sip of his water, and sighed. Cam could tell he'd prepared, had probably recited the story to himself all night, in preparation. But man, the makeup was a bit much.

"My mother, too, was very well educated, as I said, and they instilled this very, shall I say, classical ideal of education in all of us, from Pythagoras to Tennyson, though the course of study didn't necessarily take with all of the children. They were both autodidacts, my parents, teaching themselves constantly, and well enough that my Mother won a job with the city as a clerk, and my Father as an accountant with the largest black owned business in Chicago, a chain of funeral homes and restaurants, all without a hint of college, and despite a tendency to look down their noses at everyone who lacked their understanding of the Western canon—that is to say, just about everyone they came in contact with. Ours was a studious household, we never attended parties or even church socials, though of course we went to church. People were frightened of us, and resentful, which proved too great a pressure for my eldest brother, Elijah, and eldest sister, Zora, both of whom rejected the family in favor of jazz and carousing and other such earthly delights. It was very hard, we were negroes, barely noticed by white people, and then only as objects in their path, but also uppity, and so rejected by our own people. It was a bit like being in a cult, I suspect. I'm fairly sure I was the only black teenager in Chicago who could recite Horace in the original Greek. No, I can't remember any of it, I always preferred translations in any case, Greek always sounded guttural in my mind.

"So, there I was, a very young man in Chicago, and the war was going on, which, all told, was better than what came before—I never lacked for food, but the sheer stress of the Depression pressed on us surely as a pair of forceps might pinch the skull of a child reluctant to exit the birth canal. My elder brothers were all in the service, except for Elijah, who disappeared to California in 1939, I didn't hear from him again until he was dying of emphysema, 1972 or so. And my sisters were all married, except for Beverly, the youngest save me, whom we called Bee, so while the war years were scary, they were better than what came before, and Bee and I had the run of the South side, we thought. She was a funny girl, very petite, very smart but also so very naive." He stopped and took another sip of tea, settling further back into his memory, letting it wash over him.

"Ok, it was just you two and your parents, at that point?" Cam offered, trying to draw him back into the world.

"Yes, ah, yes, just us. I was a terrible brown-noser, everyone at school very quickly learned not to drink wine or smoke cigarettes anywhere near me because I would tell, I would tell any adult nearby, a teacher, a policeman, a preacher. With the perspective time grants us, I now see, or think I see, I was struggling to come to terms with my sexual orientation, or not come to terms with it, as the case may be. Regardless, I cared only about two things at the time: learning, from all the musty books I could find, and Bee, who needed protection my parents seemed unable, for all their loftiness, to offer. That may be how I first noticed my parent's weakness, in fact, as all children do at some point, noticing that their limitless power was in fact limited, and that they were weak, broken vessels, like the rest of us. So, I became her constant companion, especially when I noticed her, ah, physical development had suddenly increased quite rapidly—many sloe-eyed Lotharios suddenly took to following us home, plying her with sweets and even worse temptations, reefers and wine and stockings and all those kinds of things. And then one day I had to run an errand for my mother, and Bee was to walk home alone, and three boys took her behind a rendering plant and raped her." Tom looked down at his hands.

"That's terrible, I'm, I'm sorry," Cam said after a pause.

"Yes." Tom sat silently, and made no move to speak until Cam reached for the recorder, whereupon he waved him aside and continued.

"Yes, it was terrible, and ugly, and it made me an awful racist for a while. For a very short while, actually, I unlearned that, along with so many things, while I was in prison. But I'm getting ahead of myself. The three boys, I only remember the ringleader's name was Lester, were not, of course, arrested, no one cared much about the tribulations of a little black girl then, or now, in fact. She wouldn't leave her room for three weeks, until my Father picked her up and put on her on the doorstep, in the same clothes she'd worn for a week, and told me to take her to school. I did, and on the way home, this Lester person came sauntering up and asked her, loud enough for everyone to hear, if she liked it, and if she wanted more. I can still hear his voice, high and wheedling, in my ear, and I can still remember how it felt to pick up a piece of pipe laying at the construction site we were passing and hit Lester with it, his face was so surprised, and then hitting him and hitting him until his head was little more than a stain at the end of his neck. Close your mouth, you're going to catch flies," Tom said to Cam, who was indeed slack-jawed.

"Sorry, sorry, that's just—that's how you went—"

"Yes, that's how I ended up in prison. Joliet Correctional Center, 1944 to 1952. Manslaughter, though Lester was also just a boy. Prison was my, ah, place of self-discovery, shall we say. I prefer not to speak of it, except to give thanks for Dr. Ignacio Cordon, the prison physician and a remarkably progressive man for the time. I was twenty-four years old when I was released, my mother met me at the gate. During the time I was interred, my father and two of my brothers passed away, as did Bee, who—Bee took her own life, and my mother told me none of this until I was released, she visited me every week but never told me anything about our family."

Tom stopped and wiped a tear from his face with the back of his hand. Mrs. Treadwell offered him a tissue, which he held to his nose awkwardly.

"Are you ok?" Cam asked. "We can stop, if—"

"No, no, we're just getting to the best part! Well, almost to the best part. Before the best part, before I emerged into myself, I had to first try to; let me go back. After I was released from prison, mother found me a job driving truck, and I found a wife, more or less at random. No, that's unkind, Ella was a fine woman, deserving of much better than I. But my heart, and, other parts of me, just were not as, ah, fully engaged as was necessary, though we did manage to produce a child, my daughter, Helen. Around the time she was born, I obtained a job assisting the captain of a tug boat. Jack, ah, Jack something, I can't recall his last name, but he a was lascivious old queen who enjoyed his walks in the jungle, though I don't believe I was really dark enough for him. In any case, I learned from him about piloting tugs, and about many other things we shan't talk about in polite company, so after a year or so I was ready to both pilot my own tug and to leave Ella to find a proper man for herself and Helen. And she did, a good man, he was a good father to Helen, though he never did overcome his distaste for my presence. I suppose I goaded him a good portion of the time, but essentially we agreed to, ah, avoid the censures of the carping world, so to speak. Are you certain you want to hear all this?"

"Yes, yes," said Cam, and Mrs. Treadwell, and Frank and Constance, who had settled into chairs near enough to eavesdrop.

"My, my," Tom said, bending his neck stiffly in a failed attempt to see who was behind him, "it seems I have an audience."

"Is that ok?" Cam asked.

"Oh I don't see why not, the bag is open and cat long gone, at this point. I sought work on a tug in Cleveland, and found one running out of Ashtabula, the Norma B. It was a wonderful job, steering a cranky old lunch bucket tug around the harbor—most of my time was spent pulling barges, but there was something about spending most of my day floating that was simply wonderful. Ashtabula itself was not so wonderful, not for a budding young fairy, though really, I was always what they called, "straight-acting," or at least I tried to be. So, I began taking the train to Cleveland on my weekends off, and it was there, at the Bluebird Lounge, the only gay bar for, ahem, persons of color in the city, on the east side, that I met Hector. Oh he was a handsome man. I remember he was wearing a white cotton suit and a panama hat, he looked like a very tan version of Paul Henried. He was a professor of classics at Fenn College, which Cleveland State later swallowed up, much to Hector's chagrin. A professor of classics! All of a sudden my very rusty ability to quote Plutarch was an asset, for the first time in my life, actually. We fell in love, though of course, we couldn't express it, even in the Bluebird, no dancing, no touching—well, we did anyway, we knew who was a policeman and who was a snitch and when we could be ourselves.

"It was quite a romance. In the early 1960s, I was lucky enough to obtain a position, thanks to the AWO, our local representative was a dear, if anyone tries to tell you unions are passe, you just ask them when the last time they enjoyed a weekend off was and who they think they have to thank for that. What was I saying? Yes, I managed to get a roving position in Cleveland Harbor, piloting tugs, helping with scheduling, a great variety of things, though no tug of my own, but it was well worth it to live and make a home with the great love of my life. He loved to throw parties, we had a sumptuous old house in Glenville, before it went to the dogs—after the shoot out, I remember Hector was so frightened, he wanted to leave, I couldn't believe he was so frightened, he was from Cuba! I just assumed he had seen awful things when Castro took over, but his family were well to do and escaped very early on, I found this all out later; at the time, I sat on our front porch with a rifle on my lap and a pitcher of daiquiris on the table, and no one looked sideways at us after that. All those poor young men, looking for something to burn, something to take all their rage out on. After things calmed down, Hector made me promise to move, and we did, to University Circle, of all places, I was certain no one would rent to us but Hector used the last of his savings to buy us a tiny little house by the railroad tracks, I think technically it might have been Little Italy, but it was right on the border. A much smaller house, not a place for parties, which was fine because we were both getting older and more, ah, nesty, collecting antiques and museum memberships the way old queens do.

"And then one day I came home, and Hector told me he was sick, and he was, no, not with HIV, though it was the 80s and when he said he was ill of course that was the first thing that came to mind. But no, he merely had spots on his lungs, he always smoked like a chimney, and he fought it, he fought very hard, we both did, but the cancer won, it always does. I took an early retirement and nursed him the best I could. He wanted cremation, as do I, the body is but a cheap suitcase, and I held his hand as he breathed his last, on August 11, 1996. I was sixty-eight years old, most of my friends had died years before, as had my family, except for Helen. I sold our house to pay what I could of our medical bills, and moved to Toledo to be nearer my daughter and her family, she has three children of her own, well, they aren't quite children now but they were then, I had little use for them, small children are really so dull. Now they are much more interesting, and, of course, have no time for a stupid old Mary who can barely take care of himself, with withered old hands and a face that sags on one side like slippery tablecloth. I don't blame them at all for not visiting me. I wouldn't want to come here, if I had to visit me in such a place."

"It was better before all these stupid buildings were here," Mrs. Treadwell interjected.

"I doubt that," Tom replied. Frank and Constance were looking down in their laps, and the TV buzzed in the background. Cam reached over and shut off the recorder, Tom took another sip of tea, and tried to smile at Cam. "Was that sufficient? An honest tale speeds best, after all."

"That was, um, it was wonderful, thank you so much."

"Now is it my turn?" Mrs. Treadwell asked.

"Ha, uh, well, not right this second, Mrs. Treadwell, I need to go home and transfer this to my computer, and some other errands and stuff, but I will come back next week and record you, I promise." Cam turned to Tom and asked, "can I get you anything? Are you hungry?"

"I believe what I need most right now is a nap," Tom answered.

"Ok, well, thanks again, so much, I will try to work on this and get it online soon, and then I can show you the results, if you want to see them."

"That would be fine."

Cam thanked Tom once more, promised Mrs. Treadwell yet again that he would come back to record her, and said goodbye to Frank and Constance.

"He is a kind young man, I suspect I misjudge him," Tom said, once Cam had passed through the doors to the lobby.

"Indeed," Mrs. Treadwell answered.

"I haven't thought about some of those events for many years, he certainly has a way of making one want to tell a story."

"That's not why."

"I'm sorry?"

"He's not the reason people here want to tell stories."

"No, I suppose you're right."

****

Beverly Pinsky, returning from her gynecologist's appointment, passed Cam in the parking lot. He was older, but was surely the young orderly she'd caught smoking marijuana with a resident five or six years ago. What kind of shenanigans was he up to now? He wore no uniform, was he visiting family? Probably dealing drugs, she thought. DeFazio ran a sloppy ship, all new agey crap and patterned scrubs, she'd been a thorn in her side since she arrived, seven years ago, taking the job that was, by every correct measure, Pinsky's. Well. We'll see where this leads, after the accident with the schoolteacher she was on thin ice already. If the board had just listened to her, this tragedy would never have happened. She pushed through the door to the West Wing and was greeted by the smell, the one she hadn't gotten used to, even after thirteen years in the building, hell it was almost brand new when she took the job and it stunk then. Of rot, yes, but of sour chemicals, and metal, and brine. Oh well, who is going to die today? She wondered, nodding at Harold, who handed her the evening chart and scuttled away.

Chapter 10

Nurse Tshoke paged Carol Ann at eight p.m., after Mary checked on Mr. Zimmerman and found him deceased, laying on his bed, still fully clothed. She drove to ElderGrove, berating herself for not checking on him before she left, it was Tshoke's first double shift, after all. She tried to give the residents as much space as possible, hadn't he seemed ok at breakfast, when Chris delivered his meal? But then why did he still have all his clothes still on? Dr. Pfluke was standing in the lobby when she arrived, talking to Nurse Pinsky. Great.

"Well now, two in what, a week? Ten days? I might have to start hanging around here more often," said Pfluke. He was pale, blonde, sharp featured: Carol Ann pictured him as an extra in a Bergman film, eating fermented fish and staring at his beautiful wife, who suffered from ennui. Nurse Pinsky, on the other hand, was clearly part rodent.

"What happened?" Carol Ann asked.

"Another of your PCA's, no doubt. You really need to check their work," Pinsky said. Carol Ann ignored her, tilting her head toward Pfluke insistently.

"Uh, well, a Mr. Ernest Zimmerman died sometime yesterday, judging by the state of his body, yet the PCA," Pfluke stopped to flip the pages on a clipboard—"Mr. Chris Park? Recorded him as taking his medication this morning.

That seems a neat trick, for a dead man."

"How did he die?"

"Not sure, looks like simple heart failure, his body's been taken down, I'll check with the coroner. You have the forms for this online somewhere? Peter's on vacation, he usually does the paperwork."

"Yes, let me go send you the link." Chris Park was meticulous to the point of neuroses, he wouldn't mark the chart wrong or, god forbid, fake a med check. Pfluke followed her into the nurse's station, where Mary, Curt, the newest aide, and Nurse Tshoke all sat, huddled around a space on the floor.

"It's not such a big deal," Pfluke continued, the conversation in his head leaking out his mouth, "if your boy missed it, if there was some emergency or something, it doesn't really matter so much, does it? I mean, they guy was already dead, I'll just—" he stopped, noticing the assembled night crew for the first time. "What I mean is," he whispered to Carol Ann, "let's not get the BRC involved again, not so soon after the other one, Peter said that was a serious fuck-up."

"Whatever you think, Doctor," Carol Ann replied. She knew there was no point arguing. Pfluke had, like so many physicians, acquired a set of ear plugs along with his license. At least Peter Small gave a shit, he wasn't there just for some easy money, like Pfluke No, Carol Ann thought, Small was here for the drugs. She said hello quietly to Tshoke and Mary, and nodded to Curt as he left the room, then found the necessary documents on her computer and emailed them to Pfluke's account.

"Are you going to fill them out?" He asked, looking over her shoulder.

"I—you want me to fill them out? But I don't know what happened, and you have to sign them."

"Just fill in what you know, here are the charts, here's

the EMT report, send it to me and I'll check whatever you missed. Ok?"

Carol Ann sighed. "Yes, Doctor."

With that, Pfluke departed, and out of the corner of her eye Carol Ann saw Nurse Tshoke sag into her chair. Mary popped up out of hers and turned to face Carol Ann, in obvious panic. "It was my fault, wasn't it? I should have checked last night, after I gave him the evening meds? Am I going to get fired?"

Carol Ann sighed, sagging a bit herself. "Was he alert when you gave him his meds?"

"Um, yeah, I think," Mary said.

"I checked and signed off, it's my fault," Nurse Tshoke offered. The skin beneath her eyes was sallow and grey, making them seem blurry, indistinct against her the blue-black of her cheeks. She still wasn't used to being up all night and trying to sleep during the day, when her grand-daughter was at school.

"It's no one's fault, yet," Carol Ann said, "and you heard Dr. Pfluke, Chris Park gave him meds and breakfast this morning. Due diligence, remember. We'll get to the bottom of this."

The two women nodded, and Mary left the nurse's station. Nurse Tshoke stood and tried to let Carol Ann sit in the chair behind the desk, but Carol Ann waved her off, sitting instead in the chair Mary had abandoned. "Are you doing alright?" she asked Nurse Tshoke.

"Yes, yes, doing fine, doing fine," she replied, looking down at the table top.

"I worked overnights for a while, before I came here. I remember going a little crazy at first, trying to get used to the schedule. Pulling a double is really, really rare, I promise."

"Yes, it is a tribulation, but I'm working on it, with Jesus' help."

"Good," Carol Ann watched her clutch the cross around her neck at the mention of Jesus' name. "You know, I think I still have a book about getting used to overnights—I think that's what it's called, actually, *Getting Used to Overnights.* I can bring it in, if you think you'd read it."

Nurse Tshoke looked up from the desk. "Yes, that would be, that would be nice, thank you." Carol Ann smiled and got up to leave, then stopped at the door.

"I'm sorry, I can't believe I forgot this, but what's your first name again?"

Nurse Tshoke looked surprised, and a little wounded. "Chanelle."

"Sorry, Chanelle, won't happen again. Let me know if there's anything else you need, and I will bring that book with me tomorrow morning."

"Good night, Nurse DeFazio."

"Carol Ann."

"Yes, Carol Ann."

Carol Ann got into her car and started to cry, a burst of tears that nearly choked her. As she regained her composure and pulled out of the parking lot, she tried to reconstruct what could have happened in some more or less logical fashion. Chris Park was not the type to skip a resident and forge a chart, no matter what, and Mary was too frightened of everything to step out of line so egregiously. Or was she? In any case, even if she did blow off Mr. Zimmerman's evening meds and bed check, there's no way Chris would have done the same the next morning, that was simply too much bad behavior all at once. Maybe Mr. Zimmerman put on his clothes to go out—there was a shuttle that day, to the grocery store—lay down because he didn't feel well, and expired. That seemed to her infinitely more likely than Pfluke's eyeball autopsy pinning the time of death to yesterday evening. He was a charlatan, after all. And now, he seemed bent on "correcting" the paperwork, so no one would ever be the wiser. The thought of such unethical behavior gnawed at her, at the same a time a small voice in her head whispered words of comfort, that it would in fact take care of everything, that Mr. Zimmerman was very old and had a history of heart trouble. "Bullshit bullshit bullshit," she said aloud, parking in the street in front of her apartment. If Maggie was here, she could talk her through all this, but Maggie hadn't been back since the night they fought in front of the mullet woman, not even to fetch clothes. Maybe I could use a little Jesus myself, Carol Ann thought. If I could find a Jesus, who liked dykes, of course. Or if I had even a shred of belief, I mean, come on, the whole story was just too ridiculous. Then again, most stories were.

Carol Ann sat at her kitchen table and worried at the edge of a place mat. Place mats, china sets, frilled valances—all her idea, trying to stave off some of the avalanche of Maggie's hippy stuff, but also because she liked it, the sense of propriety involved in having good china and company china, and a spoon for the mustard only, and yes, even the occasional country girl dress, long and stiff as an oven mitt and still, somehow, sexy. How much of that feeling was simply to establish contrast with Maggie? How much of herself was formed in reaction to the sheer amount of space, physical and emotional, that Maggie had occupied? Well, it was still better than having no one at all, she told herself. She'll come back again, in a week, maybe less, asking for forgiveness, promising never to do it again, explaining all about her need to go "a little around the bend" every once in a while. And what will I do? Forgive her, ask for her forgiveness, and go back to worrying about her leaving, rather than sitting here worrying about dying and no one finding my body for a week. That's what ate Pinsky's heart, she knew, everyone did: how her husband had left her and taken their two young children, how he'd killed them both and himself during the police standoff, how she lived alone ever since, with no pets or hobbies or anything aside from work, which she hated. Carol Ann had tried to make friends with her after she was hired, and after she heard Pinsky's story, but nothing doing, Pinsky was simply mean, through and through. Maybe I'm not giving her credit, maybe she does have hobbies, maybe she has a houseful of canaries, or volunteers with the local community theater, why do I listen to all the gossips who tell me otherwise? Because that's what I want to believe, it's another way to shape my self in response to the presence of others: at least I'm not Bev Pinsky, at least I'm not so angry and disappointed that even perfect stranger could look at me and say, that woman's heart is shriveled and nearly dry, and she likes it that way. I can never be her, I must let myself be, oh Maggie, you always helped, why did I drive you away again. Such an old story, I hate that story.

****

Cam restocked the Coors Light for the third time that shift, thanks to Tink, the new night bartender who hadn't a clue but did have very large breasts and, more importantly, no qualms about using them to curry favor. She probably jiggled them at Dirwood the whole time he was having his "last one" before heading home, and that was that, no need to stock anything, or even wipe the fucking bar down. He and Andy had often talked about getting Dirwood in trouble with corporate; surely plowing your way through eight or nine beers every happy hour was not the sort of thing Store Managers were supposed to do, but even it was, he could at least pretend to pay, or tip, for Christ's sake. He served Donny, the guy he'd met at Mageaux's funeral, and whose name he now knew since Donny now believed them chums, presumably on the basis of their shared mourning for the shop teacher who thought he was a Hell's Angel. The world is filled with twats, he thought, and went down the stairs to get another case of Killian's. The prep cooks were all chattering away in Spanish, and Cam wondered if he should start recording guys like them, people who looked like they had interesting stories to tell, but who weren't all, well, so old. Not that he minded old people at all, he found ElderGrove a very sad place but also very comforting, most of the residents, and the folks who worked there too, come to think of it, were not full of shit, they weren't preoccupied by stupid drama, or with jiggling their tits at bar patrons, or with getting a glimpse of those tits between Jagerbombs. They were just living, most of them, just sitting back and feeling the last of their threads unwinding, and that wasn't sad, it was soothing, the inevitability. The conditions, the dreary poverty in which they lived, that was sad, but we're a selfish breed, after all.

Andy came back from his break as Cam stashed the last of the Killian's in the ice.

"Cops are in the back, talking to Dirwood," he said.

"Yeah? Maybe he's finally getting busted for being a total prick, " Cam replied. "I didn't even see them come in."

"Yup, one plain clothes, one uni. You holding anything?"

"Me? No, why, you think that's why they're here?"

"No idea, but if you got anything, might be time to hide it."

"No, I'm good." Andy was one of two bartenders at the Lost Lake Applebee's who dealt cocaine to customers. He dealt other party supplies as well on occasion, but for the most part, theirs was a cocaine clientele. Last year, a bus boy named Jordan had sold meth for a while, but he started using too much himself, and was fired when Dirwood found him de-liming the dishwashing machine, by hand, from the inside, wearing nothing but a speedo.

Cam nodded as Donny signaled he was going out to smoke a cigarette, and the bar was empty, as was the dining room. Happy hour would start in a little while, and all the people who thought, in their tiny, Candler City-ish way, that they were yuppies, would start filtering in from their jobs as realtors and car salesmen and medical secretaries and bank clerks, ready to laugh too loud and flirt like children and give their thoughts a bit of glow, something to buoy them for the highway, for the garage, for the prefabricated home and snotty kids. The Lost Lake Applebee's looked like every other Applebee's on the planet, which, of course, was the appeal. All the chintzy, random crap on the walls, the black and white photos of someone's mom, the gas station signs, the broken guitars, they all came from a warehouse somewhere, or maybe several warehouses, Cam knew, but it's all the same crap, and that's why people like it: here is your small dose of fun for the day, a strictly regulated amount of fun in a place that is safe and familiar, with food that tastes like it's already been chewed once for you, and the same shitty songs drone by in the background, day after day, and eleven big screen televisions, so you don't have to look like some loser, just staring off into space because you are tired and drunk and have nothing to say even when you aren't. Wow, do I need a new job, Cam told himself, for the third time that day.

"Cameron?" Cam turned and saw Dirwood standing behind him, flanked by the two policemen Andy described.

"Mr. Dirwood?" He nodded at the policemen, who said nothing.

"In my office, please?"

"Sure," he said, tossing his bar rag beside the sink. Dirwood's office was a testament to thwarted ambitions and the intractable sadness of the middle manager. Inspirational posters, fraying and curling around the masking tape that held them, jockeyed for position with certificates and awards given for perfect mediocrity: Managerial Success Course, Store of the Quarter for Fall 2002, Sensitivity

Training Program, all in plastic and fake wood frames that went yellow 30 seconds after they were exposed to air. His desk was a mess of receipts on spindles, a dirty plate or two, and photos of Dirwood with his wife and son aboard with his pride and joy, a twenty three foot fishing boat christened the *LegaSea*, though it had never been within 400 miles of an ocean. Dirwood moved to sit at the desk but the plain clothes cop stopped him.

"Nope. We can take it from here." Dirwood looked confused.

"We need to speak to him privately," the cop continued, dragging out the last word the way he did for children and idiots.

"Ah, ok, got it, sure you don't need something to drink?"

"No," the cop said, and the cop in uniform shook his head.

Once Dirwood had left, the plain clothes cop motioned for Cam to sit in the chair opposite the desk, while he sat in Dirwood's place. He was, Cam noted, the singularly most exhausted looking individual he'd ever seen, the only parts of his face that were not bags under his eyes were his eyes themselves and a moist looking mustache that the remainder of his face adhered to. His entire head, and posture, were a testament to the effects of gravity—and overeating— but his eyes nonetheless held bright, sharp points that may have been cruel, or empathetic, and were, in any case, intimidating. The other policeman looked the way beefy cops often do in uniform, as though his flesh was straining to burst free, so he could run naked down the street, feeling the chill spring air against his buzz cut as he smashed things in his path, gleefully.

"You are Cameron Wright, 2719 E. Juniper st, apartment 2?" the tired cop asked.

"Yes, that's me," he answered.

"Where were you yesterday at 11 a.m., Mr. Wright?"

"11?" Cam suddenly felt flush. What the fuck was going on here? "Um, probably at ElderGrove, the nursing home, why? What's up?"

"And why were you there?"

"I was recording someone, I make recordings of the residents, why?"

Tired cop shifted in his seat, squeaking it loudly. "And how long were you there?"

"How long, I don't know, till two or three, maybe?"

"What about before you went there? Yesterday, before 11 a.m."

"Ah, I went early and did some laundry, I dropped off cookies at a friend's house, um, I think that's all I did in the morning. Would you please tell me what's going on?"
"Do you know this woman?" He drew a photo out of his pocket and held it out for Cam. It was Angela. Oh shit, her baby daddy must've done something bad, oh no, did he see them kiss? Cam looked up, unsure what to say. "Yes, that's Angela."

"Is that who you gave the cookies to?" Cam choked, coughed, choked again. The uniform cop spoke quietly, "he asked you a question, bro."

"Yes, that's who I gave the cookies to, why, what happened? Is she, did she get hurt?

Tired cop nodded to the uniformed cop, who put a hand on Cam's shoulder and guided him up out of the chair, pulling his arms behind as he did so.

"Cameron Wright, I am charging you with the murder of Angela Padilla. You have the right to remain silent—"

"The what! What the fuck are you talking about? She's not dead, I just saw her, she—"

"Anything you say can and will—"

"No! No! She's not dead, she can't be, she..." Cam would have collapsed, but for the uniform cop holding him upright. They waited, after the Miranda reading, for him to stop sobbing and collect himself, then guided him out the door, past the bar. Cam glanced at Andy, mouthing "I told you so!", and at the first happy hour customers, each proudly bearing the privilege of witness to the evening's fount of gossip and speculation, the most exciting thing that had happened to any of them in weeks.

Chapter 11

The Candler City police station, along with the rest of the downtown municipal compound, was built in the 1970s in a fit of architectural pique, following the bulldozing of the previous station, the library, and City Hall in a misguided swell of urban renewal. The resulting building was formidably ugly, even for a police station. The tan faux-stucco walls seemed more appropriate to a fast food franchise, and the interior was a sullen maze of crooked rooms, yellowed drop ceiling, and industrial floor tile the color of cat vomit. The effect the building had on the men and women who worked there was desultory, and also self-reinforcing: it made everyone so miserable, they simply dismissed the idea that a coat of paint might brighten things up, or in fact that the place they worked could have any bearing on their state of mind. A twelve-cell jail was stuck on the back of the station, and the station's basement held two large holding cells as well, which had the small virtue of being cool in the summer and warm in the winter, and the first floor held a very infrequently used viewing room, replete with a greasy two-way mirror. It was on the other side of this mirror that Cam stood, along with three police officers, two in their street clothes, while Betty LaFalce, Angela Padilla's neighbor and occasional babysitter, sobbed while identifying Cam as the man who brought the cookies two days before.

"How could he do such a thing? What's wrong with people?" she asked Detective Heinz, blowing her nose in the kleenex he'd provided.

"If I knew that, I'd be a rich man," he offered.

Cam had been photographed and fingerprinted, all the while begging to know what was going on, and what had happened to Angela. Heinz had seen it before, of course, the feigned ignorance of the murderer, which often wasn't even feigned, but was simply a symptom of severe psychological problems. By the time they reached the interrogation room Cam had retreated into a guarded silence. He stared mutely at his hands as Heinz and patrolman Anthony entered the room and took up the same positions they'd held in Dirwood's office, Heinz across the table from Cam, Anthony behind him.

"You know what I don't get?" Heinz asked Cam, who raised his red rimmed eyes but did not answer. "I don't get why the girls, too. I mean, couldn't you go all romeo and feed the girl some spaghetti dinner and leave the kids out of it? That's pretty fucked up, don't you think so, Anthony?"

"Very fucked up, yes."

Cam felt the floor give way, felt his body being drawn downward, even as he stayed, sitting, stupidly sitting while these strange men lied at him. It simply could not happen this way, his life, the lives of the people they kept insinuating he had something to do with. It wasn't happening, he was just losing his fucking mind, and this is how the hallucination was playing out.

"I also don't understand why poison, I mean, arsenic? That's kind of old-fashioned, right? Where'd you get it? It's weird, maybe you're one of those, uh, steampunks or something."

A knock sounded at the door and it swung open. A short, plump man with a half-hearted goatee blustered in, apparently in mid-conversation with himself. "My client needs space, space, come on, come on, back away from the client..." he sat next to Cam in a chair Cam had not noticed was there.

"I'm not seeing that anyone is all that close to your client," Heinz said.

"Cameron. Cameron? Right?" Cam nodded at the man's outstretched hand. "Cameron, my name is Lee Valis, I'm your attorney."

"Ok..." Cam tried to remember asking for an attorney.

"You called your mother, your mother called my secretary, presto, I am your attorney. That's how it works. Can we have some privacy, please? And I better not hear any whirring, little motors running, little ears to the keyhole..."

"Oh Jesus," Heinz said, rising, "such drama. Don't you worry, Mr. Wright, we'll be back soon. Try not to cry anymore."

"Intimidation, intimidation, off with you, away, away," said Valis, making a little brushing motion with his hand. He swiveled in his chair and faced Cam, smoothed down his sleeves, then smiled and squinted from behind small wire-rimmed glasses. Once the door had closed, he coughed and flicked open the locks of the briefcase he'd set on the table.

"Now."

"I didn't call my Mom," Cam mumbled.

"Ah? Ah. Well, you must've called someone, and they called your mother, I assume. In whatever magical way it happened, it happened, and here I am. Now."

"I called Clyde."

"Very well, then Clyde called your mother. Look, I think you have some inkling of the trouble you find yourself in, yes yes?" Cam nodded. "Good, then let's try and sort this out so we can get you out of it." He nodded again, staring Valis' cufflinks, which were in the shape of tiny gold dice, each set showing a four and a three.

"First, to review: you have already admitted, to the police, that you brought Ms. Angela Padilla cookies on Tuesday morning. Not so smart, that. But, but, but, perhaps it simply emphasizes your innocence, to wit, you admitted this, ah, gift so readily because you had no idea the cookies were poisoned."

"I didn't, I still don't, I don't get what's going on, all of this."

"Yes, well, the full forensic analysis will take a few more days, so while the presence of poison in the cookies is confirmed, the three bodies found at the residence only show symptoms of poisoning, we need confirmation, though it may be a moot point."

"But you, wait, what?"

"The lab results, the tissue analysis, is not complete, but the cookies do in fact show high, concentrations of arsenic. And, you did in fact deliver said cookies, and were in fact witnessed doing so by a neighbor. And, you did in fact post a video on YouTube in which you question Ms. Padilla's competence as a nurse's aide, calling her an 'ignorant bitch' at one point during your screed."

"Oh shit," Cam whispered.

"Oh shit, yes," Valis said, "that is a great deal of circumstantial evidence to overcome, I must say. So, so, the first question I need to ask is—"

"I didn't fucking do it!"

"No, not that question. The first question is: from whence did you acquire the cookies in question? At a grocery, perhaps? The arsenic must have been folded into the dough, not simply dusted on. Or did you bake the cookies yourself?"

"I, oh fuck, Mrs. Treadwell." Valis scribbled her name

on a piece of paper.

"And who is Mrs. Treadwell?"

"She's an old lady, but wait, it could have been anybody at ElderGrove, I was having stomach problems, so I had to run to the bathroom a few times while we were making the batter. Anyone could have gone and put stuff in them! I mean, Mrs. Treadwell had the most chance, she, but why? What, she had nothing against Angela, she's just a senile old lady who lets me record these weird stories she makes up."

"So, the next question I should ask is: where is Elder-Grove, and why were you there?"

Cam explained about his High School job at the nursing home, about doing the first oral history as part of a Senior class project, and how he'd been going back for more than a year since he graduated college, collecting stories and then animating them, how he hoped someone would take notice and offer him a job, and at least he was building a portfolio, and how no one seemed to visit folks there much and he felt bad for them, and then he noticed Valis had stopped taking notes.

"So, yeah, that's why I was there."

"And, more specifically, why were you there making cookies?"

"Oh, um, well, it was Mrs. Treadwell's idea, I think. She makes cookies and cakes for everyone, she's made them for Angela before, and, um, Angela had lost her job and I was trying to help her."

"Help her by making her cookies?"

"No, no, I was trying to get Mrs. Treadwell to admit she'd been messing around with the med cart, see, someone died, well you saw the video, the Mageaux guy in the animation, he got the wrong meds, Angela got blamed, and she thought maybe Mrs. Treadwell had been messing with the meds."

"Why would Mrs. Treadwell touch another patient's medication?"

"She did that a lot, it was just a senile thing, like Frank trying to escape through the fire door or throwing his shit around, Mary Rose talking to her dolls, just these weird little habits the residents pick up. She would go over and take them out and try to deliver them, no idea why, after she got in trouble a few times, she stopped, or so I thought, Angela says she kept doing it." He stopped and felt the weight of using the present tense for Angela.

"That is very curious," Valis said, continuing to scribble. "So, who else could have had access to the cookies? Or to the batter, rather? Or dough, yes, it's called dough, correct?"

"Anybody, like I said, I was in the toilet most of the time."

"And, and, one more question I really should ask: the police will no doubt search your apartment soon. Are they likely to find traces of arsenic anywhere therein?"

"No! I told you, I have no idea what the fuck happened," Cam blurted, then: "um, but they will find some weed, and a bong, and, that's about it, I guess."

"Some marijuana and a smoking device are the least of your worries, Mr. Wright. I think the next step is to have my PI interview Mrs. Treadwell, and see if she will talk to him. Now, the police are rather excited, there hasn't been a murder this juicy in Candler City in quite a while, so they may try to interrogate you again, so it's very important for you to remember to tell them nothing of what we've discussed here, don't tell them about ElderGrove, or anything, if it feels like they are breaking you down, simply refuse to speak. It's your right. To not speak, I mean. In the meantime, I will have my brother visit Mrs. Treadwell and see what I can find out."

"Your brother?"

"Yes, my brother Lawrence is a licensed Private Investigator, very professional, very thorough."

"Ok, I guess, tell him to bring a recorder," Cam said.

"I'm sorry?"

"Bring a tape recorder, a digital recorder, something. I tried to write down our first interview and she said the scratching noise made her skin crawl, so she won't talk to you unless you bring a recorder."

"She?"

"Mrs. Treadwell."

"Oh yes yes, a recorder, fine, fine, very strange, all these details. In the meantime, try to rest, rest assured, I will take care of everything. These hands," he offered his hands, palm up, to Cam, "are good hands, and you are in them, my boy."

The hands in question, Cam noted, were puffy and moist with sweat. As Valis flustered his note pad back into his briefcase, he continued muttering to himself, and only stopped when he reached the door.

"Oh, and your mother is here, you will be heartened to know, though it's unlikely they'll let her speak to you," he told Cam. "I'm actually rather surprised, very surprised, they let you use the phone so soon, or at all. Such good luck!" He opened the door just enough to slide through, and was gone, leaving Cam to stare at his own hands, the tabletop, anything to keep various future scenarios from creeping into his mind and stabbing him in the back of his eye.

****

"I went in, he was sitting on his bed, in his clothes, talking to Mrs. Treadwell," Chris said, shaking his head. "I mean, I said 'hi', he said 'hi', I left his food on the table, watched him take his meds—he was fine."

"That's exactly what Mary said about evening check, the night before," Carol Ann replied.

"I don't know what else to say, I mean, why would I lie, yo?"

"I don't know either, Chris. I don't think you are lying; actually I think Mr. Zimmerman died sometime shortly after you saw him, and that, well, his time of death was terribly misdiagnosed. But, I wanted to let you know what was happening, in case anything develops further."

"Like what?"

"If his family wants to have an inquiry, for example."

"Zimmerman had no family, least that's what he said. 'Clown guns always shoot blanks', he said, I remember that one, I asked could I use it a song, and he said sure, long as when I got famous I bought him a hot dog." Carol Ann watched Chris rub his eyes.

"Well, whatever might happen. I'm sure nothing will come of it, we all just have to be very, very careful from now on, very diligent."

"Are they going to shut us down?" He asked.

Carol Ann sighed. It was the same question she'd asked herself at least once a week, since she'd begun working at ElderGrove. "I don't think so, Chris. The BRC is in no hurry to reduce the number of available apartments, we just need to be especially careful, as I said. In other words, continue doing the excellent job you've been doing, and let me worry about the rest of it."

Chris shifted in his seat. "This is probably a bad time to ask about a raise, huh?"

"You're at the top of the pay grade, Chris, you know that," Carol Ann smiled. "The rules are still the same: get a nursing degree, move up the pay scale. Not my rule, that's just the way Aames has it set up." She knew, as did Chris, that the first thing he'd do, if he ever did get his RN, would be to go find work somewhere that paid more, somewhere that didn't involve wiping quite so many bottoms. She was a little surprised he was still here, all told, most of her aides were brand new, and moved on as soon as they got some experience, or had run out of options elsewhere, in which case they were on their best behavior for a few weeks, then did something to get themselves fired, something that went askance of the Aames HR guidebook. Her willingness to maneuver Chris' schedule around his performing dates was probably the cause of his loyalty, she thought. Some bean counter at Aames would likely bristle at even that bit of flexibility, but she knew how to finagle the schedule reporting software well enough to keep the red flags to a minimum.

"Yeah, I know. When I get signed, after that, I'll have mo' money, yo," Chris said, rising to leave.

"And mo' problems," Carol Ann answered. Chris' jaw dropped in mock surprise, and he pulled it back into place with his hand, smiled, and shook his head. As the door closed, Carol Ann's phone lit up.

"Yes?" she said, glad the new hire at the front desk had finally figured out the paging system and had stopped leaving the desk to tell her every time there was a call that required her attention. Now if she could only remember his name.

"A call for you on line two, Nurse DeFazio. Someone from a lawyer's office."

Ah shit, just when the day was starting to brighten, Carol Ann thought. "Thank you, uh, thanks." She stabbed the blinking light with her middle finger.

"Hello, Carol Ann DeFazio."

"Yes, hello, I am calling representing Mr. Leland Valis, attorney at law. Mr. Valis is requesting that a Private Investigator he has contracted conduct an interview with one of your residents, a Mrs.—" Carol Ann heard the rustle of papers, "Treadwell? No first name? Do you have such a resident at your facility?"

"Ah, yes we do, may I ask what this is in regards to?"

"I'm sorry, I don't have those details at present. Mr. Valis, that is, the other Mr. Valis, can give you that information.

May I schedule an interview?" Carol Ann did not like this woman's voice at all, she sounded like she was playing the part of a schoolmarm in some community theater production.

"What do you mean, the other Mr. Valis?"

"Ah, one Mr. Valis is an attorney, the other an investigator. They are brothers."

"Alright, Mr. Valis is welcome to come speak to me, and if his reasons for wanting to interview Mrs. Treadwell seem adequate, I will see if she wants to talk with him."

"Very good, he'll be there in an hour."

"An hour? No, I don't have time in an hour, he can come tomorrow morning, at eight a.m."

The woman on the other end of the phone sighed, and rustled some more papers. "He has a previous appointment at eight, can we make it nine?"

"That's fine," Carol Ann said. "Goodbye." The woman on the other end cleared her throat, then hung up. Carol Ann had no time to take umbrage, as the alarm beside her desk went off. She jumped up and went through the day room, down the hallway to the resident's apartments. Mary held open the door to Tom Kinney's room, and Carol Ann saw Tom laying on the floor, bent awkwardly at the waist. Chris was checking his eyes with a flashlight. "I think he had a stroke," Chris said.

"I came in to see if he needed bathroom time, and he was laying there, on his face, though," Mary blurted.

"It's ok, it's ok, did you call 911?" Carol Ann replied, squatting and putting on her stethoscope in one motion.

"Yes, then I, we, rolled him over, was that ok? That was right, right?" She was holding Chris' arm now, looking very young and very small. Tom's breathing was erratic and shallow, but he was breathing. "Yes, rolling him over was fine. Mr. Kinney? Tom?" His eyes wobbled in his sockets, unfocused. "Can you hear me? Can you say 'hello'?"

Tom's head shook slightly, then stopped.

"Can you stick out your tongue for me?"

His tongue darted out suddenly, lodging in the right corner of his mouth.

"Good, very good. Mary, help me get this pillow under his head." She stayed on her knees beside him, stroking his forehead, talking softly to him until a loud bang sounded behind her head and she turned to see the EMT crew smacking the gurney against the doorjamb. She stood and backed through the door, standing beside Mary, who still clung to Chris. Residents had begun to gather, and she shooed them away. "Move aside, please, let them through." Frank stood next to Mrs. Treadwell, his eyes as flat as hers were sharp.

"He's done, then?" Frank said, laboriously. His own stroke two years ago, and regiment of medication required to keep him from constantly trying to escape out the fire door, made his speech pattern extremely deliberate, as though he was selecting each word from a shelf of possible choices, wrapping it in paper, and placing it on the ground before you. The same stroke also made him into a feces-thrower. Nature abhors a vacuum.

"Please, Mr. Gladwell, go back and sit down. I'm sure Tom will be fine. Mrs. Treadwell, please, everyone, let the emergency people do their job, and everything will be fine." She believed it herself as she said it, guiding Frank by the elbow, moving toward the day room, trying, through little more than force of will, to soothe and distract the gathered residents and brush away the cloud of fear that had risen, or at least let it settle back onto the furniture, the grey and white heads, the greasy linoleum.

"I been dead for thirty years. No big deal," Frank mumbled as he shuffled away. Well good, as long as you stop throwing shit at my employees and trying to get out the fire exit, she thought, and she didn't think about Frank again until much later, after the EMTs had left, and dinner was stumbled through, and Dr. Pfluke called to check if his presence was absolutely necessary at Thomas Kinney's hospital room, and Constance and Mary Rose both had accidents at the same time so there weren't enough PCAs so she had to take Mary Rose to the bath to clean her off, and Raheem, the new night PCA, called in sick so she had to call and beg Latrice, the other new night PCA who wasn't even due to start until day after tomorrow in to cover, and after Mrs. Treadwell made an angel food cake that put everyone in a sweet haze, and after she showed Latrice the few ropes she could show her and said a few snide things about Raheem, then left in a fog of guilt and drove home to her empty apartment and sat, fingering one of Maggie's shirts she'd found between the washer and dryer. The shirt was close to going moldy, it had been wedged in the gap so long, and dribbles of detergent and water had moistened it into a clump. Then she remembered, that she'd been glad Frank believed himself a zombie as long as he stayed put, and she wondered when it had happened, she'd become a more monstrous version of her mother, cynical for no other reason than it helped plow through the day, and then another day, and then another, until they were finally, blissfully, gone. In three years, she would be older than her mother ever was, only thirty four months from now, and she saw that the table and the shirt and the coffee maker were all numbers, things assembled from six, nine, one-point-two. One-point-one. Zero.

Chapter 12

Maureen Wright was not the typical preacher's wife, or so she liked to think. In fact, thinking she was a "preacher's wife" was one of the idiosyncrasies that made her atypical, never mind the contradiction. Her husband was Unitarian minister, which is about as far as you can get from being a preacher without entirely giving up the avocational urge to actually preach, but it suited her to think herself a preacher's wife, so she did. And a preacher's sister-in-law, twice, in fact; her husband's two eldest siblings were also Unitarian ministers, following in the footsteps of their father. The youngest was a set designer for television commercials somewhere in California, and didn't often return phone calls from the rest of the brood, but was always present for important family business, if only via telephone, which everyone involved considered a fine arrangement. The Wright family was very much an institution, she thought, broad and sturdy, well-built and of great service. Except that her son was somewhere in this awful, dank building, accused of murder—murder! Cam wouldn't cut his chicken for three years after he first saw a live one on a school trip. Her own family was a raggedy thing, her mother widowed when Maureen was three, her only brother a drug addict she lost touch with sometime during high school, no extended family that she knew of, everyone dead or invisible. She was the last thread leading back to whatever her ancestors had been, and of course, if you go back far enough, everyone is related, so she liked to think of herself as the child of Ghengis Khan, since she'd read a lot of people were, in fact, related to him, and because her eyes had a vaguely Asian pinch to them. A door opened behind her, and she turned, and felt her body suddenly want to escape itself, to scream and watch Maureen screaming from somewhere high above, as two policemen entered with her son between them, head down, hands and feet shackled together. She looked down at the table, stains on top of stains on top of peeling vinyl cover.

"Hi Mom." His voice pricked her scalp, and she heard one of the policemen shifting weight from foot to foot, jingling his keys. She resolved to bring her head up and speak to him, and not to cry, no crying, no crying.

"Oh Cameron..." she felt the tears push over the edge of her eyelids. His face was pale, and dusty, his eyes packed in dark pillows of skin, his mouth drooping open slightly. What have they done to him! She dug her nails hard into her palms and told her brain to shift into gear.

"Are—are they treating you well? I got an attorney for you, did he come? Can I bring you anything?"

Cam sighed. "I'm fine, just tired. I'm next to the cell where they put people detoxing and those guys stay up late shouting and stuff." He looked up at one of the policemen and asked for some water. Once the door had closed again, Cam allowed his eyes to meet his mother's for the first time. "Yeah, I met the lawyer, thanks for that. You could bring me a toothbrush."

She swiveled in her chair. "Can I bring him a toothbrush?"

"Yes," the lone cop answered, "but give it to the admissions sergeant and he'll check it first."

"And some toothpaste?"

"Sure, to the admissions sergeant."

She turned to face Cam once more. Her son, her youngest, her baby boy, how did this happen, stop it Maureen, get a hold of yourself.

"So, ah, um, what happened, exactly?"

"Huh?" Cam raised his eyebrows dopily.

"Why are you here, Cam? Why am I talking to you here, in a police station, why did your friend tell me on the phone you were ranting about someone getting killed? What happened?"

Cam shut his mouth in a grim line. "You know, Mom, I honestly have no goddamn idea why I'm here. I didn't do anything, and I can't go to jail for something I didn't do, so when they figure out who did it, maybe I'll know why they thought it was me."

"Did what? I don't understand."

"Neither do I. Neither do I." The policeman brought Cam a glass of tepid water, and he and his mother sat quietly for half an hour, chatting intermittently about anything but why they were there. Finally, another policeman came in to tell her it was time to go, and she stood and watched her boy dodder out of the room like an old man, shoulders hunched, head pointed at the ground. She followed the hallways in a daze, out through the front door to the parking lot, found her car and her keys, got in, rolled up the windows, and pulled out of the parking lot. When she reached the first light, she turned on the radio, turned it up as loud as it would go, and started screaming. She drove that way, slowly, down side streets, until her throat gave way and her eyes felt like they would burst. She pulled over and looked in the rear view mirror, saw a strange, beaten woman looking back, blew her nose in a kleenex, turned the radio down, and wondered what she should make for dinner.

****

At ElderGrove, Carol Ann was also inundated with policemen. There were only two of them, but they had a way of making themselves large, or taking up too much space and getting their noses into everything. She had little patience for people who seemed to take joy in making others nervous, and she still wasn't exactly sure why they were standing in the nurses station in the first place.

"You have her employment records, though?" He was asking about Angela Padilla now, after cycling through a series of vague, and vaguely intimidating, questions about practices and procedures at ElderGrove. He learned that in cop school, I'm sure, right after the lesson on how to point your fat, pastry-stuffed belly like a loaded gun at innocent people. He had a tragic, greasy comb over, a matching mustache, and dandruff that stood out even on his light yellow dress shirt. The other cop was younger, looked like he thought he was a dandy, had pressed pants and the kind of shirt wall street brokers wore in bad 1980s movies. They seemed to loathe each other, even as they communicated on some sub-verbal level.

"Yes, I do, do you have a warrant to see them?" She replied.

The younger cop smiled blandly. "Oh, we'll get one, if we need one, don't worry. Would you say Ms. Padilla was a, hmm, conscientious employee?"

"What is this all about, gentlemen? Perhaps I could serve you better if you told me why you are here." She thought about the lawyer who had called about interviewing Mrs. Treadwell. Surely not a coincidence, that.

"She was conscientious employee, yes?" He was no longer smiling.

"Yes, she was excellent."

"And then she was let go all of a sudden? Doesn't sound

so conscientious, really," added the fat cop.

"She was, ah, she made some procedural errors, and, yes, she was terminated. I'm a stickler about that kind of thing. She made a mistake that she knew, from the day she started, would result in termination. Other than that mistake, however, she was an excellent aide."

"Really," fat cop continued. "Way I heard it, she gave some old man the wrong pills and it killed him." Carol Ann's eyebrows shot up involuntarily.

"I, but," she stammered, "I don't know where you heard that, but, uh, things like that, patient's rights are inviolable—"

"Relax," young cop interjected, swinging his leg to sit on the corner of her desk. "Just something we heard, you know, gossip, word around town, that kind of thing."

"Well, I don't know who would go around spreading awful stories like that."

"Someone who didn't like her, probably," fat cop answered. They both stared at her, waiting for her to volunteer a list of enemies, or break down and spill some torrid batch of secrets. Well, there is nothing to spill, you stupid, cocksure men, so I can sit and stare just like you.

"Did you like her?" the fat man finally said.

"I liked her very well, we had an excellent professional relationship."

"Nothing more? I mean—" young cop shrugged.

"You mean what?" Carol Ann demanded.

"Nothing," young cop brushed the query away with his hand. "But really, she got along fine with everyone?"

"Yes, no problems at all."

"What about Cameron Wright? Did she like him?"

"Cam? Well, yes, I mean, he hasn't worked here in years, but he does come by often to spend time with the patients. I'm sure they got along well, I don't remember seeing them interact all that often, to be honest."

"What did he do, spending time with the patients? Spin the bingo cage for them?"

"No," she answered sharply, "he liked to hear them tell stories about their lives, and he recorded what they said, they're called oral histories."

"And then he'd put them up on YouTube and make cartoons about them, right?"

"I'm sorry?"

The fat cop tucked in a stray shirt tail and tilted his head at the young cop, motioning them both toward the door. "YouTube, he made videos, you should take a look, if you haven't already. Pretty easy to find, he used his real name. Nice to see people still do that on the internet." Young cop nodded at her as he left the office, and fat cop pulled a weathered business card out of his breast pocket.

"Thank you for your time, Ms. DeFazio," he said, "please call me if you remember anything that might be relevant to our investigation."

"I don't know what you're investigating."

He turned away from the door and let it fall closed. "Angela Padilla and her two daughters were found dead, poisoned. You didn't see it on the news, I take it. The poison was delivered to her by your former employee, Cameron Wright. We'll be back in a few days, let us know if you think of anything that might help."

He left, darting through the doorway with remarkable agility for someone built like a down pillow. Carol Ann had heard some shocking things in her life, had even seen some events whose traumatic weight might immobilize other people, but this was the first time she knew what it felt like to be stunned. Like in *Star Trek*, "set the phasers to stun," and then they pointed at the Romulan and a beam of light came out and a little glow appeared on their chest, the look on their faces as they froze, in mid-action, and fell slowly to the ground, oh and Spock mind-melding with the rock creature, that was just on last night and—

"Nurse DeFazio?" Mary's voice clacked through the intercom and broke through her daze. She shook her head.

"Yes, Mary?"

"There's a Mr. Valis here to see, um, you, I think—" she heard a voice blustering in the background, "—and Mrs. Treadwell?"

"Fine, good , fine, send him through, please."

She looked around the nurse's station, the whiteboards and cabinets and cluster of miniature teddy bears and bulletin board full of yellowing cartoons suddenly very strange, unfamiliar yet known, like things glimpsed from a past life. "Mrs. DeFazio?" She turned to see a short, pale, unhealthy-looking man wearing the kind of tiny, wire-rimmed spectacles John Lennon had made popular a very long time ago.

"Nurse DeFazio, yes, you are Mr. Valis?"

"Yes, I'll sign in here, then?" He picked up the pen chained to the guest register.

"Yes, that's right." He signed with an elaborate flourish. Perhaps he thinks he's a performance artist, she thought.

"Good, very good, ah, may I see the lady in question now?"

Carol Ann raised and lowered her chin, stretching her neck. "Shortly, yes, let me go remind her, I'm sure she's forgotten. Before you speak to her, I would like to ask you a few question myself, if you don't mind."

"Of course, of course," he said, looking at his watch, "I do have to be back downtown by 11:30 for a meeting, another meeting," he rolled eyes.

"Alright, hang on, then."

She stood and walked around the corned, back through the day room, to Mrs. Treadwell's door. She knocked gently, and the door opened almost immediately, as if Mrs. Treadwell was standing on the other side, waiting.

"Yes? Are you here for the meter?"

"No, Mrs. Treadwell, it's Nurse DeFazio. I'm here because you said you would talk to the man from the law office who wished to speak with you. Do you remember we talked about this yesterday?"

"No!" she yelled, and closed the door. Carol Ann sighed, and knocked again. Mrs. Treadwell opened it again, slightly, and peeked out.

"Does he want to take my land?" she asked.

"No," Carol Ann answered, " he just wants to ask you some questions."

"What about?"

"I'm not really sure, would you like me to ask him?"

She hesitated, scratching her nose with a yellow nail. "No," she concluded, opening the door and stepping through, "let me see what this jackass wants."

Carol Ann smiled. "That's good, but wait here, I'm going to ask him a few questions first, then he's all yours." Mrs. Treadwell looked confused, then slipped back into her room and closed the door again. Carol Ann heard her muttering on the other side.

Back at the nurse's station, Mr. Valis had made himself comfortable in Carol Ann's chair, and was chatting with Chris.

"... Aesop Rock in Chicago, really fine, really fine."

"Oh damn, that's the bomb, his shit is tight, man, damn... oh, sorry," Chris said, shuffling out of her way.

"I think it's potty check time, Chris," she said.

"Oh boy," he sighed, "highlight of the day."

Carol Ann coughed. Mr. Valis smiled. She gestured with her hand at the wooden chair beside the filing cabinet.

"Ah, sorry, so sorry, taking the most comfortable chair in the room is an instinct I picked up during my college days," he said, moving to the other chair.

"One doesn't 'pick up' an instinct, they're innate. That's

why they're instincts." Carol Ann settled into her chair and picked up the clipboard where she had jotted a list of things to ask Valis.

"No, properly said, very true. I suppose 'habit' is a better word. Is Mrs. Treadwell agreeable?"

"She is, but first, why are you here, Mr. Valis?" She crossed her legs.

"Well, that is, of course, not something I'm supposed to discuss, or rather, my brother prefers I not discuss the case, if at all possible, but if it helps, I can tell you my brother was retained by the mother of Cameron Wright to represent her son." He smiled, and all the patchy spots where his goatee wouldn't grow shone whitely.

"Ah. Yes. I just heard something about that." She looked down at her list and realized none of her questions made much sense anymore, so she put the clipboard aside. "The police were just here, perhaps you passed them in the parking lot."

"No, I didn't pass them, I waited for them to leave, then got out of my car," he smiled again.

"Why?"

"No specific reason, nothing concrete, I have found, in my years of sleuthing around, that it's best to avoid your, ah, competition as much as possible prior to the actual, er, match." He folded his hands together across his stomach.

"I'm sorry, did you say 'sleuthing'?"

"I did. That is what I do." His smile broadened. Suddenly, Carol Ann was reminded of Dr. Seusses' *Grinch*.

"I see. I think I'm beginning to understand, but I would like some assurance that my resident is not going to be made, er, upset by your line of questioning."

"I will try my best. Do you hold power of attorney for Mrs. Treadwell?"

"No, I do not."

"Are you in any other way legally entitled to prevent

me from asking her permission to interview her about this case?"

"No." Carol Ann could feel her lungs tightening. She did not like this weird little man at all.

"I didn't think so. You are welcome to be present, it might help make her feel less threatened." He took out a kleenex and blew his nose. Carol Ann raised her eyebrows, but refrained from slapping him, much as she wanted to.

"Do you have a cold, Mr. Valis?"

"No, no, springtime allergies, pollen, so forth." He put the kleenex back in his coat pocket. "Shall we?" He rose and swept his arm toward the day room. Carol Ann nodded primly, and led him to a table. "I'll go see if Mrs. Treadwell is ready."

"Very good, very good." Mr. Valis arranged himself on one of the chairs and looked around the room. A few residents were snoozing in front of the television, another was reading a book, and Dick Klickinoi was staring at Mr. Valis from one of the couches. He nodded, but Dick made no motion.

"Lovely day," Mr. Valis coughed.

"It is if you're an idiot," Dick replied, and went back to his crossword puzzle. Carol Ann appeared at the end of the hallway, leading Mrs. Treadwell, who walked with her head down and her hands clasped together, as though she were going to the principal's office.

"Mr. Valis, this is Mrs. Treadwell," Carol Ann said, and pulled out a chair.

"Hello," Mr. Valis said. Mrs. Treadwell nodded and sat in the chair Carol Ann offered. Carol Ann sat beside her and put her hand on Mrs. Treadwell's arm.

"Are you ready to answer Mr. Valis' questions?" Mrs. Treadwell nodded again, almost imperceptibly.

"I'm so glad, so glad, now, don't worry, I just want to ask you a few questions about some of the people who have worked here at—" he pulled a small note pad from his coat pocket, the same one that held the used kleenex, Carol Ann couldn't help but notice—"ah, ElderGrove."

Mrs. Treadwell stared at the tabletop.

"Is that alright with you, Mrs. Treadwell? May I call you, um," he looked at Carol Ann for help.

"Mrs. Treadwell is fine," she said, removing her hand from Mrs. Treadwell's arm and placing it in her own lap.

"Yes, ok, well. Ah, first, do you remember a Ms. Angela Padilla?"

Mrs. Treadwell continued to stare at the table top.

"Well, ok. Does she usually talk much?" Mr. Valis asked.

"To people she likes," Carol Ann replied.

"Ha. Got it, got it." He looked at his notebook, flipped the pages. "Oh, yes, yes, almost forgot," he said, rummaging around in a side pocket and withdrawing a small digital recorder, which he placed on the table. Mrs. Treadwell's eyes lit up.

"What's that?" she said, meekly curious.

"A digital recorder, is it alright with you if I record our conversation?"

"Oh yes, yes, I love telling stories," she brightened, sitting up in her chair.

"Good, so, let's get back to it," he said, pressing a button on the side of the recorder that made small green light pop on. "Ms. Angela Padilla, do you remember her?"

"Oh yes, yes, she was such a whore, it always happens like this, every year, every decade, they swim by like blind little fishies, spreading their legs and getting fat bellies and letting more babies drop out, it's just so silly, isn't it?"

Mr. Valis sat back, his brow furrowing. "Ah, yes, I think, now, hm."

Mrs. Treadwell curled her lip. Carol Ann wanted to smile as well, but wasn't sure it was appropriate.

"Right." Mr. Valis flipped through his notebook again.

"Can you tell me, Mrs. Treadwell, if you remember a Mr. Cameron Wright?"

Mrs. Treadwell made a face like an otter bearing its teeth, which allowed Mr. Valis saw that in fact she had no teeth, false or otherwise.

"Oh yes, Cameron, such a nice young man, also a whore, of course, but still, very nice, loved to listen to my stories. Angela was a nice whore too, so is Chris, and Mary, and Nurse DeFazio here, too. I bet you're a nice bloodsucking leech whore too, Mr. Vamoose, when people get to know you, right?"

"Ah—"

"Of course, Cameron would come and record my stories, I have the best stories. Do you know why?"

"Ah, no, I don't know," Mr. Valis stammered.

"Because I am a student of architecture. So many years ago, the ground came up out of the water, right over there," she pointed to a corner of the day room, "and then more ground, and when there was enough ground, there was a place for presence to land. Do know what presence is, Mr. Valis?"

"I think I do, yes," he nodded.

"Well, maybe you do and maybe you don't, but words are slippery things anyway, and when I say 'presence' I mean something that can see, hear, feel, experience things. So, there was enough land for presence, and so presence could alight, after drifting for so long, but it was such a lonely place. There was dirt and grass and ferns and bugs and little furtive animals and big stupid animals and was nice to look at for a little while, but it was lonely. Then it got cold, and then there were people, and they were much more interesting, but so much more wicked. People are wicked, so many of them, in so many ways. Over there," she gestured toward the dining room door, "twelve men snuck up on a group of women and children on their way home from picking fruit and did terrible things to them, then killed them all, which was a mercy, and ate three of the youngest children, because they were the most tender. That's wicked, yes? Over there, a ways over that way," she gestured in the direction of the West Wing, "a woman drowned her sister in a spring because she thought the sister had become a demon, when of course it was really just me! So many things, so many wicked things, and in such a small space! Now, multiply that by the size of the planet, and good lord, so much badness... but wicked ways are better than loneliness, or at least more interesting to watch. Do you know," she bent forward slightly, Mr. Valis and Carol Ann matching her incline, "on this very spot, right where this table and these chairs are, right where we're sitting, there was a house, a farmhouse, built by a very wicked and stupid man and his mother? Terrible architecture, stupid, nearly feral beams and crossbeams, but anyway, yes, it was right here. He was not smart but he was good at making things appear to be what they are not, and his mother, yes, she was a smart one, and they looked like each other, and both were broken, their heads were broken and full of wrong ideas. One of their wrong ideas was to go get the man a wife, so he went on his horse till he reached the city, and there he bought two little girls from a woman who had a home where people put their unwanted children, rather like this one," she said swept her hand across the room.

"Ok, well—" Mr. Valis began, lifting his hand for the recorder.

"I'm not finished!" Mrs. Treadwell snapped. Mr. Valis sat back, holding his hands.

"So, this man, he had a raging beard and huge bushy eyebrows, his mother had the same, well, not the beard, ha ha, you know, though she might have grown one, if she lived long enough. The man brought the two little girls back, sisters, not quite ready to bear children, but that didn't stop the man from forcing himself on them, and beating them, and the mother, too, did things like sticking sharp pieces of twig up under their toenails, laughing, laughing.

"One day, one of the little girls tried to run away, and the man caught her, and he threw her down so hard that her back snapped in two, and his mother made the other sister sleep with the body in a shed behind the barn until it started to rot. She told the girl, 'that's what you will smell like, if you try to run away.' So the girl did as she was told, but even though she became a woman, she didn't have any children, which made the man very mad, but he couldn't kill her, because his mother was so old, she couldn't do much of the housework and fieldwork anymore. So he went to the city and got another girl, a little older this time, and he put her in leg chains so she couldn't run, and soon she was pregnant. She had several children, one after the other, and the first girl helped each time, while the mother watched and cursed them both. After her third child was born, he took off the leg chains, so she could walk better, but the chains had ruined her legs and she never walked very well again after that, and both girls knew, as soon as she stopped having babies, he would kill her.

"She had two more children, and was pregnant with the sixth, when the mother drank some bad water and got very ill. The man wouldn't fetch a doctor, and it was snowing outside, and the babies and young children were all crying, and the man yelled he couldn't take the noise anymore and hit his mother on the head with a hammer. He went out into the snow, yelling at the stars. He was gone three days when the pregnant girl began having her baby, and the first girl got water and blankets and held her hands and talked quietly to her, and when she saw the babies' crown start to show between the pregnant girl's legs, she put her hand on it and pushed, and pushed it back in, and the pregnant girl pushed back and the baby pushed back and the first girl pushed back just as hard, she was strong, and there was a lot of blood and then the pregnant girl was dead, and so was her baby. She looked at all the blood, and heard all the children whimpering with hunger and she picked up the man's hammer and killed each one, then went to the barn to get kerosene.

"The man's body was swinging from a rafter in the barn, parts of him hanging out where the rats had already gotten to it. Finally found a use for those beams! Even feral architecture has its uses, I suppose. She poured some kerosene around the floor of the barn and lit it, then went inside and covered everything she could see with kerosene, laughing and splashing it everywhere, and set it aflame. The last thing she did was lay down in the floor and look through the holes the fire had eaten in the roof and watch the stars looking back at her. So many wicked things, and right underneath your feet! Hard to imagine, isn't it?"

Mr. Valis and Carol Ann both stared, dazed, at Mrs. Treadwell, who looked down, smiling, at her lap.

"What the fuck," Mr. Valis blurted out.

"Mr. Valis, please," Carol Ann said.

"Wicked, wicked," Mrs. Treadwell mumbled.

"I—I'm sorry, that was, that was just a very disturbing story, I'm not sure—" Mr. Valis fumbled in his pocket for his kleenex.

"I do have the best stories, don't I?" Mrs. Treadwell said, smiling shyly at Carol Ann.

"That was quite a tale, yes," Carol Ann answered. She had heard Mrs. Treadwell make up some very peculiar stories before, but that one was indeed a doozy. Perhaps it was time to end this interview, she decided. "Do you think you have enough answers to your questions, Mr. Valis?"

"Ah, yes, yes, I think I have it all right here," he said, palming the recorder.

"Good, then let me show you out," she continued, standing.

"Is Cameron going to come visit me soon? He's much better at this than you are," Mrs. Treadwell said, shaking her head reprovingly at Mr. Valis.

"I really can't speak for Mr. Wright, but, um, anyway, it was a pleasure to meet you," he said, extending his hand. Mrs. Treadwell looked at it, then smiled at him again.

"And you too, whore."

Mr. Valis pulled his hand back and shook his head. He had little experience with senility, all his grandparents and parents had died quite young, and he expected to follow suit, though with luck, not anytime soon. He tried to smile back at Mrs. Treadwell, but she was already staring at something in the corner of the room. He followed Carol Ann through the double doors to the lobby.

"Is she—I mean, what was that? Is that typical of, um—" he fumbled for the words.

"She suffers from a kind of dementia, yes, but I would say that the, um, manifestation of her dementia is not at all typical. She doesn't talk much otherwise, and I remember how surprised we all were when Cam first interviewed her and she just went on and on, spinning a fantastic tale. Perhaps she was a storyteller when she was young, I really can't say."

"So, most of your—"

"Residents."

"Your residents, they have some kind of senility? I mean, most of them wouldn't make good witnesses, it seems to me."

"I would venture that more than half of our current population struggles with some form of dementia, Mr. Valis—Alzheimer's, vascular dementia, sometimes both. When they reach the point where they can't take care of themselves even minimally and lose most of their contact with the outside world, they are moved to our West Wing, where they are better equipped for end-of-life care."

"Ah. Well. Too bad, too bad for my brother's client, I suppose. He had identified Mrs. Treadwell as a possible witness, though clearly putting her on the stand would not be beneficial to anyone."

"No, not likely," she said, guiding him toward the front door. "I would like to help Cam, if you think there's anything I can do."

"Yes, you could see if there were any other employees on duty on this date," he scribbled on the back of a business card, "and contact me, if so, or if any of the other residents remember anything, though I'm beginning to think that's also not likely. You see, Mr. Wright claims that the poison which killed Ms. Padilla and her children originated here."

"Here!" Carol Ann let go of the door, which drifted slowly shut.

"Yes, and that Mrs. Treadwell and he made, let me see—" he flipped the little notebook open again, "a batch of cookies. The cookies contained quite a bit of arsenic."

"Arsenic? But where would—we have no arsenic in this building!" She crossed her arms.

"No doubt, no doubt. Which does not bode well for Mr. Wright, sorry to say. In any case, if you do find anything that might be of use, please let me know."

"I will."

He stepped to the door and took the handle himself. "Ah, one more thing, Mrs.—Nurse Defazio."

"Yes?"

"Do you recall if Cameron Wright was here last Thursday, the 17th? The date I put on the card."

"I believe so, yes, he interviewed another of our residents. One who is in the hospital just now, I'm afraid."

"Really? Very good, very good, may I have his name?"

"Yes, Thomas Kinney. Last I heard he was doing well

and would be discharged back to us tomorrow. I can ask him if you would like to interview him as well."

"Yes, yes I would. I'm sure the police will also be interested in talking with him. Or not, who can tell what they're up to. And, do you remember if he did any baking while he was here? Perhaps with Mrs. Treadwell?"

"I don't remember, I'm sorry, but it's very unlikely, he has debilitating arthritis in both hands. Mrs. Treadwell bakes something for everyone at least once a week. She really is a wonder in the kitchen that way." She bit her lip, feeling like she was giving away family secrets to a stranger. But Cam was a nice young man, he was not at all the kind to do something so horrible, he wasn't even ambitious enough, actually.

"Really? Very good, very good," he said again, scribbling in his notebook. "I'll be in touch."

Carol Ann nodded as he left. She felt like sinking to the floor and sobbing, letting all her parts go slack and all the stress of the morning drool away on the tile.

"Nurse DeFazio?"

She sighed. The morning had just begun. "Yes Mary?"

"It's St. Joe's, I think about Mr. Kinney."

"Thanks, Mary, I'll take it at my desk." She pushed through the door and sat, quickly, worried she might collapse if she stood for too long. Could this really only be Monday? She caught herself wishing Maggie would be waiting when she got home, pushed the thought away, and lifted the receiver.

Chapter 13

Carol Ann stared at the half-empty bottle of chardonnay, and at the totally empty bottle beside it. She couldn't remember the last time she was drunk, but she was sure it was for pretty much the same reasons, and with pretty much the same result: one near-to-drooling nurse, in her underwear, at the kitchen table, alone. She took a sip of water, then another sip of wine. Some days just begged for this kind of bad behavior, she sneered to herself. First, the police, then the dandified private detective or whatever he thought he was, followed closely by Mrs. Treadwell's rambling Wisconsin Death Trip story, which had shaken her more than she wanted to admit. Then, the hospital called to schedule Tom Kinney's return, though his stroke had caused some "cognitive complications," which the admin she spoke with could not or would not elaborate on. No sooner had she hung up the phone then Tom's daughter, Helen Lennox, was the phone asking for directions, lost somewhere on the highway, and of course Mary patched her through because, well, why not? It was Carol Ann's job to supplant google maps now, apparently, and she tried to tell the poor woman to wait until tomorrow, but Lennox knew nothing about Tom's recent stroke, which was odd, as the hospital staff normally contacted whomever served as medical proxy first. So, when she arrived and her father was somewhere else, she flipped, which is understandable, and promised to sue ElderGrove, which is not, but Carol Ann managed to calm her down and gave her the address of St. Joe's, along with proper directions, and sent her away. At which point Mary was kind enough to tell Carol Ann she recognized Helen, that she was, in fact, a reporter for WKRT news. Yes, Carol Ann reflected, a small town talking head, hooray, with any luck they would start an investigation. Constance deciding to smear feces on the wall of her room was the most normal part of the morning.

After lunch, Carol Ann looked up Cam's YouTube page, and spent the better part of the afternoon being freaked out and saddened by the weird, amateurish animations he'd made for the oral histories he recorded for the last five or six years. Mrs. Treadwell's were easy to pick out, though he never mentioned anyone's name, because they were so bizarre, and thus fit quite well with Cam's directorial style; it looked as though his milieu was odd little movies no one but first-year film students would ever want to see. The one he made of Mr. Mageaux's story was just silly, totally unbelievable and charmless, and then, right at the end, a static image of a smiley face and Cam's voice, ranting about the ignorant bitch who killed this "authentic American wild man." Really. She tried to imagine why he'd done it, but all she could think was how damning the evidence was, even if she still couldn't quite believe him capable of murder. It was a good thing she'd used headphones, as she'd closed her browser and turned to see Chris standing behind her, pretending to sweep the floor, probably wondering why she'd been staring at a smiley face on her terminal for three minutes. Tom Kinney arrived near the end of her shift, and looked as worn out as she had expected. She hadn't expected him to giggle quite so much as she wheeled him into the day room—giggling or laughing when stressed out is a rare, but not unheard of, post-stroke symptom, she'd seen it before, but she couldn't figure out exactly what was causing the stress, the day room looked the same, the residents all looked the same, there was even a re-run of *Andy Griffith* on the television.

He went to sleep as soon as she got him in bed. She tried to find some solace in her end-of-day routine, checking boxes on her computer and on various clipboards, reviewing job applications, eating her yogurt—but something, the whole day, the whole week, was gnawing at her, Mrs. Treadwell's story, Angela and her children, the police and the imitation police and poor Helen Lennox, that twisted look of fear and confusion she'd seen too many times, in too many faces, lost in a system that worked badly at best and smelled of shit and piss and antiseptic. And then she was out, driving in circles, playing Badfinger way too loud and it nearly worked, her modest spa, until she got home and there was Maggie, sitting on the stoop, looking skinny and dark and nervous. She acted furtive, claimed she was there to pick up clothes, asked for money, of course, stuck her tongue in Carol Ann's mouth, then vanished. Fuck. Out comes the chardonnay, on goes the Nina Simone.

When she awoke at three a.m., slumped over the table, she was sure the whole day was a dream. By the time she tumbled into bed and pulled off her pants, she knew she was wrong, it was not a dream, and the weight of it fell against her, leaden, and kept her awake until morning.

****

"It was awful," Eustace said, "it was like she got turned into another person."

Tom giggled. He couldn't help it.

"It's not funny," Eustace remanded him, "she was fine one day and the next I didn't even recognize her, like the devil came and just took her soul."

"There's no devil," Tom said, and it wasn't funny to think about how fervently she believed it, so he didn't laugh. "She got old. We're all old, we're a bunch of old bodies and old bodies break down."

He wondered if the medication Carol Ann had given him was helping calm his frayed neurons. His mind was clear, he actually felt much more lucid than he had in a long time, but he couldn't seem to get the words and ideas from his brain to his mouth the right way, he felt like he had a mouthful of jelly, and he didn't want to spill any on his chin. And he couldn't help giggling at the all the wrong times.

"The hell you say. I seen him. I seen him take her, and then she got all messy and there you go, she's wheeled out of here with a sheet over her head." Constance had died during the night, and been found that morning by Chris. Carol Ann had arrived late, just in time to see the ambulance crew take her to the morgue, and she looked, Tom thought, like she was in a good bit of trouble herself. She was a strange looking woman, he decided, though most of the lesbians he'd known were either born strange looking or went out of their way to appear thus. Her head was broad at the top and very narrow at the chin, like an upside down pear, and her mouth was something of an afterthought. Her shoulders, too, were very narrow, and her hips were regular-sized but, because of her narrow hips and strange head, they looked more wide than they really were, an elongated mirror image of her head. He suddenly found himself admiring the symmetry of her creator. But oh, did she look weary this morning.

"Mr. Kinney," she nodded, circulating the day room, offering reassurances to the living, "I hope you are feeling better."

"Fine," he nodded, and he knew what sounded crisp and assured in his head sounded mealy and slow in her ears.

"Your daughter came to visit yesterday," she said. He felt an urge to giggle, stifling it by digging his fingernail into his thigh. He nodded again.

"I sent her to the hospital. Did she come see you there?"

He shook his head. For a super-competent, micro-managing, professional pain-in-the-ass, Helen sure did get lost a lot. He suspected it was why her first husband left her: navigation fatigue.

"Well, perhaps she'll come back today. Can I get you anything?" He cringed, then shook his head. He loved Helen, of course, she was his daughter. He simply couldn't stand her.

Carol Ann smiled and left him slouched in his chair. As soon as she was out of earshot, Eustace started up again. "You sound terrible. You need to get better, they'll send you over there," she said, pointing her head behind her, at the West Wing.

"So?" he replied. Anything was better than listening to this demented bible harpy.

"So, you go there, you don't come back. I went over once, just wandered over, pretending like I was lost cause I wanted to see, you know? And it was awful, just awful, nothing in there but—bodies. Devil has a playground over there, all those empty bodies with no one left inside."

Tom decided that pretending to nod off was his best strategy. He sat with his eyes closed, trying to daydream of young men with stern cocks and limpid eyes, and every time he got one in focus, his daughter's voice burst in, "Daddy! You need to get up off that couch and get to the gym," or "keep it up, blowing your seed in the wind, you sure gonna catch the bleeding disease that way." She meant well, or maybe she didn't, who could tell. She had her television voice, proper and even and loud and white enough, and then she had her other voice, wheedling and nasal and bible black—if she ever used that voice accidentally during a broadcast, she'd not only lose her job, the audience would come tear out her hair extensions and set her house on fire. He felt himself drifting toward real sleep, felt a blanket being pulled up to his chest, heard Eustace start talking about the Devil again to someone else...

"I can wake him up," Chris said to the tall woman in pink sweat pants and sweat shirt. Her hair was drawn up in a severe bun, the skin of her face ashy around worried eyes.

"Let him sleep a while, I can go outside and make some phone calls and come back in, half an hour or so, then we'll wake him," Helen told him.

"Word, I'll come out if he wakes up."

On the way toward the lobby, Carol Ann stopped her, trying to smile but aware she hadn't the energy to really pull it off. The two women regarded each other warily.

"Hello again, Ms. Lennox,"

"Hello," Helen answered.

"I see Tom is sleeping, we can wake him if you like, I know he'd be happy to see you."

"Ain't nobody in that room happy to see me," she said, crossing her arms.

"Ah, ok, well, I thought I should tell you, for when you do get a chance to visit with him, there were some complications, some behavioral complications, with his latest stroke."

"What you mean, 'behavioral'?" The last word was in the same register she used in her news broadcasts, Carol Ann noticed. It was disconcerting, listening to someone switch accents mid-sentence.

"I mean, he's displaying involuntary emotional expression disorder, specifically, a tendency to laugh or giggle when he's feeling stressed. The disorder often manifests itself in uncontrolled crying, though we haven't yet seen—"

"Giggle? Did you say giggle? My father never giggled in his life."

"Well, that may be the case, but he has been giggling

and laughing quite a bit since he got here, which seems to frustrate him, which makes him laugh even more. His speech pattern is also affected—"

"My daddy does not giggle." Her face suddenly lost it's hard angles, sagging, her lips starting to tremble.

"It may well be temporary, and certainly with therapeutic techniques, we can—"

"Oh goddamnit, wake him up. I can't take this. I couldn't take it, finding him on his kitchen floor with split pea all down his front and the gas on, I can't take care of him too, I'm just too goddamn busy..." she put a hand over her brow and looked at the floor. Carol Ann knew this swing from aggression to vulnerability well. Most people found it difficult to accept their parent's helplessness.

"It's alright, we have fine facilities here, and the staff will look after Tom very well, we have a very caring group."

Helen's head shot up. "Except for the boy you had working here who went and killed that girl and her children, right?"

Carol Ann's felt herself step back. "I wasn't aware—the person you mean didn't actually work here, well, he did at one time, but he only came to visit the patients. And I believe he's only been accused, not—"

"Yeah, yeah, I'm sorry, been working on that story this morning. Trying to get out from in front of the camera much as I can. They don't but mention this place once, cause the girl Angela worked here. She got fired for feeding someone the wrong medicine? Then got killed by another employee? Don't sound much like a caring group to me."

"She was suspended pending the Aames group investigation," Carol Ann replied. Aames had dragged their feet, as they always did, investigating what happened to Mageaux, and now she was sure some CEO was happy they wouldn't have to spend his money actually doing anything.

"I'm sorry, the reporter in me, we can talk about this

some other time. Can I have a few minutes to interview you later? Tomorrow?" She sounded suddenly like a child.

"Ah, yes, I think I might have some time tomorrow, but I need to check—I'm not sure I'm supposed to do, I don't want—"

"We can do it anonymously, that's alright, but never mind, it really ain't where the story's going. Kid was caught red-handed, they're gonna put him on a gurney and stick a needle in his arm." She turned away, facing the day room again, before Carol Ann could reply. "Can we wake my daddy up, please?"

"Certainly." Wow, she's erratic, Carol Ann thought. She led Helen into the day room. Eustace had fallen asleep beside Tom, and Dick and Mary Rose were watching an infomercial for a miniature donut maker on television. Carol Ann wondered when they would get the newest batch of residents. They had five available apartments, something she'd never seen in her years at ElderGrove. Aames certainly wasn't investigating anything, but maybe someone at the BRC had sent up a red flag.

Helen stood, her chin her hand, looking down at her sleeping father. The side of his face sagged dramatically, and a thin stream of drool leaked from the corner of his mouth. His hair stood wildly from one side of his head.

"Daddy..." she bent and whispered, once, twice, then in her regular voice, touching his arm. He snored and shifted in his chair. "Daddy, wake your ass up!" She suddenly barked, and Tom's eyes drew slowly open, his eyes glassy and wandering, gradually settling to focus on Eustace. He blinked hard and turned his head toward his daughter, squinting like the sun was behind her head.

"Ah, the bane of Troy has returned," he slurred. Helen sat beside him, tears starting to well, even as she tried to make her face hard again.

"Oh stop, waste not fresh tears," he said, dropping his

fist on her knee, petting her with it.

"I—" she looked up sharply at Carol Ann.

"I'll leave you to it, then. Please let me know if you need anything," she said, handing Helen a box of tissues and turning to leave in one motion. Eustace let out a loud fart.

"That woman is on speaking terms with the Devil," Tom said.

"I love you daddy, you know that."

"I know, peach." He wriggled in his chair.

"You, they said you, how you been feeling?" She wriggled as well, then looked down and picked at a loose thread on her pants.

"I've been better," he said, "but, I'm not dead, so there's that."

"Stop that, you know I hate that talk." She scanned the room jerkily, trying not to look at him. "I wish I could get you in a better place, this one is, uh, kinda dirty," she ran a finger along the tabletop beside her. "All greasy, everything greasy."

"It's alright," he said.

"You know Garret takes almost half my paycheck now, good for nothing, how he do that? How did that judge gonna sit up there and tell me he needed my support, fake ass painter never painted nothing good—"

"Yes, he's not the most talented artist Toledo ever spit up."

She stopped talking, and together they watched Chris wheel Mary Rose down the hall to the bathroom. "Daddy, you heard about what happened to that girl here?"

"What?"

She shifted register to her talking head voice. "One of the aides here, Angela Padilla, was poisoned, along with her two children last week. And they say another one of the aides did it." She ended with a whisper.

Tom giggled, quietly at first, then more loudly, spitting on himself.

"Daddy! It's not funny! He killed two little girls!"

He laughed aloud, snorted, and laughed again, his body shaking. Helen stared, her mouth open. He was laughing silently now, gasping for breath. She sat erect, brushed her pants, and started looking around the room again. "Stop it! Daddy!" she railed, just under her breath, and much to her surprise, he did, looking off to her right. A very slight, almost vaporous woman was standing behind one of the couches, staring at Tom. As soon as Helen looked at her, she turned and glided toward the dining room. Helen looked back at her father, who was still trembling, but no longer laughing.

"Her, she—" he started to giggle again, shook his head, and dug the nails of his right hand into his left wrist. "She did it. She made cookies."

"She what?" Helen looked back, but the woman was gone. "She makes cookies? What are you trying to tell me?"

"She... poison... made... with him..." he deflated. Helen stared at him, filled with a sense of alien apprehension, that she was looking at a person that she didn't recognize as her father, barely recognized as a person, as though someone had put a just-born baby bird in her hand and told her to crush it.

"Oh daddy..." she took his hand and thrust her thumb between the fingers, massaging his arthritic joints as best she could. "I—I need to go, but I'm gonna come back, I'll bring some of that tea that you like, and some good magazines, and—I love you, I love you, I love you..." she ended in a whisper choked by a sob. This is how we end, she thought. I hope I die before I get all broken and used up like this. His own damn fault for living the way he did, she remembered the first time she went to went to stay with him after he'd left momma, she was seventeen and he was, well, she thought they were all out of their minds, men wearing makeup and dancing together and daddy presiding over the whole affair from his throne by the little kitchen bar. Sick, all sick, just like her momma warned her. And that's what you get, oh daddy—she felt herself starting to cry again and realized she was standing beside her car, keys in hand, and no idea how she'd gotten there. That's how it starts, she thought, I'm losing my goddamned mind already.

Inside ElderGrove, Tom had watched her drift away, and felt a sense of calm wash over him in her wake. Mrs. Treadwell emerged from the dining room with Eddie, the cook, in tow, face red above his bushy beard. They both stood at the counter, and Tom caught snatches of Eddie's frustrated dialogue "can't work... always underfoot.. find anything..." Carol Ann emerged from the nurses' station and stood between the two of them and Tom, trying to soothe everyone. He heard the back door bang open, and a small, dark woman with a serious mustache came rushing past the day room and joined the three of them, talking loudly, waving her arms... all the activity worked on Tom's psyche like the white noise that used to come out of the television after the station signed off, and he flickered back to sleep.

****

"I don't care, it's your responsibility, the pipe is on your side of the facility," Nurse Pinsky barked.

"I understand, I've called the water authority, they said they'd send somebody," Carol Ann replied.

"Called them? When? Three hours ago, when the water went off?"

"Was it three hours?" she asked Eddie.

"Yeah, something like that, when I told you," he scratched his face and tried not to notice Mrs. Treadwell. She gave him the creeps, and wouldn't get out of his way, either. He'd been trying to pour enough bottled water into the pot to boil potatoes when she came in and pushed the potatoes and peeler into a corner and started measuring flour. It wasn't her kitchen, it was his, he tried to hard to be good and Christian and helpful but lord she worked his nerves, always popping out of nowhere and taking over his things.

"You don't even know? You don't even know, for Christ's sake, what kind of place are you running? I've had enough, time to make some phone calls. I got people over there need water just so they don't smell so goddamn bad, and you're over here, picking your nose—"

"ENOUGH! Please, you aren't helping anything," Carol Ann said, immediately regretting her outburst, as she new it would just make Pinsky get louder. Which it did.

"Enough? Enough what? I've had enough! I've had enough of trying to cover your mistakes, trying to pretend I don't see what's going on here! How many empty beds do you have! Empty beds! How can you have empty beds when every other facility has a waiting list? Oh, I know, because your residents keep dying, and no one seems to know why!"

She spun on her heel and took a few steps, then spun again to face them. "I'm calling Bernadette when I get back to my office. She needs to do something, the company needs to do something, and oh they will, I promise you." Her shoes squeaked on the tile as she marched down the hall and out the back door. Carol Ann noted the alarm had not gone off. She sighed.

"I just need her to stay out of the kitchen unless she asks permission first," Eddie said, gesturing over his shoulder at Mrs. Treadwell.

"Ok, ok Eddie, Mrs. Treadwell, let's have a seat over in the station and have a chat," she replied. Mrs. Treadwell walked around the counter and sat without a word. Carol Ann nodded once to Eddie, who shook his head and shuffled back through the dining room door.

Carol Ann sat and looked at the ceiling.

"He's a blowhard," Mrs. Treadwell offered, "and the

rat lady is rude."

"Yes," Carol Ann sighed, "he can be blustery, but he means well."

"No, he doesn't." Carol Ann tilted her head back down and looked at her tiny head. Her face had wrinkles inside of wrinkles, yet seemed oddly smooth at the same time. Her eyes were round, nearly black, and full of something that crackled.

"Can we make a deal? Will you please just ask Eddie if he's busy before you use the kitchen?"

"Bernice doesn't care," she answered. Bernice cooked the occasional evening and some weekends, and was the worst cook Carol Ann had ever known, but she'd never missed a day.

"Yes, but Eddie does," she said.

"Arnold never cared, Sue never cared, Susie never cared, even Malik never cared, and he hated white people," she said.

"Those folks are all before my time, dear. And again, it doesn't matter, because Eddie cares."

"Is she going to get you fired?"

"What? Who?"

"That nurse from next door," she said, touching the end of her nose as if to make sure it was still attached.

"Oh, ha, no, I don't think so. Maybe. I don't know, I don't know if I care, at this point. She's a very unhappy woman," Carol Ann answered.

"So she's in the right place."

"What do you mean?"

"Over there, the other building. Everyone there wants to die."

"Oh, no, I don't think so."

"It's true, I've been there."

"When?"

"Many times. I float. I'm a bird and an angel too, some of the time. I go up in the eaves." She made a little set of wings with her crossed thumbs, waving her fingers. Carol Ann smiled.

"I know you are. Maybe you're right, maybe some of the people in the West Wing really are so unhappy they would like to die. Sometimes I wonder why we have to keep people alive, no matter what. Why can't we let them go? Let them go back to—" she caught the end of her sweater, shocked she was speaking like this to a resident. She really was losing her shit. No more chardonnay.

"Why do you keep the bodies going, when their souls are gone, or trapped?"

"Just remember," Carol Ann said, shifting gears, "to please ask Eddie's permission before you go and use the kitchen. I love your baking, everyone does, we just need to be considerate. Men are children, you know."

"I know. Bad children." She rose to leave.

"No, just children." Carol Ann watched her glide away. All those cooks, she didn't know any of those names, she thought. She rose from her chair and went to the cabinet where the active resident files were kept. Mrs. Treadwell's was remarkably slim, noting her surprisingly fit physical condition, a few handwritten notes about her baking, her tendency to lock herself in her apartment for days at a time... there were no other records to speak of, and Carol Ann sighed again. They'd lost several hundred records when a crate full fell out of the truck bringing them to Aames to be digitized, but those were whole records, not just pieces. The admitting address was smudged, and Carol Ann realized the whole thing had been typed on a type-writer. The date of admission was also almost unreadable, though Carol Ann thought the year read '1972', which was clearly impossible. Oh well, she thought, sliding the folder back into the cabinet. Some relative dumped her here, or maybe she had no family and some policeman found her wandering the streets, lost, unable to remember her own address. All I ever wanted was to help, to give these poor, decaying bodies the sense that they belonged here, alive, together, but how can someone belong to a zoo? They're trapped, and they know they're trapped, just like they know I could walk away anytime I wanted to. This isn't how it was supposed to be. I watched my Nana slowly forget everyone and everything she cared about, steered her toward bed every night, woke to steer her back to bed when she got lost in the dark, looking for god knows what, that's how my father decided to deal with the dyke his wife spat out before she died: send her off to begin her spinsterhood taking care of the mother he couldn't deal with himself. And it worked, I found a purpose and compassion and even joy, and rode them all the way through grad school, driven, surfing all the high-sounding gerontological theories and concepts. I came here armed with Dannefer, with Bengston and Allen and cumulative advantage/disadvantage theory, ready to analyze the speech communities of the dispossessed in my care, and none of it made me ready for this, for the constant death and decay and loss, every day I lose something, someone, we all do. And the first thing I lost was the illusion that compassion meant loving everyone. I can't love everyone here, I hate some of these people, the ones who stamp around, children in run-down bodies, the bigots, the ones who think they are clever and have never been clever a day in their lives—but they, too, deserve compassion, and I search for ways to give it to them, even as I hate the sight of them. They never learned how to live, and so have no idea how to die. That's what we should be doing, teaching people how to die, teaching them as children, as soon as they understand the concept, what a meaningful death is. That's the only way anyone can have a meaningful life, and it's clear to me now that most of us go into the grave having wasted our lives on less than nothing. But we keep on, out of habit, out of fear. Yes, habit, most of us are nothing more than aggregations of habit, she thought, and took down the evening med checklist to scan and mark.

Chapter 14

The sandwiches Maureen left on the seat had surely grown soggy, and the car probably reeked of mayonnaise by now, but she couldn't muster the energy to get up, walk 20 feet, and open the door and check. She'd stopped to get a pack of cigarettes on the way to visit Cam and became transfixed by the television blaring overhead, detailing the "cookie killer" who'd poisoned a woman and her two children. Where did they get that awful picture of him? His hair was a mess and he looked half asleep, or drunk, couldn't they have chosen something nicer, like his high school graduation photos? She remembered how they'd fought over that, he wanted nothing to do with it, being a teenager, but she insisted, and they really did turn out so nicely, not tacky like a lot of those pictures can be. The story probably only lasted two minutes, but as she floated out the door, she found she'd lost all sense of time, and sat on a bench to smoke one of the cigarettes. Charles wouldn't approve, of course, nor would he approve of the small fortune she'd spent over the years on air fresheners and mouthwash to mask the smell of her tawdry little habit, but so what, to hell with Charles, he wouldn't even visit his own son in jail. He'd written Cam a letter—a letter!—and asked her to deliver it, it sat even now in the back seat, cold and dry and useless, like her husband. The toothbrush and toothpaste were more comforting than he ever would be.

Why wasn't he here? He said he needed time and distance and prayer first, and that he would visit Cam "when the time was right." He's in jail, about to be tried for murder, is that not a good time for you, Chuck? She dragged heavily on the cigarette and looked around at the decaying neighborhood that surrounded the mini-mart: old, illegible graffiti on flaking brick, boarded windows, collapsed fences around scabby vacant lots. She'd grown up in places like this, then tried to make herself into someone new, to erase all this squalor from her inner landscape, and here she was, puffing on a Marlboro, sitting on a bench, part of the scene once again.

She ground the butt into the sidewalk and watched two skinny kids on bicycles tear by, laughing. Joy, even here, she thought, and stood, brushing ash off the front of her blouse. The car did reek of mayonnaise, but the sandwiches were still good, better than anything they're giving him there, she told herself. She turned in her seat to touch the other bag, the one with the toothpaste and toothbrush and shampoo and conditioner and deodorant and, yes, the awful letter, part of her had hoped it was never there, that Charles was already at the jail, waiting. He could have at least come to the bail hearing, that stupid judge saying Cam was a danger, the stupid lawyer talking a lot of mumble-jumble about plea bargains, she'd felt like a little girl again, tiny and scared and confused by all the big-talking people everywhere. Her boy wouldn't hurt anyone, she knew him too well, he was gentle and, really, too wishy washy to ever kill someone, too cerebral, like his father, obviously someone had set him up.

She teetered crookedly up the steps to the jail. She knew now to go around back and avoid having to walk the gauntlet of cops in the station, glaring at her, judging her every move. The desk sergeant here was a nice enough man, grey haired and round faced, he seemed like one of those people who had found their place in life, and took it as it came. He looked at the bag of toiletries, unwrapped the sandwiches and touched them strangely, then handed them back to her with a smile. Then she was in the visitation room, dirty and reeking of disinfectant. Cam waited for her, staring at his lap. He seemed to shrink each time she saw him.

"Hi sweetie, here, I brought you some of the things you asked for," she said, passing the bag over the table. Cam dragged the bag over the table and looked inside.

"Thanks mom, I think I'm set on toothbrushes, now."

"Oh, that's right, I brought you one already, didn't I?"

"This makes four, mom." He took the envelope out and looked at it.

"Ah, a note, from your father," she said, trying to keep the disgust from her voice. Cam nodded, and put it back in the bag.

"So, Mr. Valis said there might some kind of deal in the works? Is that right?"

Cam nodded.

"So, tell me, I mean, he told me, but what do you think about it?"

"I think—" he stopped, took a deep breath, and finally raised his head to look at her. "I think it means I'll go to jail for twenty-five years instead of going straight to death row."

Maureen nodded, and kept on nodding, the motion prevented her from screaming. "Yes, well, that's a start, right?"

"Right," he said

Cam watched his mother prattle on, watched her lips move and heard words come out and tried to make the correct gestures at the correct time. Last night, someone had walked by his cell and thrown a jar of piss on him as he lay on his cot. At least the choruses of "baby killer" had started to wane, but threats had increased in both number and creativity, it was like the other inmates were trying to best each other with more and more graphic promises of torture. It would have made a good short, actually, and

Cam smiled to himself: "gonna ram a knife up your dick," have uber-cute big eyed bunnies and kitties and puppies mouthing the words, "peel your ball sack open and make you wear it like a hat," said the little pink koala in a tutu. His mother had stopped talking, so he nodded.

"No, honey, are you listening? I said, your father promises to come, as soon as he thinks the time is right, do you want me to tell him anything?"

"Tell him not to worry," Cam said blankly. His mother's eyes quivered, then let go the tears, like clockwork. She put her hand in the center of the table for him to hold. "No touching, remember?" he told her.

"I forgot. Oh Cam..."

"Don't worry mom. Everything will be ok."

"I know, I know honey," she said, taking out another tissue, wiping her face and honking her nose loudly.

"Please don't cry."

"I'm sorry." She gave her head a little shake, trying to convince them both she was pulling herself together and staying positive. Or at least that she wasn't about to collapse in a heap. "Is there anything else I can bring you tomorrow? More sandwiches? Some chocolate?"

"I'm fine, mom. Just take care of everyone, ok?"

"What do you mean?"

"Dad, and Uncle Garret, and Uncle Tobias and Dylan, and—well, just please take care of everyone. Everyone needs help, even dad, he doesn't mean to be, um, distant, he just doesn't know how to deal. Give them help, you are the best one of everyone at helping, just keep on trying, even if they seem like they don't want your help, they really do."

Maureen felt a strange sense of calm. "I will, yes, I will dear. And I'm going right over to Mr. Valis' office after this, we're going to do a whole lot better than the stupid deal he's talking about!"

"Great, Mom, that's really great."

He watched her turn back three, four times as she left the visiting room, then the fat necked guard who put his cuffs and ankle chains on way too tight tugged him back to his cell.

It was midnight before the baby killer chorus stopped, which was early, and the torture description competition began. They sounded like birds if you listened in the right way, Cam thought, a field of birds chirping from treetops on a summer morning. When he was a boy, he and his brother would "camp" in a tent in the back yard of their house in Pikeville, and Dylan would spend the night trying to scare him with spooky stories about the Pumpkin Man and the Bloody Claw, and then he would wait till Cam fell asleep and put his hand in a bowl of warm water, trying to get him to pee in his sleeping bag. Cam figured it out after the first time, so he'd stay awake until Dylan fell asleep, waking as soon as the sun came over the ridge, and he'd lay perfectly still and listen to all those birds, there must have been thousands of them. Dylan never woke until someone shook him awake, so Cam would open the tent door and creep out into the dewy lawn and watch the sun come up, always at the same steady pace. He tried to count how long it took for the top edge to reach the big oak tree at the end of their property, but he'd always get distracted and lose track, and when he looked back, it was too bright and hurt his eyes. They moved into Candler City when Cam was eleven and Dylan was fifteen, to a street full of houses and cars and other kids and no clear view of the sunrise, and they never camped in the yard again. Cam went back to film the old house years later, as part of a school project, 2113 Etheridge Road, and he drove back and forth, looking for the number, and he finally stopped at 2111 and walked down to where his house used to be, but it was gone, no grain silo, no old oak tree, not even a foundation, just a field of weeds and clover. He filmed it anyway, the space where his house had been, tattered swatches of memory drifting through as he wandered the lot: breaking his arm by jumping off the top of the porch railing; eating so much birthday cake he puked and how colorful the puke was, blue and orange and white; his mother waking him to see the new snow covering everything; his father showing him how to make a snowman, was that really him? Or was it Uncle Garret? Or Dylan? All the memories started to run together and he took the camera from his face and looked down and there, in the dirt, was the arm from an action figure, maybe G.I. Joe or Masters of the Universe, muscled and ready to grasp some tiny plastic weapon. He picked up the arm and stuck it in the top of a small mound of dirt, curled fingers pointing upward, and filmed it, and that was the end of his project, he remembered, the little arm pointing up and then a slow pan to the left, to the field where his house used to be.

The torture descriptions tailed off, and the snoring began in earnest, punctuated with the occasional mid-dream shout. Cam took the strips of blanket he'd slowly torn loose over the last few nights and braided them together, knotting them every so often, until he had a long, thin, but sturdy length of fabric with a loop at one end. The cot squeaked sharply as he stood, tied one end of the braid to the pipe that joined his toilet to the water system, and ran the looped end over the top of the horizontal bars of his cell door. He put his neck through the loop, took a deep breath, and let himself drop, forward, toward the floor. His weight was enough to bruise his neck but not enough to snap it, and he struggled briefly, clawing at the homemade rope, before lack of oxygen dulled him and his body slumped, sideways, against the bars.

* * * * * * * * * * *

From the shower, Carol Ann heard her phone ringing, and wished she hadn't trained herself quite so well to recognize the sound. She stepped out and wrapped herself in a towel and got her phone from the night stand in her bed room. The screen announced the number for ElderGrove. Of course.

"Yes?" she said, trying to sound just annoyed enough that whoever was calling would remember the next time they called this early.

"Nurse DeFazio?" It sounded like a very rattled Nurse Tshoke.

"Yes?"

"Hi, um, hi, this is, um, Chanelle Tshoke, at ElderGrove—" was she crying? Carol Ann couldn't tell. She had certainly taken the phone away from her mouth. "You need to get down here, please, I mean, right away."

"Ok, listen, Chanelle, it's 5:40 in the morning. I have a dentist's appointment at 7:30, remember I put it on the calendar? So, I will be in right after that, I'm sure you can—"

"No, really, please, you need to get down here right away." She was now, without a doubt, definitely crying.

"What is it? What's the problem?"

"Please, just come down here. The police are on their way and—"

"The police? Why are the police—oh shit shit shit. Ok, I'm on my way." She threw the phone down on the bed and pulled on her clothes, tripped over the ottoman twice looking for her other shoe, and got to the car before realizing she'd left her keys on the kitchen table. What in the hell can possibly have gone wrong now, she asked a perfectly silent and increasingly incomprehensible universe. She blew through a red light and jabbed the public radio news feed off. Her first instinct was that Frank had gone off his meds and fled into the night, but he'd never really gone anywhere when he took off, he just wanted the attention of setting the door alarm ringing. The only time he'd gone out the front door—which he was certainly allowed to do, anytime he wanted, as long as someone was there to help him when he got confused—they found him at the end of the driveway, sitting the in the grass, crying. So why the police? A fire? No, that would mean firemen, stupid. The only possibility was someone else dying, someone who wasn't supposed to. Maybe Cam was innocent after all, someone had killed one of the residents, or tried to kill them, it was that Mary girl, she always seemed about like she was hearing voices or something, but no, she was off yesterday, was it Chris? Kyle? Eddie? Jennifer? She'd just come back, she'd worked at ElderGrove for four years, she was a great PCA but she had young kids to deal with, one of them developmentally disabled, now she was back and Carol Ann had re-hired her without question. Maybe something happened to her, maybe her kid died, and now she flipped out and—this is ridiculous, what has happened to me that I'm even entertaining these ideas. She pulled down the driveway of ElderGrove and saw three police cars and two ambulances parked in the fire lane and on the sidewalk. She thought about pulling back out of the driveway and hitting the highway and never looking back, but the younger cop who'd visited her on Monday caught her eye. Monday, and today was Thursday? What a week.

"Nurse DeFazio," he said, walking toward her as she locked her car door.

"Yes, sorry, I don't remember your name," she said.

"Merrill. Detective Merrill, my partner and I—"

"I remember, it wasn't that long ago."

His face hardened. "I was going to say, my partner and I have done our best to calm your folks down, but we aren't so good at that kind of thing. Did the night nurse brief you?"

"Brief me? No, she just said to get down here."

"Ok, let's go inside."

They walked past groups of cops and paramedics talking quietly, in clusters. The whole scene was oddly quiet, and Carol Ann realized none of the sirens were going off, no radios barked, no lights were dancing and blaring at her. Inside the lobby, Chanelle Tshoke sat on one of the visitor's benches, her face both puffy and deflated, like a raccoon rotting by the side of the highway. When she saw Carol Ann, she looked at the floor. Merrill took Carol Ann's elbow and led her through the door to the day room. It seemed all of the residents were gathered, talking quietly just as the police and EMT clusters had been. No one paid any attention to Carol Ann and Merrill as they went around to the nurses' station and sat. Carol Ann wiggled her computer's mouse reflexively to snap it out of screen saver mode. She looked at Merrill, who was leaning forward, elbows on his knees, hands pressed together.

"How well do you know Beverly Pinsky?" he asked, just as Carol Ann decided she would get up and make coffee if he wasn't going to speak.

"Pinsky? Ah, professionally, that is, not particularly well. Well enough, I suppose. Why, what happened to her?"

"Well, we're not quite sure. What we do know is that all 13 residents of the West Wing of ElderGrove died last night, all more or less within and hour of each other, and when the morning crew arrived, they found Ms. Pinsky in a storage closet, rambling incoherently. The other two people working that shift, the, what do you call them—"

"The PCAs," Carol Ann answered flatly.

"The PCAs, right, Tamara Johnson and Bobby Flume, were both asleep in chairs in the main room, the one like that," he said, gesturing at the day room.

"The day room."

"Right, ok, the day room. They were asleep, sound asleep, we figured they were doing some dope or what have you, they swear they were not, they allowed us to take blood so we'll know for sure when the lab gets the results back." He sat back and tilted his head toward Carol Ann. Like a dog, she thought, now he wants me to tell him what to do, what ball to fetch, or offer to take him for a walk. She sighed, and wished she hadn't, as it seemed to reassure Merrill.

"I'm sorry, this is a lot to process. You're telling me all the residents, all thirteen people in the West Wing, died? All at the same time?"

"Looks like it, yes, again, we need to do proper autopsies, but the Doc was here and he says it looks like time of death was sometime between three and four a.m. for everyone."

"Holy mother of god," she said.

"Yeah," he answered. "My grandmother was in a place like this, she had Alzheimer's, lost most of her mind at sixty-six and lived to be eighty four. She couldn't even roll over herself by the end." Oh shut up, Carol Ann thought.

"Why—why was Pinsky even here? She isn't the night nurse, Nurse Banhoff is."

"Right, Banhoff told us they switched shifts because Pinsky's going on vacation tomorrow. A cruise, I think she said. Well, she was going to go on vacation tomorrow..."

"I just, I can't—" they sat and listened to the clock on the filing cabinet tick. Merrill stood, opened his mouth to say something, and Jennifer poked her head around the corner:

"Nurse DeFazio?"

"Yes, Jennifer, hello." Her head felt like bottle of soda pop someone had left the top off.

"Hi, um, what's going on? Nurse Tshoke is getting into a cop car, and there are a lot of cop cars, like, what's up?"

"Come in and sit down, Jennifer, I'll tell you about it." She looked back at Merrill. "Why is Tshoke in a police car?"

"Probably just giving her a ride home. She's pretty

shook up," he said.

"I'm sure."

"When you're done here, would you mind coming out front? Pinsky was asking for you earlier, the Doc sedated her, she isn't, uh, screaming anymore."

"Screaming?"

"Yeah, every time we tried to get her out of the closet, she started screaming, Doc gave her a sedative."

"Right, you said that, ok, give me a minute to talk to the staff and to my residents."

"Okey doke." Did he really say that, she wondered, watching him stride off, utterly lost but sure he needed to project an air of confidence nonetheless. Jennifer sat where Merrill had been sitting. As she retold what she knew of the events of the previous evening, Carol Ann wavered between wanting to cry and remembering what a crush she'd had on Jennifer, how they'd flirted in a harmless way until her husband Dave, or was it Dan? had come to work one day to take her to lunch, he strode around looking threatening, hiking up his pants at men who were fifty years older than he. Jennifer was more distant after that, still friendly, but no longer did Carol Ann drive home fantasizing about her shoulders, her hands undressing her. After the initial shock, she took the news about as well as anyone could, as well as Carol Ann did, that is, with a sense that the utter disbelief she felt would soon crumble, and she would sit staring down a hole, trying desperately not to fall in.

She left Jennifer thumbing frantically at her phone and went to the day room. The quiet chatter had ceased, and she felt a sea of rheumy eyes peeking up at her. She nodded at Tom, at Eustace, Dick, Mary Rose, even Godfrey had come out of his room, for the first time in months. She saw now only about half the residents were gathered; Frank was folding and unfolding a piece of paper, beside poor Sara Israel, who'd only been here two weeks and whose dementia had broadened drastically in that time—she's been on the list of potential West Wing transfers, as had Tom, as had Frank, and Godfrey, and Mary Rose, and most of the others, come to think of it. Who knows where they might go now.

"Well." She knew she shouldn't smile, but she tried anyway. No one moved.

"They wanted to die, then they did, so what" came a wispy voice from the back, and she saws Mrs. Treadwell, standing against the wall, trying, it seemed, to become part of it. Eustace gasped, Tom giggled into his blanket.

"That, no, I don't think we can say anyone wanted to, to pass, Mrs. Treadwell. What happened next door is, was, very sudden, and we won't likely know exactly what happened for a long time, if ever. But I am sure that no one can say what another person wants, no matter how we might think they feel."

"They all wanted to die, that's what happened," she repeated, more loudly.

"Please stop saying that, Mrs. Treadwell."

"Well it's true."

"May-may-maybe you went over and helped them," Tom said, stifling his laughter, then gently sobbing.

"Maybe I did. Maybe you did. Maybe Frank did. Maybe we all did," Mrs. Treadwell answered.

"Now just stop!" Carol Ann blurted. "No one here had anything to do with what happened in the West Wing last night, let's get that straight! That is beyond silly. Now, I strongly suggest we do our best to get on with our days. I'm sure there will be a memorial service soon for the residents next—of West Wing, we can all plan to attend and talk about it more then. But really, people! We're better than this." As she prepared to turn and attend to her morning routine, she saw Tom waving his hands at her, gesturing for something, she couldn't quite tell what as his hands were so gnarled, but she thought he wanted to tell her something.

"Yes, Tom?" His hands fell motionless, and he stared at them. "Ok, perhaps Jennifer can take you. Or Chris, I know you prefer Chris to take you, he just got here." Tom looked up to his left, at Mrs. Treadwell, still leaning against the wall. She smiled at him, the first time he'd ever seen her really smile, and he prayed to every god he could think of that he might never see it again.

****

After describing the situation to Chris, who clearly had already heard it from Jennifer but was enjoying the details a little too much for comfort, Carol Ann went out to the parking lot. A single police cruiser remained, and beside it sat a single ambulance, it's back doors open, Beverly Pinsky laying on a gurney within, an IV stuck in her right arm. Carol Ann nodded at Merrill as she went past and stood behind the ambulance, hands clasped in front of her, wondering what sort of chemical reaction had set this poor woman's mind down the path to madness. It was palpable, her face, though sedated, was like a drawer full of mixed knives and forks, all pointing in different directions.

"Hello, Bev," she said, trying to stop Pinsky's eyes from rolling back and forth. The focused on Carol Ann and hardened to points.

"Ha, you," she said, and tried vainly to sit up on an elbow.

"Yes, it's Carol Ann. How are you, Bev? Can you tell me what happened?" She asked, feeling more foolish the more she spoke.

"How did you do it? I mean, that woman, what is she? Not a woman, ha, what, did you tell her, it, that I was a nuisance? That I didn't eat pussy, maybe? Fucking unbelievable..." the last word trailed into a mumble, but Carol

Ann got the gist.

"I'm so sorry," she replied. What could she say? She'd never though much about Pinsky, she knew she resented her for getting the East Wing job, but could this poor, mean little woman really be a monster? A mass murderer? Her mind wouldn't accept it, but couldn't accept any other explanation, so it danced a pirouette, staring up at the stars, wishing it was anywhere but here.

"Ha, I fucking bet—" Pinsky suddenly focused again. "You don't even know, do you? You will, stupid dyke bitch, you will...." her eyes rolled back again, then closed, then popped open again. "And your Jesus, your stink finger Jesus can eat me...Johnny cockaroo, whatever. Bad blood, bad blood..." she dissolved again into mumbling, her eyes again closing, but twitching madly under their lids

Carol Ann sighed. She'd been, she thought, on the precipice of collapse before herself, had worried herself to sleep wondering if she was going insane, but whenever she'd been confronted with the real thing, she was reminded just how close to the ground she lived. Whatever happened in the West Wing, whether Bev Pinsky had snapped and taken all those poor souls with her, or if someone else had broken in and done things to her before going from room to room, killing—whatever happened broke this woman into shards, and Carol Ann found herself feeling oddly jealous, knowing she would never so completely lose her mind, and because it was a state denied her, it seemed like a kind of release from the state she was in now: being herself, Nurse Carol Ann DeFazio, steady, a bit prudish, weird looking, unable to let herself go, even for an instant.

Chapter 15

In the days that followed the West Wing tragedy, it became clear to the employees of ElderGrove that the West Wing would not re-open as an assisted living facility anytime soon. Police tape drooped from the doors, and forensic crews shuttled in and out at all hours. This led to a creeping, pervasive, and entirely reasonable fear that the East Wing, too, would be closed down. Carol Ann tried her best to find hours for the West Wing PCAs, but a surplus of aides was not something she was used to dealing with, and the tenuous shift situations only increased the general sense that things would end badly. There were pins and needles everywhere, and no one had any shoes.

The police detectives returned Friday morning, though not before a news truck had camped in the parking lot, so Merrill found himself giving an impromptu press conference while Heinz lumbered in to speak with Carol Ann. He found her at the front desk, explaining something to a tiny brown woman with very short hair and enormous glasses that hid most of her face. When she saw Heinz, Carol Ann stiffened, raised her index finger to hold him in check, and continued her demonstration.

"It's just like the system in the other building, Gwen, except the extension numbers are slightly different."

"I understand, I just never did the phones over there."

"Oh, ok, well, what happened if someone was busy and you had to cover the front desk?"

The woman sighed. "We only had one job, that's just the way we did it. Everybody had the one job, I was potty and pills."

"You were what, now?" Carol Ann's hands went to her hips.

"Potty and pills. Take folks to the head, feed'em their pills."

"What did you do when no one needed the bathroom and there were no pills to distribute?"

"Waited, mostly." She put a finger under her glasses and rubbed her eye.

"Wow, ok. Well. I'll go get Mary, she can get you up to speed with the phone, right now I have to speak with this gentleman," she said, tilting her head in Heinz's direction.

"Right, ok m'am."

"And please, stop calling me m'am."

"Ok m'a—miss. Nurse DeFazio?"

"Either of those last two is fine." She gestured for Heinz to follow and went through the door to the nurses' station. Heinz went through the main door, and waited while Carol Ann talked to Mary, then came around the counter to sit across from her.

"So," he said, settling his bulk around itself.

"So, can you get the news truck out of my parking lot?"

Heinz snorted, which made him cough, which made him choke. Carol Ann went to the water cooler and got him a cup of water. He nodded and sipped, still coughing, his cheeks the pallor of an uncooked hot dog. "Ha," he finally blurted, "believe me, I wish I could." Merrill appeared and came around the counter to join them, nodding at both.

"What do they think they're going to find? It's ridiculous," Carol Ann said.

"What they always hope to find, some dirt exposing the general foulness of the human condition that they can peddle to couch potatoes everywhere," Merrill said, adding quickly, "the news crew, you mean?"

"Yes, them," Carol Ann said. "The woman in charge, her father is a resident, she tried to come in with the camera crew and everything, said she had a right to visit her father. Yes, but she can't come in with her cameras, right? These are private residences, she can't just invade."

"Right," Heinz answered, "but if he gives her permission to ask questions or interview him, she can bring them in."

"Well, he's asleep, and I don't see that happening, in any case. But really..."

"Really, she has a right to report on what happened, too, you may want to get a statement ready, get them off your back for a minute, anyway. They're trying to connect it to the suicide," Merrill told her. Heinz did a poor job hiding his sneer.

"Ah, yes, Cameron Wright," Carol Ann said. She'd seen the news the night before, but she still hadn't had time to sit and process what had gone on with Cam and Angela, and every time she started to try, she pictured him, alone in his cell, putting a rope around his neck, and then she heard a great buzzing noise deep in her ear, as though her brain were simply censoring the experience, removing it from what was real.

"We're not smart enough to do all that," Heinz said, "but we do have a warrant—"

"I remember, yes, you called yesterday and said you would be coming with it." Heinz looked up at Merrill sharply, who shrugged.

"We're not trying to get the drop on some gang banger here, Claude," he said. Heinz snorted again, but did not choke.

"As I was saying, we have a warrant for the building,

all records, and right now we're gonna look in three of your, ah, places—"

"Residences," Carol Ann corrected.

"Right, whatever, three of them, Gladwell, Kinney, Treadwell. So, whenever you're ready, go wake them up, whatever." He hoisted himself out of the chair by his arms.

"Fine, though I really don't see the point of all this."

"We'd also like to see your schedule for that might, medication schedules, the—"

"I got them already, Claude, I left them in your box," Merrill interrupted.

"Oh, right, good, ok," he said, and swept his arm to the left dramatically, offering Carol Ann egress. She gave him her worst fake smile and proceeded. All three residents were already waiting in the day room: Mrs. Treadwell staring at Tom, Tom staring at a book in his lap, and Frank nodding off on the couch, his hand down the front of his pants. The detectives surveyed the scene, looking hard at Tom and Treadwell, causing Tom to let out a tiny giggle that could well have been a burp, which in turn caused Mrs. Treadwell to turn her head toward the policemen:

"You here to send us all away?"

"No ma'm," Heinz said.

"Yes you are. I want to go to Florida, with my niece," Mrs. Treadwell replied, then went back to staring at Tom.

As Merrill had explained it to Carol Ann the previous evening, they were at a loss for suspects, the forensics team had found nothing, not even fingerprints, and every one of the residents had died of natural causes, albeit within an hour of one another. Both Bev Pinsky and Tamara Johnson claimed they'd seen someone walking down the main hallway between the apartments, and Pinsky swore up and down that it was Mrs. Treadwell. The other PCA, Bobby Flume, had seen nothing, and was, according to Merrill, "doing his best to stay drunk ever since." So, they managed to convince the Police Chief that Mrs. Treadwell might be a suspect because of Pinsky's assertions, that Tom might be because he'd already been to jail for killing someone, and Frank, because he had a history of "escaping" ElderGrove and wandering away. All extremely tenuous connections indeed, and all made, Carol Ann assumed, to help the detectives seem like they were actually doing something. She remained convinced that Pinsky had gone off the deep end, and she got the sense that Merrill did as well, but it would be very difficult to prove, unless the more detailed forensic reports came back with something clear cut. At the very least, Pinsky would never work as a nurse again. Well, not in Ohio, Carol Ann thought. Maybe in Alabama.

Mary waved from the nurses' station and Carol Ann joined her. "It's the corporation people," she whispered, holding the phone to her chest.

"Who?

"From the Aames place, the corporate people," she whispered, more desperately. She was nearly jumping up and down, Carol Ann noticed. Gwen was squinting at her skeptically. She took the phone from Mary and pressed the orange button.

"Nurse DeFazio," she said.

"Ah, hello DeFazio, Todd Ambrose here, Aames New York," a booming voice replied.

"Yes, yes, hello, I expected you would be calling," she said, feeling her ear growing hot.

"Of course you did, and you were right on with that one. I see you have a crisis management situation down there, correct?"

"Ah, yes, that's one way to put it."

"Media there?"

"Yes, there's a truck outside."

"There'll be more, just don't say anything to them, not a peep, our crisis team will be there tomorrow morning, eight a.m. sharp," his voice began to crackle and fade. "Going into a tunnel here, just—tomorrow—wait—k?" And then Carol Ann was holding the phone, listening to the dial tone.

"Shit," she said, hanging up the receiver and noticing Mary in the corner, chewing her lip.

"Are they gonna close us down?" Mary asked, looking somewhere to the left of Carol Ann's eyes.

"I have no idea, Mary. Sorry."

Carol Ann tried to immerse herself in work, but every time she nearly lost herself in some mundane task, she would spot Merrill and Heinz coming out of one of the residences, or standing in the hallway mumbling furtively to each other. Or, the circus outside would leak in: the shuttle that came weekly to take residents to the mall left empty, after the news crews buffeted the driver with questions. Carol Ann shooed them away, but the damage was done. There were now three news trucks at the edge of the parking lot, including one from CNN, bustling behind the cordons the police set up that morning: enough to scare not only residents, but visitors as well, if any ever came, Carol Ann thought.

Merrill stopped by Carol Ann's desk as Heinz shuffled by, out the door.

"Find lots of skeletons?" Carol Ann asked, peering over her monitor.

"Ha, well, no, nothing, really. But, when was this place built?" He asked.

"Early 1970s, why?"

"Well, there is a—let me just show you," he answered, turning toward the day room.

They walked down the hall until they reached Mrs. Treadwell's room and went in. Carol Ann wondered for a moment at the smell, which she'd never noticed before, and realized it was the absence of the usual smells—feces, urine, disinfectant, cheap perfume—that gave her pause.

How had this never struck her before? "Over here," Merrill gestured toward the closet. The room was spartan, something Carol Ann had noticed before, but it now seemed even more bleak, given the heightened awareness Merrill's attention to the room had awakened in her. He opened the closet door.

"1970s, that's a long time to never finish the floor," he said, stepping aside. The closet was clean and totally empty, not a single blouse or sweater hanging from the pole, and not single shoe on the floor, which Carol Ann saw, was dirt. It was a good few inches lower than the floor outside the closet, and tightly packed, even tidy, but was dirt nonetheless. She stared, her mind trying to form words, the words scuttling away like roaches when a light is thrown on.

"What do you make of that? I mean, who was here before, how did no one complain about something like that?" he said, stepping back.

"I—I really don't know," she said. "It's been her room for as long as I've been here, perhaps the previous tenant pulled the flooring out."

"Thought about that, but in all the other rooms, the closet floor and apartment floor are all one piece, the closet framing is done on top of it, to pull the floor out like this you'd have to use a saw or something. A really, really sharp saw."

They wandered back to the nurses' station, fumbling together for some explanation, finding none, gradually drifting away from the oddness of the discovery into bland niceties.

"Thanks for being so accommodating."

"Of course, thank you for the cordon, keeping the trucks a bit further away will help."

"Please call, if you remember anything that might help, we'll be in touch."

"Call if I remember anything, up to date..."

They spoke detached from their voices, in a shared haze, and then both turned their heads at the same time to see Mrs. Treadwell, sitting at a table in the day room, staring at them. They both blinked, looked again, and her eyes were closed, her head pointing slightly downward, asleep. Before either could speak again, the intercom buzzed, Gwen announcing to Carol Ann she had a visitor.

"Who is it, Gwen?"

"A Mrs. Wright? She says her son used to work here."

****

Tom watched the young cop back out of the nurses' station, try to glance at Treadwell surreptitiously, and fail miserably, tripping over a chair leg, nearly knocking over a washed out white lady coming through the door the other way. Then he was gone, and Tom felt his breathing start to return to normal. He couldn't help it, cops made him nervous. He wheeled himself toward the nurses' station, hoping to overhear something that would give him a clue about what was going on. Why had the police searched his room? Carol Ann had tried to reassure him the night before, claiming it was simply routine, they were grasping at straws, blah blah blah but why would they search an old black fairies' room after all those people died, unless they thought he had something to do with it, in which case someone dropped a dime, and since there was no dime to drop, someone set him up, and someone was Treadwell, he knew she was the one and now she trying to set him up, dirty old cunt.

He managed to get to the nurses' station counter without being intercepted by one of the aides, or by Treadwell, who was pretending to sleep. He gestured to Carol Ann, who gestured to the woman, her back to Tom, and came to see what he needed.

"Some water and some Advil?" he asked, laboring to get the words out.

"Of course, Tom," she answered, returning with a two plastic cups. He drank them down and settled into his chair, pretending he was drifting off, trying catch some of their conversation. The woman was crying, quietly, but definitely crying, Tom gathered she was some relation to the young man who had recorded Tom a while back, weeks or months or years ago, the one the aides said poisoned another aide and her children, the one the news said had hung himself in his jail cell. Why she was here, he couldn't quite catch, and then he felt a hand on the back of his chair, one of the aides, one of the ones from the other place, young, black, stupid, acting the little girl though she looked a hard forty. "Come on, now, let's get you back over here, you can take a nap with your girlfriend," she said, and of course she meant Treadwell, and of course he giggled, it made him mad enough to bite through his lip but he couldn't help it, felt the sensation welling up through his chest and popping out his mouth. She wheeled him over near Treadwell, who was still pretending to sleep, and he giggled harder, gesturing toward the TV. She turned him so he could see it, locked his wheels, chattered something inane, and left him, face to the Wheel of Fortune, back to a murderous bitch. He thought he heard her speaking to him, in snatches, "they wanted to die," and "I'm here, indeed, indeed," but it was so hushed, indistinct, he couldn't tell if his mind was playing tricks on him or if it was really happening, and then he was truly asleep, dreaming of Hector, wearing a chiton, holding a wound-up scroll before him like a ward, wolves and bears and white policemen snarling and drooling and clamoring in the darkness he held at bay.

****

Carol Ann saw Maggie sitting on the steps as she pulled into the driveway later that evening. The sight of her, looking thin and ragged and slightly feral, was enough to snap her out of the dreamy, dissociated fog she'd been in for much of the day. This might not be the absolute last thing she needed to deal with today, but it certainly deserved a nomination. She watched as Maggie waved nervously, twitching, brushing her clothes and her arms and generally raising every possible strung out flag she could before Carol Ann even got out of the car.

"Hey, babe," she warbled, tottering down the stairs.

"What do you want, Maggie?"

"Oh, ok, I'm sorry, can I just come in for a minute? I'm sorry, I just need someone to talk to." Her knees bulged in legs crossed over from willowy to gaunt, Carol Ann noticed. She'd never looked this bad before.

"Right, come on," she answered, sliding past her to unlock the door. She flipped on the lights and saw that Maggie was actually dirty, sleeping-under-a-bridge dirty.

"Changed the locks, huh," Maggie said, dangling her set of keys and wagging her head.

"I told you I was going to."

"Yeah, yeah you did, babe." She fell into a chair as Carol Ann got a glass of water and put it in front of her, then sat down as well.

"So what's going on, you look terrible."

"I know, right? But I'm getting myself back together, you know, just lost it a little, kinda, went overboard, you know how I can be, but I'm getting myself together now, I just need a place to crash—"

"No, not—"

"No, babe, I know, not here, I'm going to a hotel tonight and then gonna check in the clinic tomorrow, just tonight

I need, a little cash, you know? Just enough for the hotel..." she grabbed a piece of her hair and started chewing it.

"So that's why you're here," Carol Ann said, sitting back and crossing her arms.

"Well, yeah, and to see what's up with my girl, right? So what's up?"

"A lot, actually, and I'm really tired and I don't have time for this, so, let me go see what's in the cat." She stood and went back to her bedroom and pulled the cork out of the ceramic cat where she put change and small bills to save for the vacations she never took. She counted out twenty five dollars in ones and came back to the kitchen to find Maggie rocking beside the counter. Her purse lay on its side in front of her.

"Did you just go in my fucking purse?" she yelled. Maggie cowered for a moment, then coiled herself forward.

"Fuck you, no, I didn't go through your purse. God you're a fucking slag sometimes."

"Take this and get out of my house and don't come back here ever again or I'll call the fucking cops," she said, flinging the wad of bills at Maggie. A few fell on the floor, and Maggie scooped them up and pushed the wad into bra.

"Yeah, don't worry, I won't. Jesus," she said, walking past Carol Ann, putting her hand on the knob. "But I gotta tell you, babe," she said, nearly whispering, "You need to go get yourself tested, you know? Get your shit swabbed out, get a blood test, cause all the years I lived in this shit hole with you, I was fucking everything I could, wherever I could, just so I could stomach your pasty little hands on me. Yeah, your friends, everybody, and we laughed at you, poor sad little alien looking weird tight ass bitch, liked old people and dead people better than the people right in front of her. Yeah, you better make that call, get you an appointment," she said, finishing with a middle finger, snapping it out of her fist like a knife. She left the screen door swaying shut and ambled down the driveway, still muttering.

Carol Ann couldn't muster the energy to cry, she felt like a giant straw had extended from the sky and sucked out her insides, she had no idea how to do anything, she didn't even know if she knew how to breathe and then she couldn't and she was gasping, banging a fist on her chest, her vision blurring and twinkling with little spots of color. Her breath came back in a gust, and she began counting: one inhale, two exhale, three inhale, four exhale, until she got to twenty and reached over and took a sip of the water she'd given Maggie. She suddenly thought of Cam, how his mother had come today to tell her thanks for all Carol Ann had done for him, though she'd done nothing except let him record the stories of people who almost never had another visitor. She knew now he couldn't have killed Angela and her kids, and she could picture him in his cell, what he must have felt, like there was no way anything would ever get better, that it would just get worse and worse and more and more painful until it was so unbearable that you wanted to die but couldn't, because you were too worn out to do it, and too scared, and all your will had dried up and blown away. That's why her own father drank himself to death, that's why Maggie did what she did, even, they knew what was coming, but they were too scared to just do it, so they wore their bodies down until there was nothing left for their souls to hold onto. But I'm strong, she thought, stronger than them, strong enough to face it head on. I'm not going to let you beat me. I'm going to go on because there's no reason not to, ha, there's no reason to go on and none to stop so what the hell, it's just so ridiculous you've got to laugh, and she did, until her face hurt and tears finally came.

Chapter 16

When Tom awoke, he couldn't remember where he was. He felt his mind surface, rising up through waves of sleep and dream, and when he broke through to air, he was in a small, dark, awkward little room somewhere, and someone was with him. "Hector?" he creaked, and managed to roll up on one elbow.

"No," they replied.

Recognition swept over him. He was in an old folk's home, a tawdry one, for people with no money, like him, and the devil really did exist and she was sitting in a chair at the foot of his bed.

"You've come for me, now, I suppose." He noticed he wasn't giggling. He also wasn't sure if his mouth was actually moving, or, in fact, if he was really awake.

"What do you mean, Thomas?" she said.

"To kill me too, though you'll have no one to pin it on, if you do. Can't kill the fall guy, you see."

"I don't understand you, any of you. You want nothing more than to cease, yet you cling to life like fleas to a rat."

"I don't want to cease, not at all, you really don't understand." He sighed. "Why, how, I mean—how did you do it? All those people, sleeping away, how?"

"They wanted to die. Most of them could not find

words to say what they wanted, most of them had wasted their meager time here and could barely find words for anything, they had only the most dim awareness of their own lives, and that awareness grew dimmer everyday of their lives until all they had left was a desire to snuff it out. You think I am bad for helping them answer the call of their own desire?"

"But how? How did you manage—"

"I have been here so long, I am so much more than you can possibly comprehend. To answer you in a way you might understand: it's easy, so very easy, whatever is the simplest thing you can do, reading one of your books, chewing your tasteless nutrients, it's like that, easy peasy."

He felt like he should shudder, but his body was perfectly calm and relaxed, his mind clear.

"So, why? What are you? Eustace said the devil was here—"

She shook her head. "Just another story, your little red man, you know more of the real than that. Nothing to him, nor to God, nor to any of the stories you sing yourselves to sleep with. So many stories! That's the only thing truly delightful about you, the way you make everything out of stories, yourselves, your buildings, your world, all from stories. Truly remarkable, that, the only thing worth studying."

"So you're, what, here to study us?"

"I am here, that is what I know, and I have been here a very long time."

"But why here?"

"I cannot leave."

"Why not? Where did you come from?"

"More stories. I cannot tell, I know but I cannot tell, I am in this body, one of your bodies, and I use its architecture to tell stories, to learn how to tell them, but I have so much to learn, I'm not very accomplished yet. I look through the scaffolding and find words, pickaninny, sambo, nigger, faggot, words I am not supposed to use with you, the censoring is also part of the, the structure, and I take the words and make a frame and lay the words upon it and try to make a story with them. Would you like me to tell you a story?"

"No. Yes."

"Which?"

"Tell me what happens, what happens to me now. You've said there's no God, no devil, I think I've always known that, but what now? Am I to blow away, a little puff of wind in a great gust?"

"Ha, that story, everyone wants to know that story. Why? What does it matter? When you are dead, you are no longer concerned with such things. Is that not enough?"

Well that takes it, Tom thought. Meet some kind of supernatural being and all they can say is the same old agnostic crap. "No, it's not. And it's not enough that you seem to think people want to die, most people, in my experience, sometimes want to die and sometimes want to live, and most of the time feel both simultaneously. Do you read minds or something? Because you might want to tell yourself the story where you don't know what you are doing, where you're getting it all wrong."

There was a sound that might have been a laugh. "I know, I understand, and sometimes people die who don't want to, and I have made a mistake. When I take a body, this one, for now, I also take all the bodies' architecture, as I told you. And sometimes that architecture gets in the way—"

"So, you're not really in control all the time."

"Correct. I cannot be, if I am to learn anything. I need to let this, person, be, her, me, sometimes, and that means I am not entirely in control all the time."

"And that's why you poisoned that poor girl and her children? Because I think you made a serious mistake there, they didn't want to die, did they?"

"I have no idea, and yes, that was an error, this body

is very jealous, she was, how might I say, in love with the young man, and she was jealous of her."

"So you let her, no helped her, murder two children? And what about the young man? The news said he hung himself in prison. Does that seem just? What is the point, how do you rationalize such cruelty? Do you even recognize cruelty? Is there something resembling morality in your 'architecture'?"

"They are not here anymore, how is that wrong? A mistake, but they are not suffering for it. If they had lived, damaged and forever in pain, would that not be worse? In what way are their deaths wrong? How is any death wrong? How is any death anything but what it is?"

"Because you, or her, or whoever you want to say is to blame, chose for them, instead of letting them choose themselves. We must all strive to go as Dido: 'But let us die: for this! and in this sort it liketh us to seek the shadows dark!'"

"And now, having died, their selves have never been, and have never cared about such a decision."

"Oh stop, now you sound like a Hare Krishna." They sat still for a while and listened to the night.

"Why poison, why not just snuff them, like you did in the other building?"

"As I said, I am not always directing this bodies' actions. And, because I cannot leave here, I cannot go beyond my home. And it was your idea."

"My idea!"

"Yes, to bake something nice for them. Very clever, I applaud your creativity."

"My idea was to make them something sweet, you pervert everything. And now the boy your body loved is dead too. You are too ugly for words." He closed his eyes. He wanted to cry, but nothing rose through the still water upon which he floated.

"Ok, fine, if you won't tell me the story of what happens next, tell me the story of what you've learned about, people, I guess, and then if it doesn't help me, if it doesn't make me see why the horrible things you have done are acceptable, if it doesn't comfort me, then you must promise to leave me alone."

"I understand, very interesting, it will be a good test of my skill. Let me worry at it for a moment."

Tom looked at the ceiling. There were brown and yellow stains on the drop panels, and one had a missing corner.

"Alright. First, I must tell you that many people have been here, right where you are laying now, right where I sit, many people have wandered across this patch of ground. People with architecture that seemed more crude, but which I now see was simply elegant, it was much less encumbered with the barnacles and baffles and buttresses and things your species has acquired, because you have, you are the product of everyone who came before you, all the architecture is within you as well, like coral growing atop itself, or a cancer. And even then they killed one another, and even then, some of them wanted to die. One of the first minds I came to know was an old man, left here to die, perfectly accepting of that fact, but frightened all the same. He had little language, and he was perhaps half your age in years, but his body was as worn down as yours."

"Well gosh, thanks," Tom said.

"Hush. Many other people crossed here. I watched as some of them built mounds of earth and stone and killed animals near them and sat on the mounds and burned their fat and saw stories in the smoke. I saw others who thought God had given them the right to come and kill anyone who did not believe as they did; in fact, more of your people seem to think they have been given special dispensation over the lives of others by some imaginary being than do not. And you think me ugly! But you do not bear this affliction, I have found this charming, and unusual. I have seen many of you kill each other here. I have helped many die here, who wanted to die, and I have heard so many, many stories. But one man always stands out in my architecture, a man who did not want to die or to live, in fact, he seemed unconcerned with whether he did either. He came following a stream that once ran near here, he would follow streams and catch animals and kill them and use their skin to buy other things, and he made a small building where the parking lot now stands, and lived there for two years. Not once did I feel him caring if he lived or died, though he did all the things he needed to in order to persist: he made his toilet far from his house, he killed animals and ate them, he ate berries and other things from the woods, he traded his skins for plants to smoke and plants to eat, he did all the things he needed to. I looked in his mind, and saw he had once loved a woman, and how she died, and how he had once loved books and stories and wanted to make his own, and that his mind was now like a piece of glass. When I could stand it no longer, when my curiosity would not relent, I waited until another person came near, a young girl from a group of people, Indians, you call them, who had strayed near the stream, and I took her body to him and told him I had been watching, and that I was not truly a young girl, and I asked him why he lived as he did.

"He did not question, as you have, he did not even doubt, for a moment, that I was speaking the truth. He looked at the forest behind my body, and asked if I had ever put such questions to a tree, or a stream, or a stone. I said I had not, that their architecture was too strange for me to ask such things of them. 'So,' he said, 'you are also strange, and apart from the world,' and he was right, and at that moment, I stopped, to use words you will understand, being a child. And I saw my own existence, without end in sight, without any understanding of how I had come to be, chained to this little plot of land, watching, collecting stories until there was no one left to hear any of them, and the small body I was in began to cry, and the man began to cry, and I picked up the knife he used to skin the animals and put it in his neck, in the place where so much of your blood passes through. As he died, I saw his eyes, and I saw the whole story, as he began changing from body to earth, from earth to the star dust to galaxy, to galaxies colliding and romping like young deer in a field and then—I cannot tell you the rest of what I saw, but I can tell you that this moment is the only comfort I have felt, the only time I am not alone, because it is this story that finally includes me, that takes me with it and shows me that someday, I will no longer be so alone.

"There. Does that comfort you?"

"Dear god, no! Why would that comfort me?" Tom felt his body shimmering.

"You kill people because it makes you feel less lonely? Why not just take your own medicine and kill yourself?"

"I don't know how, even if I wanted to, and I do not. I don't understand wanting to die, or even what death is in a way you could understand, I am only able to taste it."

"Taste it? Look, the ending that you won't reveal, what happens to consciousness after we die, if I will someday see the man I love again in some form I recognize, if all this means nothing or something or if it's all just a dream—tell me one of those stories, maybe I would feel comfort, but no ma'm, that story did not comfort me one bit."

"I need to work harder on my storytelling."

"Yes, you do, you most certainly do." They sat again in silence. Tom wondered if the moon was out.

"Can you roll me over to the window? I mean, can you make that body roll my bed? I'd like to look at the moon."

"Yes," she said, and he was beneath the window. The

moon was not quite full, a sliver at the bottom edge hid in darkness.

"Let me tell you a story," Tom said.

"I would like that," she answered.

"You know, when I was a boy, I killed a man. Another boy."

"Yes, I know that story."

"Well, like you, I saw his eyes when died, and all I saw was a story dwindling to a point and going out, like a light. I felt his body go limp, felt his breath leave him, and I looked around and the world was still there, the same as is had been. How many stories might he have told? How many choices could he have made, good and bad? I have no right to decide such things, and neither do you, no matter what kind of thing you are. I also thought that killing him was what would make me belong, he'd hurt someone I loved and I thought that's what men did, when someone else hurt those you cared about, and that I might be more part of the tribe, one of the men, if I did what was expected of me. And it did the opposite: I was a murderer, and all murderers are alone, you get nothing from those you kill, this little story you've told yourself is a lie, a lie to sing yourself to sleep with, as you said, I have spent my life wishing I could go back and find that boy and take him in my arms and whisper 'it's all right' in his ear, and hold him until the pain was gone, but I can't, and that has made me more alone than anything. The only way I found my way out of the hole I'd dug was through love, I found a man worthy of my love and admiration, and he felt the same as I, and though we could never be inside each others' minds, we trusted enough, we knew enough of the rhythms of each other's being that we were more than just ourselves, alone, we were more than you can ever hope to be, imagining yourself a part of someone else's death rattle. You will never be anything more than alone, until you understand that."

"You may be right," she said. They sat together, looking at the moon, at the clouds, thin and dark, sailing past it. Tom turned and looked at her, her yellowing face, hands, all perfectly still. Her eyes caught him.

"So, you didn't comfort me at all. That means I win, you have to leave me alone."

"No, it does not," she replied. "Did you really think your bargain held sway over any of my actions? You have been a very unusual man, Thomas. I almost understand what you mean by 'love', and maybe someday I will."

She leaned over and put her hand to the side of his face. It was surprisingly warm, he thought, and then he saw her eyes again, and they grew to fill the room, and he heard someone whispering something he couldn't quite make out, and then his arms began to rise of their own accord.

Chapter 17

The ambulance arriving Sunday morning drove the news trucks into a frenzy. Carol Ann stood in the lobby and watched as the crew from WKRT arrived first, hunkering down in front of the door like a pack of beggar children in Mumbai. She smiled as Grant and Lauren, the regular EMT crew, ignored the questions the reporters flung at them. She held the door open for the gurney.

"Sorry about all the noise," she said to Grant.

"Nah, no worries. I just tune'em out."

Tom Kinney's face looked composed, the drooping his strokes had imposed gone, his lips taut. He looked calm, and even handsome. Carol Ann was glad. He would appreciate it. Hell, wouldn't we all, she thought.

She signed the paperwork and went to hold the front door again. In such situations, protocol indicated the back door was preferable, but Carol Ann asked if they wouldn't mind using the front, this time.

"Really? Out into the feeding frenzy?" Lauren asked.

"Yes, I'll come with you," she said, holding the door open.

The noise swept over her like heat on a summer day. "Excuse me, is that another one? Are there more in there? Is this another mass suicide? Can you comment on reports of a cult operating in..."

She ignored them until they reached the ambulance, then turned to regard the gaggle as Grant and Lauren hefted Tom's body into the back door. Helen Lennox was standing three feet away, holding her microphone like a sword.

"Nurse DeFazio, can you please comment on the situation at ElderGrove? Is that another body?"

"Yes, Helen, the EMTs are removing the remains of one of our deceased residents."

"Another one? Will there be many more? Can we expect another mass episode?"

"Just one, this time, Helen. He died in the night, of natural causes."

"You're certain of that? Has that been confirmed by the coroner? Will there be a thorough autopsy?"

"Well, that's really up to you, it's your father," she said, smiled, and pushed past Helen to the East Wing.

A year ago, I would have thought that cruel, she thought. A year ago, I would have been scared to speak to her at all. She smiled at Gwen, who'd taken to front desk duty with flair.

"Thank you, yes, Werdigo Funeral home. Nurse DeFazio?" Gwen called.

"Yes, Gwen?"

"The people from Aames corporate called while you were outside. They said they'd be here in half an hour."

"Lovely."

"Nurse DeFazio?"

"Yes, Gwen?"

"Do you like poetry?' She took a book out from under the desk calendar.

"Ah, I suppose, I can't say I've read much of it since college," she replied.

"Here, you might like these," she said, offering the book to Carol Ann. *Men, Women, and Ghosts*, Amy Lowell. It rang a bell, but the bell was clanging on some hilltop somewhere in another part of the world.

"Thank you, Gwen, I'm sure I'll enjoy it."

"We just read it in the poetry class I'm taking. Well, we read one of them, 'Patterns,' that's the bookmark there, they're very moving, and we read some about her life, too, and—I just think you'll like it." she said, looking down at her hands.

What a strange little creature, Carol Ann thought. I do believe she's trying to flirt with me. "Thanks. That means a lot."

She took the book and went around through the door to the nurses' station. Mrs. Treadwell was waiting at the counter.

"I want to make cookies and Eddie is being an ass."

"I'll speak to him in a moment, Mrs. Treadwell." she said, and watched the woman turn and glide away. Beyond her, in the day room, Dick Klickinoi was doing his exercises, which consisted of lifting a small bag of sand with each arm, then with each leg, while sitting in the middle of the floor. It drove Frank crazy for some reason, which usually led to shit being flung at Dick, so Frank usually stayed in his room until Dick was done, at Carol Ann's request. Eustace was up too, flipping through the TV channels with the remote. Another day in paradise.

The Aames crisis management team arrived at 8:30, in a black SUV that they steered into one of the handicapped parking spots. The three men and one woman who emerged wore similarly cut dark grey suits, sunglasses, and, weirdly, black sneakers. The men blew past the news horde, while the woman removed her sunglasses and read something to them from a clipboard that appeared from somewhere on her person. Two of the men had similar bags, black canvas bicycle messenger style satchels slung over their shoulders. Oh this is going to be very sad, Carol Ann thought, watching them through the lobby window. The men reached the door and pushed through. They were just kids, Carol Ann thought, couldn't be older then their mid-twenties, each wearing a conservative, 1950s-style haircut meant to make them look older.

"Bill Tagget," the shortest of the three said, breathing hard, reaching his hand out to Carol Ann. She took it, shook, and successfully resisted the urge to wipe the sweat off on her pants.

"Nurse Carol Ann DeFazio, at your service."

"Great, great, this is Miles McGill," he paused so Carol Ann could shake a second, sweat-soaked hand, "and Larry, sorry, Lawrence Maschevski." It was funny, that he forgot how Lawrence wanted to be addressed, it must have been, since they laughed, all three, loudly.

"Gentlemen." They stood, smiling at her, then not smiling so much, then not at all, unsure how to proceed. The door behind them swung open, and the woman who had disembarked with them came through the door. She seemed a bit older, though not by much, but it was clear from the way they reacted to her entrance that she was in charge.

"Well that sucked," she said, walking toward Carol Ann, hand extended. "Nina Roy, Aames Corporate, Crisis Management and Response."

"Nurse Carol Ann DeFazio." At least her hand wasn't clammy, she thought.

"Ok, we need to get recon on the building where the incident took place, Bill and Miles, you got that?"

"Got it," they said in unison, and retreated to a corner of the lobby, where they opened their bags and withdrew several manila folders.

"They can go use the nurses' station, or the dining room, I think everyone has had breakfast," Carol Ann said.

"Great, great, Miles, Bill, dining room," Nina said. Carol Ann led them all to the dining room, empty but for Chris, who was stacking trays for Eddie to run through the dishwasher.

"Ah, this is Chris Park, one of our star PCAs," she said,

introducing each of them. Bill and Miles commandeered a table and spread out some of the documents from their folders, including a floor plan of the whole facility. "Great, great," Bill said, to no one in particular.

"Very good, well, is there anything else I can help you with?" Carol Ann asked.

"Yes!" Miles said, smiling broadly. "Three things: First, a master key for the other building. Second, some coffee, cola, or other caffeinated beverage that isn't tea. Third, you can tell me what they are cooking in here, it smells absolutely fantastic."

Carol Ann sniffed the air. "Ah, yes, that would be one of our residents, Mrs. Treadwell. We let her use the kitchen occasionally because she's such a great baker."

"Mm, mm, mm!" Miles replied. "Well, you tell Mrs. Trestell I would love to have one of whatever it is she's making when they're done."

"I'm sure she'll offer you one, and it's Treadwell," Carol Ann said, turning to Chris. "Chris, can you get these gentlemen the keys, while I ask Eddie to start the coffeepot?"

"Aiight Nurse D," he said, doing his best pimp walk, which wasn't very good, to the dining room door.

"Chris is an aspiring rapper," Carol Ann explained. The men both nodded, brows furrowed with concentration, eyes turning back to the maze of documents their black canvas bags had unleashed.

At the nurses' station, Nina was standing over Lawrence, who was typing frantically on Carol Ann's computer. Mary was standing off to the side, looking worried. "Mary, why don't you go help Clint give Sarah her bath. He needs help getting used to it, you know,."

"Ok, I'll go help. Sorry," she said. Carol Ann turned toward Nina and Lawrence's clenched backs. "Excuse me, are you going to be long? I have work I need to do on that."

Nina swiveled. "On this PC? Nope, gotta take it back

with us. We have a nice, sparkly new one out in the truck for you, Lawrence is getting ready to migrate your data, should only take a few hours."

"You're taking my computer?"

"Yeah, procedure. Would be even faster if you followed the directions in the email and got it ready, but whatever."

"What email would that be?" Carol Ann crossed her arms. This was getting seriously old.

Nina took what was either a very small tablet or a very large smart phone out of her pocket and scrolled on it with her finger for a few seconds.

"Right here, email subject 'Process 226e, computer removal', sent Saturday, April the 20th. To this computer."

"No, I never got any such email."

Nina made an uncomfortable noise, shrugged, and thrust the tablet phone thingy under Carol Ann's nose. "Right here, see? Sent mail, to you, from me."

"Ah, no, that email is addressed to Cdispenza at aames dot com. I'm DeFazio."

Nina sniffed and stared at the screen. "DeFazio?"

"DeFazio."

"Like *Laverne and Shirley*?"

"Right, and you know, I've never heard that before."

"Really?" Nina asked, suddenly curious.

"No, I'm being sarcastic."

"Oh," Nina said, "well, never mind, like I said, prepping would just make it easier. Let's go over here and let Lawrence do his thing, I need to do a debrief with you."

"What exactly does that mean?" Carol Ann said, not moving.

"Just talk, honey, just talk. Stop worrying." Now Carol Ann really was worried. They sat in the two folding chairs that usually leaned by the utility closet. A copy of *People* sat on the low table between them, featuring a smiling Channing Tatum on the cover. "Ooh, Channing, baby," Nina cooed.

"Can you give me some idea—" Carol Ann began.

"Oh sure, we're gonna give you lots of ideas, I promise. But first, let me pull up this form, and we can run through the debriefing." She scrolled more with her finger, making a series of faces at the screen. She thinks she's on television, Carol Ann thought, she thinks someone's filming her so she's posing. Jesus, maybe they are, she thought, and peered around nervously.

"Right, ok, great, great," Nina said at last, and looked up at Carol Ann, squinting her eyes. "Honey, you look tired," she said.

"Yes, well—"

"Ok, here we go, standard 113-B debrief form. Painless and completely non-fattening."

"Uh-huh."

"The incident in question, in which thirteen residents PO'd,"

"I'm sorry, what?"

"The incident, why we're here? April seventeen slash eighteen, thirteen residents PO'd—"

"I know what happened, but what is 'PO'd'?"

Nina let out a breath like she'd been holding it in for quite a while. "Ah, PO, passed on, passed over, put out, it actually means 'post-occupancy' but you know, fun with acronyms!"

"'Post-occupancy'? That's what you call a resident who died?"

"Well. I wouldn't say we call them that, I mean, it's just a category, like, if someone moves to a different Aames facility but doesn't, well, pass on, they're classified MO, moved occupancy. LO is left occupancy, I mean, come on, you know all this, it's part of orientation."

"Ah, right. Whatever, let's move on." Carol Ann decided not to tell Nina she'd never had orientation, that this was the first visit anyone from Aames had ever made to Elder-

Grove, and that she wished beyond hope that it was the last time she would ever have to deal with them again.

The debriefing continued for the next hour, in part because of the sheer number of redundant questions Nina asked, but also because of her excruciatingly slow screen tapping skills. She completed the entire form using a pink stylus, typing one letter at a time, and each time her eyes roved over the virtual keypad as though someone had dumped a Scrabble set on the floor. Carol Ann was about to start writing her answers out on a legal pad when Nina suddenly piped, "all done!"

"Wonderful, now, I really do have so many things I need to attend to. Is Lawrence bringing my new computer in soon?"

"Yes, he should be back any second. He also went to get us coffee."

"There's coffee in the dining room, per your associate's request," Carol Ann frowned.

"Sweet! More coffee. I love coffee. Ok, great, great, I'll go fetch me a cuppa, then we can start debriefing the residents." Carol Ann coughed, then felt the walls suddenly grow close.

"You ok, honey?" Nina asked.

"Yes, yes, I'm fine, I just—are you going to debrief them all with, um, that thing?" she asked, pointing at the tablet/phone.

"Sure, these babies really have a kick-ass amount of memory, so the IT guys told me, and anyway, I'm just saving it all to the Aames cloud, so no worries." She breezed out of the nurses' station, passing Frank on the way. Carol Ann tried to smile at him, but only managed to grimace and twitch her eyes nervously.

"I can't find my hands," he said. She came around the counter and took his hands in hers and held them up to his face.

"Those are mine?" He looked closer. "Oh yeah," he said, and walked back to the day room, shaking his head.

****

The debriefing of the residents stretched on well into the afternoon. Bill and Miles finished their sweep of the West Wing, filling the SUV with several well-taped, obscurely marked cardboard boxes of junk, then left for several hours, returning with bags of sandwiches from Subway. After eating, the crisis response team gathered and watched Nina tap things into her device, occasionally muttering snarky things to each other, or tapping into their own phones. By 4:30, they'd debriefed everyone except Frank, Eustace, and Mrs. Treadwell.

"Great, great, three more on the list, then we can wrap this up," Nina said to Carol Ann, who'd come to ask when they thought they might be done for the day. "Who's next? Um, is there a Mr. Frank Gladwell? Bill? Which one is he?"

Bill went over to where Frank was sleeping. "Must be this guy, the last two are women." He tapped Frank on the shoulder. Frank opened one blood-red eye, stared at Bill, then closed it and resumed snoring.

"Let me," Carol Ann said. She went to Frank and took one of his hands and began rubbing the back of it. He started awake, snatching his hand back. "Oh, it's you. Dinner time?"

"Very soon, Frank. Right now, these people have some questions they need to ask you."

"Oh. Ah shit. Do I have to?"

"Well, no, you don't have to, but it would be very nice and would mean a lot to them. And to me."

"Alright," he muttered, rolling the wheeled chair over to the table where Nina held court.

"Ok, shoot me," he said.

"Ah, ha ha," Nina laughed flatly, "no shooting, just a few questions, Mr. Gladwell."

"You gonna poke me with that?" He gestured at her pink stylus.

"No, no shooting, no poking, are you ready to start?" Carol Ann had enjoyed listening to Nina's voice grow grittier over the course of the day, shorter, more clipped, more, her face growing more, how had she put it? 'Tired looking'.

"Good, ok, well," she continued, as Frank began rubbing his belly. "Let's start with last Wednesday, ok?"

"What?"

"Last Wednesday, April seventeenth. Do you remember April seventeenth, last week?"

"Yeah, yeah, last week."

"Good, great, great," she said, tapping away on the screen. "And do you remember anything unusual about April seventeenth?"

Frank though a moment, then put this hand all the way down his pants. It occurred to Carol Ann that he'd slept through bathroom break. "Sure, that one over there went and killed all the retards in West Wing," he said, groping toward Mrs. Treadwell with his other hand.

"Ah. Yes. Well." Tap tap tap. "And what about April eighteenth? Do you remember anything special about April eighteenth?"

"No, wait, yes, it's my son's birthday."

"Oh, really, that's nice. Did you get to see him that day?"

"No, he's been along with the rodeo for twenty years, I don't make it onto a horse much anymore," he said. As Nina tried to figure out how to tap that response into the form, Frank sat forward, brought the hand in his pants around back, and drew out a hand covered with very wet shit. Nina gave him a curious smile, caught a whiff of his excrement, and vomited on her pants and shirt, narrowly missing her tablet, which she held at arm's length.

The sudden proliferation of bodily fluids served as the de facto conclusion of the crisis management team's action plan. After getting cleaned up and outfitted in a worn blue scrub top, Nina assured Carol Ann that they had everything they needed, and that Aames would let her know asap what further processes would be in place. She also gave Carol Ann a script to follow, should she encounter anymore media types. As she was giving Carol Ann the script, Detective Merrill knocked on the nurses' station counter.

"Hi, got a minute?" He said, talking to Carol Ann, but staring at Nina. Carol Ann realized Nina, once hosed off and wild-looking, was just the kind of hotsy totsy little blonde girl that men like Detective Merrill would commit perjury for.

"Yes, hello Detective, I'll be done here in a moment." He nodded, gave Nina a goofy grin, and melted back into the day room.

"Ooh, hotty," Nina said.

"If you like that sort of thing, yes," Carol Ann agreed. Nina gave her an odd look, then soldiered on. "Look, maybe it's my encounter with Mr. Poopy Pants there, but I feel like I should just tell you what's what, and stop all the business stuff for a minute. Girl to girl, ok?"

"Whatever you like."

"Ok, so, this place," she waved her hand around the nurses' station, "is old. I mean, yeah, old people, all that, but the facility is old, like, too old, the company wants to move forward and get rid of these old holdings, build some more state-of-the-art stuff. Look, like I have this brochure for a place we put together in Summervale—"

"I saw it, yes."

"Right, so, that's the direction Aames wants to go. Newer places, better appointed, more things for residents to do, and at the same price point, so—" And, Carol Ann thought, because you got more money every time you "upgraded," whether it was necessary or not. Maybe you should pay your PCAs a living wage instead.

"Look, I can tell you like it here, it's your place, mama hen and all that. But when my guys and I show up, it's because, well, we're getting things ready to take it down. Now I checked, well, ok, my boss told me I needed to check on your resume and boy, you have some impressive shit on here, you've really kicked ass."

"Well," she replied.

"So, and my boss is totally down with this, we can find you a place anywhere you want, anywhere Aames has a facility, have you checked out the company job postings at all?"

"I have not."

"Oh you need to! There are a bunch of sites you would totally kick ass at, I know it, and really, basically what I'm saying is, and what my boss is saying is, once all this stuff is in boxes, and the bulldozers come and take this shanty town down, well, all we really want to save is you. You are just the kind of employee Aames wants to keep hold of! So use me as a reference, ok! You have my card, just use all the info from there!" She stood and extended her hand to Carol Ann, who returned the gesture.

Nina turned and flipped Carol Ann a "bye" and a hair toss that was surely flirtatious. Took her long enough to figure that out, she thought. Detective Merrill watched her walk away, then turned to Carol Ann, his hand pointing at the chair Nina had just left.

"May I?"

"Of course," she replied, sighing.

"So, just an update," he said, pressing his fingertips together. "The Wright case, pretty much closed, the suicide is as good an admission of guilt as any for most people."

"That's—ok." Carol Ann felt her internal censor weakening. She had to get out of here, soon.

"Incident over in the other building, forensics has nothing. The Pinsky woman was let go on her own recognizance after a day in the hospital, and we found her last night, about 2 in the morning, in the Denny's parking lot, the one near the old paper mill, naked."

"Oh dear."

"Yeah, she's pretty much lost it. But she's admitted everything, gave us the names of everyone she, um-"

"Killed? Murdered?"

"Well, yeah, and the list of names includes all the residents over there, but it also includes her own mother, Osama Bin Laden, and JFK."

"Ah."

"Yep. So, in effect, that case can come to a kind of close—what I mean is, we're going to keep looking into it, but in an effort to get the folks off your lawn, we're going to let her, uh, confessions be made public." And, in an effort to close a difficult case as quickly as possible, so you can get back to shaking down Craigslist hookers, she thought.

"So. Thought you'd like to know."

"I appreciate it, Detective Merrill. Please say hello to Detective Heinz for me." Merrill winced, then smiled, though his smile could not quite get out of the way of his wince and ended up slightly mangled. Well, he tried, Carol Ann told herself. He must be the new breed of policeman, nothing like her father. She tried to imagine her father at a sensitivity training session, and laughed out loud.

****

The following morning, Carol Ann called a voluntary meeting with the PCAs and other staff. Chris, Mary, Jennifer, Gwen, Eddie, and Eric, the new janitor, all managed to show up, and they sat in the kitchen, drinking coffee and talking quietly. Carol Ann came in, poured herself a coffee, added some creamer, and sat down.

"Thank you all so much for coming, and for all that you do. I'm sure you all have some idea why I've called this meeting—"

"They're closing us down, yo," Chris said.

"Yes," she nodded, "no one had given me a date yet, but I'm sure it will be fairly soon. Of course, there will be a lot to do, helping the residents get ready for the transfer, packing things, so there will plenty of hours for everyone—"

"Ha!" Eddie interjected. "For a week, maybe two, then what?"

"Unemployment, for me, I need a damn rest," Eric said.

"You only been here like three weeks, dog," Chris said.

"No matter, last job I was at six years. I'm taking off, brother."

"I need a job!" Gwen burst out crying.

"Now listen, I'm sure we'll be able to find everyone jobs, I'll write letters for everyone, I can help with your resumes, with job searches, come on! You are all excellent workers in an industry that needs them! You will all find jobs, I promise." Mary rubbed Gwen's shoulder.

"I get to retire in two more years," Eddie said.

"Well whoop-de-do," Jennifer said.

"Come one now, really, I understand the frustration, but let's be supportive of one another, let's help each other they way we helped all the residents we've seen pass through these walls."

They grew quiet, remembering, or picking their nails, in Eric's case.

"Now. Let's not say anything to the residents just yet, lets wait until we get official word, then we will have transfer sites for all of them, and we can all be encouraging and try to show them how wonderful their new homes will be." This time Mary started weeping, softly, but she also nodded.

"Let's go. Lots to do." She stood and cradled her coffee

in both hands, and followed as everyone but Eddie filed out of the dining room. She turned to watch Eddie pass through the kitchen door, then turned back to find Mrs. Treadwell standing behind her.

"They're going to close this place down," Mrs. Treadwell said.

"Yes, Mrs. Treadwell, I think you're right."

"Where will everyone go?"

"You'll all be given residences at other facilities, like this one. Not to worry."

"Not me, I mean the others."

"Yes, you will also be given a new home."

"No I won't." She walked back toward the door and looked up at the ceiling. "This place is all shoddy architecture, anyway," she said. "Good riddance."

Carol Ann felt suddenly like knocking her down and throttling her, then found herself transfixed, unable to look away from the old woman's face. She shook her head, wondering how long she'd been staring. She wondered when she had sit down again, and saw that Mrs. Treadwell was not by the door any longer, but standing close beside Carol Ann. Out of the corner of her hand, she saw the old woman reach out a hand, and felt it touch her face, and with a burst of cognition, Carol Ann saw, saw everything Mrs. Treadwell had done at ElderGrove and before ElderGrove, all the people whose lives she ended, and all those people's lives, she saw them all, flashing through her mind, searing themselves into her.

"Mr. Kinney suggested I try love," Mrs. Treadwell said.

"What—what are you?" Carol Ann felt all the knowledge settling into her mind, unable to process it all at once, but latching on to stray details: Mr. Mageaux helping a fellow sailor cover up the man's rape of a young girl, Mr. Zimmerman weeping when Tilda the elephant died...

"I am," she paused, folding her fingers together, "I am

an emissary," Mrs. Treadwell said. "I know I must have a title, Mr. Kinney helped me with that, too. Your words are titles for actions."

"So, now, me too? Will you take me too?"

"No, dear, as I said, Mr. Kinney suggested I try love. And your craving is so pitifully small. But of course, I will help everyone anyway I can," she said, and turned and walked through the dining room, through the day room, down the hall, toward her own room. Carol Ann watched her walk away, then stood up drained her coffee in a gulp, and flung the mug at the wall, where it shattered and fell to the floor.

Chapter 18

The demolition crews arrived at ElderGrove on a steaming summer morning in late July. An excavator and a dump truck appeared first, just as the sun came up through the trees. Fitted with a rotating grapple, the excavator rolled down off the transport trailer and approached the southern side of the west wing tentatively, rocking slightly over bumps in the yard. It sat for a few minutes, arm poised, then opened the grapple and punched through the roof, clenching shards of metal and wood and wire and dropping them into the truck bed. As it tore the roofs from both buildings, two bulldozers appeared and sat in the parking lot, waiting their turn. After lunch, the crew swapped the grapple for a hoe rammer, and the operator punched hole after hole in the concrete walls, the glass brick windows, collapsing the day room, the kitchen, the nurses' station, and all the little rooms the residents had lived in. Once the walls were down, the bulldozers went to work, pushing the rubble into piles as the crew changed the excavator attachment once more to the grapple.

Rodney Kinsch, the foreman of the crew, was having a typically bad day. His wife, who had begun loathing him shortly after they missed the flight for their honeymoon because he wrote down the wrong departure time, had again threatened to leave him that morning if he didn't find a way to get her a new car, as the old one was "too ratty" to be seen in. The night before, his eldest daughter had revealed to him that she was pregnant for the second time, at age eighteen. His gout was shrieking in his left toe, his allergies were flooding his eyes and nose with what felt like a million tiny bees, and he now owed Carmen, his bookie, twenty-three thousand dollars, after the Indians once again failed to cover the spread last night. In short, had he been offered the choice, he might well have accepted the spike of rebar that bent under the weight of a chunk of concrete and then snapped free, flying a few yards before burying itself in his upper back, severing his aorta very near his heart, killing him almost instantly.

The suddenness and severity of the accident halted demolition for the rest of the day. The next morning, one of the bulldozers pushed dirt over the dark spot where Rodney breathed his last, and demolition resumed. The project was complete the next afternoon, and all that remained of the ElderGrove Residential Living Community was a gouged out spot of earth lined with tread tracks, amid a field of grass and clover and burdock and chickweed. Killdeer, Pheobes, and Whippoorwills kept up their songs, moths and earwigs flourished, and a colony of wasps dug a home in an old log. Then came the cold, and the snow, and the world burrowed in for the season.

Prior to demolition, the transfer of residents to other facilities was relatively painless, if rather hectic. All the remaining residents of the East Wing, except for Eustace and Dick, found lodging at the GentlePond Care Center of Greater Toledo, which did indeed have a small pond outside its day room window. Eustace made a series of frantic phone calls to her grand-niece, a devout Baptist, who found her a place in the Briarwood Christian Home. Though she died of heart failure a week after moving in, she did so confident that she had at last found a home that was a sanctuary from the devil. Dick cried for days and swore he wouldn't go anywhere, that he wanted to stay and be knocked down along with the building, then relented at the last minute after discovering his former business partner now lived at the Cody Home for Retirees, an independently operated retirement community near Cincinnati. Mrs. Treadwell was absent the final days of packing up and shipping out, and a thorough search through the records revealed that no one by that name ever resided at ElderGrove. This fact puzzled Chris Park, the only PCA to notice her absence from the list of transferees, and he meant to ask Carol Ann about it several times, but in the blur of activity, he forgot, though he would often wonder, as his career as an A&R man for True Dog records took him all over the country, where the hell she went.

Spring arrived, and shoots of green sprung up from the dirt and tread tracks. Once the meltwater had subsided and the mud hardened enough to support their weight, a new fleet of machines appeared. Excavators came and dug trenches for plumbing lines, and bulldozers shaped the outlines of a series of interconnected cul-de-sacs. The dirt sprouted again, this time with the ends of white and green and black tubes, stubbed in conduits for water, sewage, electricity, and gas. Concrete pads were poured and roadways scratched in the earth. The walls and floors came in great stacks and were fitted together like children's toys, and the roofs were roughed in, then finished speedily, under the first hot sun of early summer, by crews of small brown men who traveled around Ohio for eight months slapping on shingles before going home to their families in Mexico. Finishing crews hung drywall and painted and lay carpeting as the roads were poured outside, and men in short-sleeved shirts and ties walked through each building with clipboards, turning taps and flicking light switches.

Thus did the Thorn Hollow condominiums appear at the northern edge of Candler City. The owners of the strip mall across the street put a new coat of paint on the fake stucco walls and rubbed their hands together, dreaming of Florida.

****

Maggie stood in front of number 11/12, Briar Run Way, and wondered if she should ring the bell. Then she wondered if the flowers she brought, a bundle of carnations and babies' breath purchased at the Market Basket, were even close to appropriate. Then she looked at her dress, tie-dyed, spaghetti-strapped, and her short sleeved undershirt, her worn brown sandals, and despaired, the sun at her back going down, her beat up Accura beckoning to her: come, let's run away! Leave this place! These people live in McDonalds containers! But before she could move, the door flew open, and Carol Ann smiled at her. She'd let her hair grow, Maggie had remarked how much she liked it when they'd bumped into each other at Rose's Cantina. That it made her look much less alien was the first thought that sprung to Maggie's mind, but she held it in, probably not the best foot to get off on, after everything that happened.

"Maggie, hi!" she said, beaming. She really did look good.

"Hi, sorry I'm late, I just, it's hard not to get lost out here, it all looks—" she caught herself again.

"I know, it all looks the same, cookie cutter buildings and cul-de-sacs, but look, my tree is doing well." She pointed at a sapling tethered to the ground to Maggie's left.

"Oh, yeah, nice, you planted that?"

"Yes, with my own hands," she answered, and stood to the side so Maggie could enter.

The small atrium had two more doors in it, one marked eleven, the other twelve.

"Come on, this is me," Carol Ann said, pushing on the

door to number eleven. They entered a small landing, with stairs going leading both up and down. "Oh, here," Maggie said, thrusting the flowers at Carol Ann.

"Mm, lovely, thanks, come on in, I'll put them in some water." She led Maggie upstairs to the dining room. To the left was a living room, puffy couches in an L shape around a TV, and behind them a small kitchen. To the rear, behind the kitchen and dining room, down a few steps, was an office with a desk and computer, and another set of stairs at the very back, leading upward.

"Interesting layout, it's all so, um, vertical," Maggie said.

"Yes, I like it, I get to sleep at the top of a tower, like Rapunzel," Carol Ann said from the kitchen. She emerged with the flowers in a vase, and in the other hand, a bottle of white zinfandel.

"Would you mind? I'll get glasses," she said, pointing with the bottom of the bottle at a corkscrew on the table before placing the bottle beside it. Maggie pulled the cork and sat in one of the chairs. Carol Ann came out again from the kitchen with a tray of cheese and crackers, and sat across from her.

"So," she said. "Thanks for coming, it's good to see you again."

"Oh yeah, you too," Maggie said. "I—when I saw you at Rose's, I was pretty sure you wouldn't want anything to do with me, but..." Carol Ann smiled reassuringly.

"Sometimes the best way to get over something is to get over it. I feel ok where I am, with what happened with us, and seeing you reminded me of that. And I think we can be friends, I mean, we had some really fun times, didn't we."

Maggie laughed. "We sure did, Annie."

Carol Ann poured two glasses of wine, gave one to Maggie, and raised hers in a toast.

"To old friends," she said.

"Chin chin," Maggie replied. They sat quietly for a time, sipping wine.

"So, tell me what you've been doing," Carol Ann said, taking a piece of cheddar from the plate.

"Oh, well, I guess you know some of it, or maybe you know the start, anyway," Maggie took piece of cheese as well, popping it into her mouth. "That last time I saw you, I was, well, you know, I was pretty fucked up." Carol Ann nodded. "I don't know how it happened, I just, I started smoking, um, smoking meth with this chick, and it was really good, I mean, it was really fun and she was—well, anyway, next thing I know, I'm all fucked up. I didn't know where I was half the time. When I saw you was about rock bottom. And I—I'm really so sorry about, I just don't know how I could have done that, no matter how fucked up I was."

"It's ok. Lucky for both of us the credit card company called to ask why I was taking cash advances at all those gas stations."

"Yeah, well," her eyes grew moist, "I'm just really sorry, and I'm going to pay you back every penny, my job is going really well and—"

"Right, what are you doing? You said something about it at Rose's but I can't remember."

"Working in the upholstery shop, the one down on Clinton, you remember Fat Barb?"

"Sure, yes."

"Um, yeah, she bought the place from some old chinese guy, his kids all moved somewhere else, I think she said, so he wanted to retire and so he sold her everything, tools, fabric, everything, for pretty much a song, and she heard I was working at Family Dollar and knew I did the seamstress thing way back when—"

"Yes, when we met, you were working at the flamenco dry cleaners," Carol Ann laughed.

"Oh god, remember them? Stamping around in their shoes to get them comfortable? The noise drove me nuts."

"They were a nice couple, just a little obsessed."

"Ha, wonder what happened to them, there's a chain in that spot now."

"Yes, I drive by every day on my way to work." Carol Ann poured them both more wine.

"Right, so you said, what, you work the emergency room now? Shit, that's got to be hectic." She almost said "babe," but caught herself. It was too easy, old rhythms taking over her speech, her fingers, her lips.

"You know, after ElderGrove, the ER is almost soothing."

Maggie slurped down her wine and grabbed another piece of cheese and a cracker. "Yeah, it got kind of crazy there, right? I heard about, on the news, all those people dying, that must have been a mess."

"Yes, it was bad, but let's not talk about that. Are you seeing anyone?"

Maggie smiled, suddenly sheepish. "Yeah, I've been dating this one femme girl, a little young for me, not even thirty yet, but man is she cute. And she makes these wild paintings, like collages but with house paint over them, and pieces of fur and stuff pressed into them. She's gonna have an opening in September, I'll send you an invite. Did you ever get on Facebook?"

"No, not for me," Carol Ann said, rising. "I'll grab another bottle," she called over her shoulder.

"Yeah, so, Susan, this chick, and I went up to Cleveland last weekend, saw some jazz band, I don't remember who, but it made me think of you."

"Oh yes. That's sweet." She screwed the top off the second bottle and poured them both another glass.

"And you? That chick you were with at Rose's, that somebody special?"

"Yes, I think, Lauren, we've been seeing each other for a few months now. She's an EMT, I knew her from ElderGrove, started seeing her a lot more at St. Joe's, and we hit it off. Not too serious yet, taking it slow, you know?"

"Cheers to that," Maggie said, raising her glass. "I like this place, I didn't think I would, but the inside is actually pretty cool."

"Thanks, I do too. It's little weird, I know, ElderGrove was right here, after all, maybe I'm being sloppy and sentimental, but once I saw the way it was laid out, I knew I wanted to be here. And the trees keep the highway noise out."

"How long you been here?"

"Almost two years."

"Wow, it has been a long time."

"Yes, it really has. What about you?"

"I, uh, I'm staying above the upholstery shop, actually, it's kinda cool cause I can just roll out and go to work, but I also can't call in sick, ha, and I get tired of being in the same block all the time. But it's a cool block, there's a Greek diner up the street, a coffee shop, a cool little furniture place—hey, you remember Chad and Dan, right?"

"Chad and Dan?"

"Yeah, Chad tended bar at Flaherty's, we all went to Cincy that time to see Madame George—"

"Oh my, yes, of course!" Carol Ann's face lit up with recognition. "Oh yes, I remember," she said again, face darkening.

"Yeah, well," Maggie continued, "they opened this place, Chi Chi's Parlor, don't worry, there's no Chi Chi, they just made the name up, but it's the coolest little design store, you should come down, get a few things to spice it up in here a little, just a little, I mean—"

"I remember, I remember because I was in the hotel bar with Chad, yes, we were going to see Madame George, and I had to run back to get something from the room and walked in and you and Dan were snorting coke off the coffee table."

"Oh, yeah, well—"

"And I remember because I got angry, and so of course you got angry, and you vanished before the show was even over, you didn't come back till the next morning, right when we were about to call the police to look for your body."

Maggie looked down at her lap. Fucking bitch. Always guiding the conversation back to the negative.

"But, look here we are now," Carol Ann suddenly chirped. "Let's not talk about that either," she said, filling their glasses again.

From the landing below came a knock at the door.

"Whoops, either I forgot to lock the front door, or it's my neighbor," Carol Ann said, getting up from the table. Maggie slammed the rest of her wine and poured herself another glass. She wasn't exactly nervous, just unsteady, unsure of what she was supposed to do—did Carol Ann expect her to make a pass at her? Were they going to eat anything besides cheese and crackers? If she'd known, she would have grabbed something at Market Basket. This was all so weird, why did Carol Ann always have to be so weird! So proper, so—the unsettling sensation was the thing Maggie had, at first, mistaken for love. Now she knew better. Finish this wine and go, sister, she told herself, making a fist with her other hand.

Carol Ann came up the stairs helping a very small, very old lady, who was carrying a tupperware container.

"Ok?" she asked the woman as they conquered the final stair. The woman nodded, and Carol Ann guided her to another chair.

"Maggie, this is my neighbor, Mrs. Treadwell," Carol Ann said.

"Indeed," Mrs. Treadwell cooed, nodding her head. She peered back down the stairwell. "The front door was hard and heavy, it shut behind me on the house of ghosts."

"What?" Maggie said.

"So sorry dear, someone has been giving me poetry to read and it addles my architecture. Hello!"

"Hi, nice to meet you," Maggie replied.

"Carol Ann has told me so many things about you," Mrs. Treadwell said.

"Really? Well, that can't be good," Maggie laughed.

"Oh, no, Carol Ann is very nice. My," she said, peering hard at Maggie, "and she is right, you have very sad architecture."

"Uh, what?" Maggie said, looking at Carol Ann in a mild panic. Carol Ann smiled and gave a slight shake of her head, seeming to give Maggie permission to dismiss whatever doddering thing might come wandering out of the old woman's mouth.

"Ah, I see. I know what you want!" she continued.

"Uh, what's that?" Maggie played along.

"A cookie!" she said, prying the top off the tupperware. She must have just baked them, Maggie thought, the smell was intoxicating, she could almost feel it caressing her nose.

"Wow, well, um, yeah, they do smell really great."

"Go ahead, take one," Mrs. Treadwell said. Maggie felt a sudden chill, and her stomach did a flip. She drained the rest of the wine in her glass.

"They smell awesome, but really, I need to get going, I would, but—"

"Oh go ahead, they'll help."

Carol Ann smiled and sipped her wine. "She really makes the most wonderful cookies. And cakes, and soda bread, and—" they both laughed, Carol Ann's deep and throaty, Mrs. Treadwell's sounding like someone walking through deep leaves. Maggie felt dizzy.

"Ok, well, can I use you john before I go? Maybe I'll take one for the road."

"Sure, right down there, toward the desk, take a right," Carol Ann said.

Maggie stumbled into the bathroom and fumbled in the dark for the light. It came on by suddenly, and she heard Carol Ann laugh again, outside the door. "It's on the outside."

She looked at herself in the mirror. Her face was white and sweaty, her eyes red from wine. She felt sick from all the booze and not enough to eat, she thought. Get home and smoke a quick J and feel better, lie down with Tookie, her mutt, watch some TV... she flushed the toilet and splashed cold water on her face. There. Much better. Bring on the cookies, you freaks.

Carol Ann sat alone at the table, rubbing her finger along the edge of the wine glass.

"The old, your neighbor, that was fast! Did I insult her?"

"No, no, she's impossible to insult. She really just came to bring you some cookies, she loves to bake but she can't eat the stuff she makes, and I sure can't eat it all..." she laughed again, more softly this time. "But really, take them with you, give one to Susan, I promise you, they are the best goddamn cookies you ever had."

Maggie started. Carol Ann rarely swore, maybe it was the wine, or maybe it was all the memories washing over her, after spending time with an old lover.

"Ok, I'll bring back her tupperware," she said, picking up the container.

"No, you won't" Carol Ann said softly.

"Ok, look," Maggie said, one hand on her hip, "I had a really nice time, so, so don't spoil it, I don't want to fight, not now."

"Me neither, sorry," Carol Ann answered, standing to kiss Maggie's cheek and guide her downstairs.

"Drive safe," she called from the doorway. Maggie waved a reply, fumbled with her keys, and got in her car. She turned the key and put it in drive, her foot on the gas, then popped it in neutral and opened the tupperware, The smell wafted out again. She turned on the radio, smiled to hear "Love Roller Coaster" ease out of the speakers, then reached over and took a cookie. She noticed it was still warm, sniffed at it, then bit off half, melted chocolate chips dribbling on her chin. "Oh my fucking god," she said, stuffed the other half in her mouth, wiped with the back of her wrist, and drove out into the night.

Marc Pietrzykowski lives and works in Niagara County, NY.

You can visit Marc virtually at **www.marcpski.com**

Pski's Porch Publishing was formed July 2012, to make books for people who like people who like books. We hope we to have some small successes. **www.pskisporch.com.**

323 East Avenue
Lockport, NY 14094
www.pskisporch.com